More praise for I'D RATHER BE IN PHILADELPHIA

"This new case for schoolteacher Amanda Pepper sparkles with wit on every page and may be the most amusing mystery of the summer. . . . Roberts generates more witty one-liners and pithy social commentary than many authors achieve in a lifetime of trying, as well as a respectable number of deliciously loony secondary characters."

—*The Denver Post*

"Here's the Dorothy Parker of mystery writers, laughing even when—especially when—it hurts, and giving more wit per page than most writers give per book."

—NANCY PICKARD

"Chilling and warm, heartbreaking and sidesplitting. From the unfolding of its intriguing premise, it shines with the narrator's sensitivity, charm, and intelligence. The author has worked a rare and satisfying magic that makes us think and makes us laugh. Gillian Roberts is a mystery reader's dream come true."

—LIA MATERA

Please turn the page for more reviews.

"Roberts has mixed us a light and tasty mystery, garnished with a message of social and moral significance that will leave readers gently stirred, but not shaken."

—*Mostly Murder*

"A tightly plotted, constantly spry series . . . I'D RATHER BE IN PHILADELPHIA moves along at a brisk clip."

—*The Philadelphia Inquirer*

"Witty and humorous . . . Fast paced . . . The author handles a serious subject with compassion and intelligence, creating a successful blend of a murder mystery, tragedy, and humor."

—*The Journal* (IL)

"Amusing and entertaining, this is nice addition to the earlier books in this series. Roberts keeps it light and spins a complicated but plausible tale. She also makes some tellingly chilling observations on domestic violence and abused women. . . . This book is a good candidate for a cold day and a cozy fire. Let's hope Amanda has further adventures in the city of Brotherly Love."

—*The Louisville Courier-Journal*

"Roberts' prose is wry and witty, and the likably nosy Amanda is a gem of a heroine."

—*The Baltimore Sun*

"Entirely plausible and terrifying."

—*Philadelphia Daily News*

Also by Gillian Roberts
Published by Ballantine Books:

CAUGHT DEAD IN PHILADELPHIA
PHILLY STAKES

I'd Rather Be in Philadelphia

An Amanda Pepper Mystery

Gillian Roberts

BALLANTINE BOOKS • NEW YORK

This book is dedicated to the woman who wrote in the library book.
I hope you have found safety, peace, and joy.
I wish I could have found you.

 Published in the United States by Ballantine Books, a division of Random House, Inc., New York, and simultaneously in Canada by Random House of Canada Limited, Toronto.

Library of Congress Catalog Card Number: 91-58641

ISBN 0-345-37782-6

Manufactured in the United States of America

First Hardcover Edition: August 1992
First Mass Market Edition: August 1993

One

T.S. ELIOT SAID APRIL WAS THE CRUELLEST MONTH, WHICH proves he never experienced February in Philadelphia.

February is when Mother Nature has PMS, and I didn't feel terrific either. On a Monday afternoon, enduring a standard-issue winter cold, with only one of the five teaching days completed, I considered the nasty little month the longest one on the calendar. Winter could come and spring be agonizingly far behind, no matter what a dizzily optimistic poet had claimed.

Several stories below my classroom, students poured out of school, emitting happy noises that floated up to me while I tidied my room and let the VCR rewind. Above the blackboard, the likenesses of Willie Shakespeare, Virginia Woolf, and Mark Twain looked annoyed or disdainful.

Perhaps they were offended by my declining standards of teaching. The shorter the days, the longer my cold, the less enthusiasm I was able to muster.

The VCR whirred in reverse. My seniors, suffering last-semester ennui, had received their final transfusion of Shakespeare intravenously, through film. I didn't even feel guilty about it.

I would someday like to meet the warped curriculum designer who inflicted halting, amateur readings of *Hamlet* on English teachers already coping with seniors and February.

If I ever find him, I'll make him sit through Moose Moscowitz's portrayal of the Prince of Denmark. That'll give him a new definition of tragedy.

I had tried to present Shakespeare in the orthodox manner. Nevertheless, after a few wretched scenes, during which Moose's classmates rolled their eyes like dying horses, we switched to the Couch Potato version. Moose was replaced by Laurence Olivier. I did it all for the Bard.

But then, because we had zipped through Shakespeare and because I was still coughing and sneezing, I tossed in a "bonus" play, a comedy this time, *The Taming of the Shrew*, which happened to be available in the resource library. Now I waited as it rewound itself.

"I'll do a better job tomorrow," I muttered to the literary icons above the board. Tonight, however, was devoted to feeling sorry for myself. I'd drink chicken soup and mint tea and wear woolly socks and contemplate the fact that my gentleman friend was occupied with a former girlfriend and that it was still February. In fact, there was no need to wait until tonight. I started pitying myself on the spot.

My delicious wallow was interrupted by discreet throat-clearing. I turned and saw two senior girls, each standing with one hip out, head tilted, waiting for me.

I knew I was on the verge of having even more to feel rotten about. Seniors didn't linger after school to share glad tidings. "Hi," I said, "I didn't realize you were still here. What's up?"

Rita, the more aggressive of the two, stood with hands on hips and chin in the air in eloquent and challenging body language.

I steeled myself.

She nodded, head bobbling forward in preagreement with whatever she had to say. "Wanted to talk about . . ."

"About your paper, I guess." Every senior had to write a research paper in order to graduate. No senior wanted to.

"No," she said, shaking her head. "About *that*." She pointed her thumb toward the VCR. "That shrew play. You like it, Miss Pepper?"

Truth is, *The Taming of the Shrew* makes me queasy. I

have trouble with the premise that there's something wrong with a headstrong woman. Is a headweak woman the ideal? I wouldn't have chosen the play if it hadn't been sitting on the English Department shelf.

"He's a *pig*!" Rita said.

"You mean Petruchio?" I asked.

"*Shakespeare!* He's the pig." Rita looked to her companion and yesperson, Colleen, for confirmation, but got none, because Colleen was busy shoving papers into a lime folder ornamented with the metallic stars elementary teachers award spelling tests. Gold for perfection. Silver for one error. Red for two, as I recall, but Colleen's stars spelled an Anglo-Saxon word that never appears on vocabulary lists.

Shakespeare is a pig. I mulled this over. I hadn't expected my seniors to stay awake through the movie, let alone react to its philosophic nuances. Bad enough that the class met the last period of the day, but it was also suffering advanced senioritis, an affliction of those about to be sprung, or graduated, as we prefer to put it. Grades had been sent to less selective colleges everywhere. Nothing mattered from here on except not getting thrown out of school, and it's nearly impossible to be thrown out of Philly Prep if your parents have already paid your tuition. Our seniors know that if they remain in suspended animation, the finish line will come to them.

"I coulda puked when Kate says nice wives should put their hands below their husbands' feet!" Rita could talk and growl at the same time. "A perfect wife my—! I wouldn't get married if that's how it was. Right? Am I right or what, Coll?"

"Well . . ." Colleen said noncommittally.

I felt obliged to present the official academic defense. "It's a farce. Light, funny, not to be taken seriously."

Rita's hands balled into fists. "But it's *not* funny what he does to her! And what kind of happy ending is that supposed to be? She's got no spirit left—no mind, even. He says it's night, so she says it's night. He changes his mind and says it's day, so she says it's day. He breaks her, and that's supposed to be funny? Am I right or what, Coll?"

"Well . . ." Colleen looked wistfully toward the gray out-of-doors.

Despite Colleen's indifference, I felt light-headed, and not from my cold. Philly Prep is where people who don't want to go to school *do* go to school, so an after-hours, voluntary debate of Shakespearean sexism was cause for giddiness.

"If a guy ever treated me like that—" Only a suicidal male would treat Rita any way she didn't want to be treated. For starters, she had a large housefly tattooed on her face. For whatever comes after starters, she acted and dressed the way you'd expect somebody to who etches an insect on her cheek. "I been telling Colleen." Bad English was Rita's second language. Her father was a lawyer, her mother a professor of education at Penn. Sometimes, when agitated, Rita accidentally slipped into English Queen Elizabeth would envy.

"Colleen's boyfriend's so tough," Rita continued. "Macho, you know? She lets him get away with murder. He pushes her around and says he ought to teach her a lesson, like the creep in the play."

Colleen shrugged and finally looked directly at me. "Maybe you could explain to Rita how guys are," she said.

"Me?" I didn't know whether to laugh or cry. "I'm not certified in that subject area." Thirty years old and I still didn't have a handle. It was embarrassing to be such a slow learner.

I busied myself tidying the desk. Philly Prep is easy on its students, exacting of its physical plant. We stand for the highest educational values: clean blackboards, neatly aligned window shades, cleared desks.

"I'm sure your guy isn't a wimp," Colleen said to me.

"Well, I'm sure Miss Pepper doesn't let him push her around and tell her what to do like you let Ronny," Rita said.

"About whom are we talking?" I asked.

"Ronny Spingle." Colleen looked honored to say his name. "He doesn't go here. He's twenty and—"

"No. I meant you were asking me about somebody who doesn't tell me how to act. Who?"

"Hell, Miss Pepper, we know teachers are people, too." Rita sniggered, as if despite her words, she considered the idea ludicrous. "And we know that you and the cop, the cute one who was here that time . . . well, you know."

I didn't know much—not even the cute cop's given name.

But one thing I did know was that I wasn't about to discuss C. K. Mackenzie or my romantic life with a seventeen-year-old in black lipstick and a woodpecker hairdo.

In any case, my shaky lovelife didn't include the kind of testosterone-poisoned man the girls were talking about. I had never been attracted to Rambo types, the Stanley Kowalskis who look likely to knock around their women. Besides, we had wandered far afield from the play Rita had stayed to discuss. "Don't forget," I said, packing papers into my briefcase, "circumstances were different in Shakespeare's time. Women were chattel."

"They were *cows*?" Colleen's mouth hung slightly askew.

Rita sneered. "She didn't say cattle, stupido. No wonder Ronny says you're dumb. No wonder—"

"Chattel," I repeated. "Personal, movable property. Husbands owned their wives." I thumbed through the text of the play, still thunderstruck that an idea had outlasted a class period. I found the spot and read:

> "She is my goods, my chattels; she is my house,
> My household-stuff, my field, my barn,
> My horse, my ox, my ass, my any thing . . ."

"My ass, *my ass*! I mean *really*!" Rita waved a menacing fist and cracked her gum. "Where does that pig get off calling her a shrew?"

"And what is a shrew, anyway?" Colleen sounded whiny, like a child afraid of being called stupid again.

"It's a tiny animal. Kind of like a mouse. A fierce fighter who takes on animals bigger than itself."

"Is that why they call Kate a shrew?" Rita's hands were back on her hips. "The big animal she takes on is a man? Is that what it means?"

We were talking semantics. We were upset about etymology. Incredible. "She takes him on with words," I said. "Nagging, temper tantrums." The weapons of the weak and hopeless.

"Why shouldn't she get angry?" Rita's gum cracked. "Her

father was selling her to whoever paid! You wouldn't treat your dog that way!"

"I agree one hundred percent." These girls had hibernated in my class for seven months, and the abrupt activation of their dormant gray matter was awe-inspiring. I would have gone on admiring the transformation had not the wall clock advanced with a hiss and a click. I checked it and realized I had to leave. "Let's talk about this in class tomorrow, and after school, too, if you like." I buckled my briefcase and moved toward the door.

The Shakespearean scholars stayed in place. They looked at each other, then at me, gulping, sighing, shuffling their feet. Maybe I had been too abrupt. "I want you to know something," I said. "It's been a genuine thrill talking about ideas instead of hearing complaints about term papers!" I wasn't kidding. My mood had lifted, my head felt clearer, and even the sun seemed to come out of retirement.

Colleen bit at her lip and stuck a finger into the recesses of her hair to scratch. "Yeah," she said. "Well actually, now that you mention term papers . . ." She nudged Rita and swallowed hard.

A few seconds passed while I absorbed the fact that my lovely after-school encounter had been carefully orchestrated with me in the role of dupe. The illusion of sun dissipated and my sinuses reclogged. I had been set up, softened with Shakespeare, and now I was ready for the kill.

"No offense," Rita said, "but the subjects you suggested? They're no good."

I had tried to be innovative and untraditional, to make the idea of research fun, to provide unscholarly, unanswered questions for which the students could formulate theories. I had obviously failed. My spirits sank even lower.

"They're like for idiots," Rita added.

Could she be right and publishing empires and supermarket checkout stands wrong? Did only idiots care about the existence of Bigfoot, pregnant ninety-six-year-old women, UFOs landing in Wichita backyards, and—the number-one concern of America—whether or not Elvis was actually dead?

"Boring," Colleen said.

"You said we should pick what interests us," Rita said. "No offense, but that junk doesn't."

I mourned those innocent moments when I'd thought they'd stayed for Shakespeare's sake. "What would you rather research?" I asked softly.

They shook their heads. One looked like Woody Woodpecker in a snit, the other like an inverted skunk. Colleen had dyed her hair a while back and was in need of a touch-up, which made her the only person I knew with blonde roots.

They were using standard senior strategy, dithering and dawdling until June happened and they won through erosion, battle fatigue, and the faculty's desire to see them gone. But it was only February. There was still life and fight in me.

"I have to leave." I popped the rewound tape out of the VCR while I searched for a way to head them off at the pass. And suddenly I realized I held the solution in my palm. Literally. "But there *is* something that interests you!" They cringed at my cheery response, as well they might. "You said so yourself!"

Their eyes slitted. They knew they'd wandered onto a mine field, one they themselves had planted. But they didn't know how or where to get to safety.

I waved the tape of *The Taming of the Shrew*. "We've been talking about what interests you. Uppity women. Abuse. Chattel. Marriage customs. Male Chauvinist Pigs. What it means to be a perfect wife. What it means to be pushed around."

"But—" Rita said.

"No buts about it! You yourself told me you cared about those issues, so go to it!"

They looked like doomed woodland creatures paralyzed by oncoming headlights.

Which was fine with me. You get hard in this line of work. I pushed my advantage, and by the time the three of us left the classroom, one of us was researching the rights of married women, one of us was investigating spousal abuse, and one of us was as happy as an English teacher can be, given that she has a head cold and no idea what she just set in motion.

Two

I WALKED INTO THE AUDITORIUM, MY CONVERSATION WITH the two girls reverberating in my head. I convinced myself that Rita had been honestly upset by the sexism and abuse in *The Taming of the Shrew* and that her agitation hadn't been pure performance art. I felt a little better psychologically, if not physically.

"There's Amanda now," someone onstage said. I was late for my afternoon of so-called volunteer work for the annual flea market, called, since it was held inside the school, the Not-a-Garage Sale. The stage, serving as temporary storage space for donations, resembled a set for a play about the absurd meaninglessness—or messiness—of just about everything. Positioned between and on randomly placed and mismatched items—a lamp with a tiger-striped shade, a wicker bird cage, a wagon, a file cabinet with skis propped against it, misshapen chairs, and gawky clothing-strewn tables—other faculty volunteers slumped over, examined, and tagged castoffs.

"Sorry I'm late," I said as I joined them onstage. "Some of my seniors stayed after class to talk about a film we saw."

My not exactly accurate announcement produced astonishment and envy, except from Caroline Finney, the ever-pleasant Latin and ancient history teacher, who behaved as if such after-school intellectual encounters were common. She smiled greetings as she sorted through a pile of clothes and pulled out a threadbare burgundy velvet cape I recognized as a longtime companion of my friend Sasha.

I had encouraged Sasha to use the sale as an excuse for weeding through her eccentric wardrobe, but as soon as I saw the familiar cape, I decided to buy it and give it to her next Christmas, by which time she'd be missing it.

Rachel Leary, the school counselor, held a clipboard and seemed to be in charge. "Could you do the books?" she asked me.

"Bookkeeping? Me? Numbers are not my—"

Rachel blinked. "It's really not hard. All the hardbacks are a dollar. One zero-zero. Paperbacks twenty-five cents."

"Oh, the *books*!"

She looked at me quizzically. "Sort them into categories and put them in separate cartons. When we move the stuff into the gym, we'll shelve them that way. They sell better if they seem organized. But don't go crazy or Dewey decimalize them."

I put Sasha's cape on will-call, which is to say I took it and promised to pay ten dollars when the sale opened.

I settled in the middle of several dozen cartons. On my left, Neil Quigley sorted board games, checking for missing parts. On my right, Edie Friedman glued price stickers to the underside of a bilious snack set with bubblegum-pink hearts on both the plates and cups.

Edie sighed. "For romantic nibbles, I guess."

Edie was a congenital yearner. She was attractive and clever, but the only quality men seemed to notice—just before they ran away—was her desperation. Edie subscribed to *Modern Bride* and had a full hope chest and detailed wedding plans and an unshakable trust that soon, True Love would find her.

I didn't offer my opinion of the nauseating snack set. I sorted books instead, delegating cartons for general fiction, mysteries, science fiction, diet, and love-help. Men who couldn't, or wouldn't. Women who shouldn't.

Eventually, I was surrounded by half-full cartons. I put aside a few books for myself—an Agatha Christie, a tome on the no longer so new female psychology, a slender novel whose title, *Trust*, intrigued me. Hoarding was the volunteers' perk. As long as we didn't set the price of the object, we could have first dibs on whatever appealed to us.

"Look." Edie held up a small crystal lamp with a gathered, pouffy shade. Even in the gloom of the stage, its facets glittered. "It's for the boudoir," she said wistfully.

I had an image of eighteenth-century ladies in wigs reclining on satin lounges, and I wondered how Edie, a gym teacher with Nikes and a whistle on a chain, fit herself into a picture that belonged on a Regency romance. "Boudoir originally meant a place for pouting," I said. "Who needs a lamp for that? It's more fun in the dark."

"A lamp like this is for grand seductions." Sometimes she seemed like a mythical character under a spell. The next single male to turn the corner would be her destiny. And it was never too soon to stock up on the proper crystal love accessories. "Wish I could afford it." Edie put the lamp down.

Wish I could afford it could be every teacher's motto. Maybe Caroline Finney could translate it into Latin, and we'd have a crest made. Crossed chalk and red pencil above, those words below. The subject of personal finances had occupied a lot of my thinking lately. February does that to a person. Money can't buy happiness, but it can definitely lease a beach during winter break. A warm, adolescent-free zone with industrial-strength sunshine. Give me the beach; I'll take care of the happiness part.

After hallucinating about the tropical escape, I had finally decided to earn it by moonlighting. The next hurdle was finding a moon to light. I vetoed the idea of parties where I'd demonstrate makeup, plastic containers, or sexual aids, and that left doing overtime with the academically impaired. I therefore had an appointment tomorrow after school at the headquarters of TLC, which ran tutoring centers all over the city and suburbs.

I continued sorting and discovered a cache of Little Golden Books. I suspected that my niece was too old for these, and I knew that my newborn nephew was definitely too young, but I nonetheless put them aside for somebody. Then I studied a nice edition of *Fanny Hill* and debated whether removing Victorian pornography from a high school sale constituted censorship. I decided to solve the issue by buying the book myself.

Next to me, Neil Quigley stood and stretched his long frame. "They give me eight-hundred-piece jigsaw puzzles. How am I supposed to know whether or not they're intact?"

I smiled in sympathy, but his attention was elsewhere. He cracked his knuckles and sat back down.

"I have an appointment at TLC headquarters tomorrow," I told him. "I haven't interviewed for anything in years. Any advice?"

His expression became direct, surprised and unhappy. "Only to stay away from them. Don't be stupid the way I was." He picked up a game box and dropped it back down. "No timer," he said. He looked at me again. "I'm serious. I'm sorry I ever got involved with TLC."

"Why? I thought you were doing so well. What's wrong?"

"Do whatever you want, okay?" Neil sounded almost angry.

"I'm only interviewing for a tutoring position." Neil, on the other hand, had become one of their franchisees, running a center in South Philadelphia.

"I shouldn't have said anything. It's your life." His voice was flat.

Neil was a history teacher in love with his wife and Benjamin Franklin. He was writing a biography about the latter. He was also a great dancer, and he played the banjo, or had, until recently, when he stopped having much to sing or dance about. First, his wife Angie developed environmental allergies which forced her out of teaching and into specially designed and expensive new quarters. Now she was very pregnant with their first child and having a bedridden time of it. Given his burdens and bills, popular wisdom had it that he was lucky to have a second income from his franchise of one of the Teller-Schmidt Learning Centers, more commonly known as TLC.

"I wish you'd explain," I said.

"If you had any idea what I've been through, what they—" Neil clamped his jaw so tightly the socket bone pressed against his skin. He was a long, thin man with a brand new tic at the side of his eye. He made me think of a stick of dynamite, counting down to detonation. "Sorry," he said. "I'm tired. Angela had a bad night again. Forget it."

"How is dear Angela?" Caroline Finney asked. Everyone was dear to her and by and large the feeling was reciprocated, even if her heart belonged to Ovid, as she'd once confessed, blushing.

She and Neil discussed, in properly vague terms, Angela's tortuous progress toward delivery, and the many alterations to their home that had been necessary to alleviate her allergies.

I once again returned to my chores and realized that *Fanny Hill* had been only a sample nugget. I'd hit the Mother Lode of erotica: slender volumes with plain white covers by Anonymous, and racy contemporary soft-core best-sellers, all hardcover first editions, and all the way back to *Peyton Place*.

I furtively thumbed through the collection, sure that any minute the principal would find me out and haul me away. Consequently, I gasped when Neil tapped my shoulder.

"Sorry," he said. "Sorry twice. Didn't mean to scare you now or snap at you earlier. I only meant . . . I'm not the person to talk to about TLC. I'm sure Teller and Schmidt would agree. They'd be the first to say I'm biased—and a bad businessman."

"Why?"

He shook his head. "I'm not supposed to talk about— Some other time," he said firmly.

It was true that Neil was not my idea of a tycoon. Ferreting out odd facts about Ben Franklin was one thing. He'd been really excited the day he'd discovered that old Ben developed the idea of street cleaning, for example. Research delighted Neil, not receipts and bills. However, it shouldn't have mattered. TLC's literature promised that the main office handled the paperwork for their franchises. I had lots more questions but, as he obviously didn't want any further discussion of the subject, we returned to our tasks.

I peeked into another racy number called *M'lady's Boudoir* and put it in a carton with its X-rated brethren. Then, for all his determination to be silent, Neil spoke. "They send us those letters inviting us to be a part of their team. Probably every teacher in the Delaware Valley hears their pitch every year. But they never mention how much you *won't* make. How much will go to advertising,'' he said. ''You know what television time costs? And brochures and the building and the furniture? Not a clue.''

On my other side, Edie moaned. It appeared that the donor of the crystal lamp had shucked an entire boudoir's worth of bibelots: a powder box, a mirrored tray with crystal handles, a bud vase, and a votive holder. I wondered what dreadful change of fate had made the crystal's owner give her treasures away, and whether it was the same person who'd gotten rid of all the steamy literature. Edie, on the other hand, appeared to be wondering only about what would be possible in a room full of these objects.

She blushed, as if I'd seen through the cut glass into her fantasies. She put down the candle holder.

''They make it sound great,'' Neil continued as he examined a flimsy-looking toy train set. ''You should read the article *Philadelphia Magazine* did about the place.'' He shook his head.

''Oooh,'' Edie said. ''I meant to tell you I saw it—the article and the picture of you.'' She turned to me. ''Neil looks soooo *handsome*,'' she said.

Neil's expression grew darker and more strained. ''I didn't notice. All I could see is how good they made Wynn Teller look.''

''Neil!'' Edie squealed. ''You shouldn't be jealous! The man's adorable, true, but you're cute, too.''

''I didn't mean that.'' Neil looked ready to explode.

Caroline Finney's gentle voice intervened. ''Wynn Teller,'' she said. ''His son Hugh was here, wasn't he? Such an interesting child. He was in my ancient history class. A good mind, but then he left so abruptly. Has his father ever said where Hugh is now, Neil?''

Neil shook his head. ''We don't talk about things like . . . Anyway, I never met Hugh, so I never asked.''

Hugh Teller had been in my ninth grade class several years back, a bubble of a boy whose unfortunate name and shape prompted Baby Huey jokes. However, as if he were a character in one of the Broadway shows he adored, Huey Teller triumphed and became a star. The little boy had an enormous voice, an overwhelming, clear bellow designed for hard-of-hearing folk in the top balcony. He'd been the hit of our annual show and then, almost immediately, in midsemester, he'd transferred out. Whenever I saw an ad for a Broadway opening, I searched for Hugh Teller's name.

"I heard he went to boarding school," Edie said. "Out of state. Several boarding schools, in fact." She didn't sound interested. Hugh was too far away, young, and unavailable to be her True Love at Last.

I kept sorting, and discovered several accounts of exotic expeditions involving rough terrain, native guides, and derring-do. I envisioned the person who'd donated them, jettisoning their weight before setting off for the unknown again.

However, as the sorting wore on, I wore out, tossing increasing numbers into the miscellaneous carton. In went a tattered Dr. Spock, a dictionary of firearms, an out-of-date *Guide to American Antiques*. I belatedly realized that I could create a reference category, but that seemed too much trouble. Tomorrow's volunteer could do it. I wanted out of this dithering and commotion and into my sweatsuit and a pot of chicken soup.

Reader's Digest Condensed Books landed in the to-be-sorted carton along with the World Book, Volume 18, So–Sz; a collection of poems about unicorns; a zip-code directory; a photographic homage to fireplugs; and a paperback about battered women.

I stared at this last one. Rita, much to her own surprise, was now researching spousal abuse. I picked up the book again. For twenty-five cents I could be a sport, jumpstart her project. If, of course, the book was worth anything in the first place. I opened it and scowled.

It was underlined and there was graffiti in the margins. I detest hacking through thickets of other people's markings, and I was sure Rita would be equally annoyed. Or worse, she'd use this stranger's underlines as a study guide. I tossed the book back in the box.

Still. For a quarter. I picked it up again, flipped through to see the extent of the damage, then paused at a notated passage.

I all but stopped breathing. *He put a gun to my head*, the text quoted an abused wife. Terrible. But still worse was the margin note, in minuscule, fastidious printing: *He did this and does this to me. I am so afraid.*

Tiny letters, tidily printed. A small voice, pitched low, deliberately insignificant, as if cowering. Plain language, making her message horribly clear.

The noise and bustle around me, the slap of articles dropped, the thunk of pieces moved, the blur of talk, faded, and I was alone with the quiet voice, the hand that had underlined the passage in neat, true lines. She'd used a ruler. To be safe.

I could see her trying not to move, not to breathe as he held a gun pointed at her head. *He did this and does this to me. I am so afraid.*

I looked in front of the book for a name, but there was none there or at the back, or on any of the pages I flipped through. Then I went through the book again, slowly this time, stopping at her careful underlines that together told her life history and secrets.

> Battered women often survive by behaving in unusual manners that wind up misdiagnosed as schizophrenia, paranoia, or severe depression. They may even be institutionalized for the condition and undergo therapy, never revealing the real root of their problem.

Yes, she'd printed in the margin next to this passage. *But I am not crazy, only afraid, and even if I could dare to tell somebody, nobody really wants to hear the truth.*

Battering crosses all socioeconomic lines was underlined. *Batterers are found in every profession and walk of life*. Her note made it clear that her husband was a successful, respected man in his community. Nothing like the undershirt and bottle of beer stereotype I'd automatically summoned, but a financially comfortable, well-tailored man who battered his woman in a well-appointed house.

Sometimes there was only a poignant *this is true* in the margin.

> Often the beatings and therefore any telltale marks stop before the wife is going to do business entertaining.

This is true.

> Battered women often isolate themselves because the batterer perceives anyone who is kind to her as a threat.

This is true.

> The batterer is often also violent with the children.

This is true.

Bit by bit, in a mosaic of sad fragments, a picture emerged from the underlined segments and marginalia.

I looked around, almost surprised not to find her onstage with me, because I could hear her so clearly, calling for help. An hour ago, I had casually mentioned abuse to the girls, but now it had changed from an abstraction into one bright woman so terrorized and with so little hope, she'd sent an anonymous cry out into the world, like a marooned sailor floating a note in a bottle.

I am alone and terrified. Listen. Help me.

There were long unmarked segments about the history of violence in America. I skimmed through them until, near the end, I found another underline.

> . . . sooner or later the violence escalates. Many times, the batterer kills either himself or his spouse.

And in the margin, her whisper, cramped letters half trying to hide themselves and their message: *I know he will kill me. He says so. I believe him. He will kill me soon.*

I put the book on my knees and lowered my head, nauseous and disoriented, wondering if she was still alive or already murdered.

Who are you? I checked every single page again, but still found no name. She had probably even been afraid to use her handwriting, choosing instead unidentifiable printing.

Why? I asked her. You want to be heard, need to be heard, want to be saved, but you're making it impossible. Which school donor are you? Do you have a child here? Will I see you the day of the sale and not recognize you? Will you watch to see who buys your book?

And as I sat, head down, wondering, I noticed a mailing label on the carton from which I'd pulled the book. I leaned closer. The label had Sasha Berg's name on it.

Sasha? Impossible. She wasn't even married. But then, all it really took was a man, not a wedding ring.

Sasha. I squinted at the notes in the margin again. I'd recognize her handwriting, not this anonymous printing. *Sasha?* She was wild, took too many chances. Lots of times I'd been cast as her rescuer, but not this secret, furtive way. It didn't make sense. But then, neither did a man's terrorizing and brutalizing a woman make sense. And it was true, what was written there in the margin. *Nobody wants to hear.* Maybe I'd never listened.

This very afternoon, when Rita insisted that Colleen's boyfriend was or could be abusive, had I asked questions, intervened, helped out? No, I'd busied myself with classroom detail. I didn't want to hear.

In fact, to be completely honest, most of me still didn't want to. In truth, I wished I'd never opened that book.

But now that I had, I couldn't ignore it. I gathered up Sasha's cape, as well as my Agatha Christie, psychology, erotica, and Little Golden Books, and I made my farewells. The rules said the merchandise had to stay onstage until Friday, when it could be paid for. I decided a private niche backstage qualified. That way, no other volunteer could forget the cape was already sold.

Back in the confusion of ropes and props, dusky light filtering through a small window helped me spot a chair on which to store my treasures. I moved to do so and tripped over my own fool feet, splatting spread-eagled on the floor.

One more reason to feel sorry for myself. Or rather, two, as in sore knees. I dusted myself, tossed my purchases on the chair, and limped off. Only the underlined book traveled with me.

It had already told me more than I felt prepared to know. Now it had to tell me what to do about it.

Three

SASHA'S APARTMENT IS NEAR THE RIVER, ON THE FRINGE OF Society Hill's smartly restored Colonial streets. I could and would have walked there if the weather, my sinuses, or my spirits had been in better shape.

Which is to say I drove, and which isn't to say I was thereby warm or insulated. I have a '65 Mustang. Wine-red burgundy. Convertible. Classic. Once upon a time, it was a part of my brother-in-law Sam's brief youth. When he mutated into corporate lawyerhood, a secondhand sporty car no longer fit his image, but there I was, without an image and with tongue hanging out.

That was many years and payments ago. Both the buggy and I had aged considerably in the interim. In the case of the car, it was most obvious in the cracked and gaping plastic rear window, which I could not afford to repair, and which turned the car into a mobile wind tunnel as I drove. The only reason I kept the top up was to fool pedestrians into thinking I was sane and snug.

I didn't lock up when I parked. Why irritate thieves too dumb to notice that they could stroll in through the back window?

The foyer of Sasha's building was marvelously overheated, and I bathed in the hot dry air. With one hand I pushed the

Berg button. With the other and a tissue, I ministered to my nose.

"It's me," I said into the little grill.

"Bea who?"

"*Mandy!* Remember? From third grade on?"

"Your ridiculous ailment is getting boring," she said, but she took pity and buzzed me in.

As my head warmed up, it attempted to function again, which wasn't good news. I didn't want to think about the book and the questions that had brought me here.

"Mulled wine," Sasha said as she opened the door. She wore a hooded robe Merlin would have coveted. Her jet-black hair was pulled to the side and held with silver spirals of ribbon.

"Is that the secret password?" I asked.

"It'll cure what ails you." I followed her into her kitchen and watched her pour wine and spices into a pot. Almost instantly, the long narrow room was perfumed with lemon and cinnamon. The scents were its only decor. The rest of Sasha's apartment was a lush confusion of art deco, Victorian whatnots, poufs, jukeboxes, and anything else that caught her fancy. But the kitchen doubled as her darkroom, a spartan and utilitarian laboratory. You could roll up the blackout shades and perform an emergency appendectomy on the counters any time they didn't sport trays of developer.

"Do you always have mulling spices on hand?" I asked. Another reason the kitchen was generally pristine was that Sasha was as domesticated as an aardvark.

"Doesn't everybody?" We hovered around the little caldron. "So. What brings you to my door on such a miserable evening? Don't you have anything better to do? Where's Eliot Ness?"

"He's, um, expecting company. A friend from out of town."

"What kind of friend?"

"The goes-way-back kind." I cleared my throat. "You know, I was sorting for that stupid Not-a-Garage Sale and—"

"I dropped off a ton of things," she said.

"Actually, that's what I—"

"I don't work there or have kids there, but I did it for the greater good of Philly Prep. Is that unselfish or what?"

"Very impressive, and since you mentioned it, there was a donation I wanted to ask about, but it's a little awkward."

It's hard for a six foot tall, voluptuous woman dressed in a medieval sweep of embroidered velvet to look embarrassed, but Sasha managed. "Look," she said, "I was going to say . . . you know how much I brought in, but there was one thing . . ."

"Yes?"

"Oh, it's too . . . never mind." She bent over the saucepan and inhaled. "Do this," she said. "The steam will cure you. Hot air's the secret. Honestly."

I complied. It wasn't possible to imitate Sasha's deep breath. It also wasn't possible to say much in that position. I stood up. Sasha was setting out glass mugs and rooting in her pantry. "I met a plant man today," she said. "Not the kind who comes to your house and waters things. The kind who studies them."

"We were talking about your donation," I reminded her.

"It'll wait. Inhale again." She'd found an open box of Oreos. I hoped they were soggy or ant-ridden. I swore that even if they were in perfect crunchy condition, I wouldn't so much as open one to lick the filling. I had to be bikini-ready for that beach next month. I bent over and let more warm fragrance work on me.

"This guy's field is safe sex for plants," Sasha said.

I stood back up again. "It's hard to imagine a daisy playing around. What do they do about those roots?"

"No, no—it's the birds and the bees. Or the birds and the moths. They spread anther smut—is that a great name or what? Can you imagine a mother daisy warning her daughter about *anther smut*? You keep your petals closed, you hear? You want to be an anther smut slut like that gladiola nobody talks to anymore?"

"Why aren't we talking about the thing you brought for the Not-a-Garage Sale?"

"Because it's too stupid and I'm really embarrassed. Forget it."

"Look, Sasha, I know."

"You do?" Her eyes widened.

"That's why I'm here."

"How on earth did you find out?"

"Didn't you expect me to? Or somebody?"

She fiddled with a silver earring. "I'm sorry I did it."

"Don't be. It's nothing to be ashamed of."

"I didn't say ashamed. I said sorry."

"I . . ." This was new and frightening turf I was trodding. No matter what the book said, people I knew didn't get involved with lowlife woman-beaters, certainly not a smart Amazon like Sasha.

I watched her unearth a tarnished silver tray, a souvenir of one of her marriages. She filled the mugs and put them and the Oreo box on the tray, then regally carried it into the living room, where we settled on opposite ends of a forest-green sofa covered with enormous down pillows.

I was suddenly suspicious of my old friend's long, draped sleeves. I had thought of the velvet caftan as eccentric, as was most of her wardrobe, but now I realized it hid every bit of her except hands, face, and the bare feet she tucked under her.

"So, how did you find out so quickly?" she asked.

"I, er . . ." My tongue felt as large as the sofa pillows, and, too late, I remembered that you weren't to mix antihistamines, even of the non-drowsy-making variety, and alcohol, even of the quasi-medicinal sort.

"Looks like I'm in real trouble."

I credited her jokey tone to nervousness. "I'm here to help," I said.

She stood up. "Okay, I confess and repent. I'll turn it over. I have it here."

Alcoholic antihistamine toxicity had rotted my mind. What *it* could she turn over? The *it* was in my briefcase.

Sasha went to a draped table near the window and lifted something. "I swear I was going to tell you and give a donation. It's not like I'm stealing."

It was a carved wooden picture frame burdened with cherubs and grape leaves and tiny birds with open beaks, all so diminutive they blurred into lumps, like mahogany acne.

"*That's* what you're talking about?"

"Mrs. O'Roarke upstairs donated it, but I couldn't resist."

"You could have said you wanted it, Sash."

"You said teachers got first pick. I'm not a teacher."

"Honestly, who on earth besides you would want the thing?"

She sat back down. "Are you kidding?" She eyed the frame lovingly.

"It's yours," I said. "Consider it a gift from Mrs. O'Roarke." With that nonissue resolved, the unspoken topic again loomed. Just because she'd lifted a picture frame didn't mean she hadn't also donated a frightening book. I risked further pharmaceutical danger by downing more spicy wine for courage. Then I made my voice as casual as I could manage. "Still seeing Mr. Marvelous?" Her latest reminded me of Bluto, with pecs larger than his IQ.

"You are insufferably prejudiced," she said.

A real bruiser, she'd called him a while back. Only an expression, of course, but suddenly an ominous and perverse way to describe a man.

"And the answer is no."

"Why? What did he do to you?" It blurted out. Stupid, I silently shouted at myself.

Sasha looked understandably confused. "He did a lot of extremely interesting things to me," she said. "You want lascivious details?"

"I meant . . . why aren't you still seeing him?"

"Because I'm not farsighted enough. He went home to Wisconsin. To study nursing. Easy come, easy go."

"Sasha, tell the truth. Did he hurt you?"

She shook her head. "He always said he was going to leave. I expected it."

"I don't mean your feelings. I mean you. Your body."

"On purpose?"

"Yes. Did he ever hold a gun to your head?"

"Are you nuts? He's studying to be a *nurse*, Mandy. Besides, no man ever lifted a—" Her eyes narrowed over the rim of her cup. "What's really eating you? You've been edgy since you walked in. I thought it was your cold, but honestly—" She stopped for a second. "Oh, Mandy," she moaned. "Oh, my. I had no idea. But I've read about it. They get desensitized. You can understand, after what they see. But my God, to put his gun to your head!"

"*My* head? Who?"

"You can't let him push you around. He's used to criminals. I see movies. I know. Good cop, bad cop, all that business; but you aren't one of his—"

"I'm not talking about Mackenzie!"

"Who else are you seeing? I thought—"

"Stop thinking. Nobody's hurting me." Even though I'd assumed that Sasha might be the victim, I was, in truth, insulted that she thought I could be. Even though the book had specified that violent men were in every walk of life and in every profession, I had added a small footnote that exempted any man I'd date. "I asked a question," I said. "My class read *Taming of the Shrew* and it led to a discussion of that kind of behavior."

"Abuse?"

I nodded. "But only in general. I don't know anybody like that, do you?"

"How would I know? It's not something people discuss. I remember a cousin of the second or third or once-removed type." She poured us more glog. "She showed up at a family wedding with a black eye. I was about nine and I asked her what happened. She said she'd fallen, and I couldn't figure out how she'd hit her eye, so I asked more questions and everybody shushed me, said I was rude. The family considered her a clumsy woman, always tripping and banging herself up. She looked so sad all the time and her husband was an angry, mean guy."

"Did she—what happened to her?"

"I don't know. They moved away and we never heard from them again and nobody tried to find out. I think we not only had a family skeleton, but we had one with bruises. But who knows what's really happening to anybody?" She looked at me intently. "So okay, Mackenzie doesn't beat up on you. What does he do? And by the way, who's this gal enjoying his Southern hospitality?"

"How did you know it was a—"

"Who is she?"

I refilled my cup until it nearly did runneth over. The more I drank, the less either Mackenzie's guest or my cold symptoms troubled me. "Old friend of the family."

"Not nearly old enough, I bet. You look miserable."

"I'm sick."

"Just barely. You're man-miserable."

"Well, okay, they were involved in college."

Sasha sat up straighter. "An item?"

"Fifteen years ago. Long since and completely over." I was parroting his words, trying to make them believable.

"Why's she visiting after a decade and a half?"

I shook my head. "Just got divorced. They've stayed in touch. Families know each other, or something."

"I don't like the sound of it," Sasha said. "Not that you couldn't do better than a homicide cop who is never around when you need him but who makes time for a Southern belle. Is she? Southern?"

I nodded.

"So Scarlett—" Sasha said.

"Her name's Jinx. As in bad luck."

"Don't worry about her. She's undoubtedly a fluttery dimwit who gets the vapors."

"She's an MBA management consultant." Mention of Jinx's résumé had the same effect on my system as a germ. My throat burned raw and painfully.

"Oh, then she's the hard-as-nails type." I admired Sasha's loyalty, particularly given her disapproval of Mackenzie, or more accurately, of what she saw as my overattachment to him. "A bitch," Sasha said. "A shrew."

Shrew. The word started a headache all over my skull. I didn't want to think beyond this warm overstuffed room, the pleasant haze of wine. But part of me had defected back to the conversation after school, the research project, and then, inevitably, the book. My entire head, even my nose, felt arthritic.

Sasha wasn't the woman crying for help, but that didn't make everything sugar and spice. "There's a book in my briefcase," I said just before I sneezed again. I pulled tissues out of my pocket.

Sasha extracted a volume. "What on earth?" Her voice was heavy with scorn. *"A Million Ways to Meet Men?"*

I blew my nose. "Not that book!" I said, but she was already engrossed, eyes wide, voice astonished.

" 'Smile a lot,' " she read out loud. " 'Try to get on the *Dating Game*.' Honest to God, Mandy! Just because the fuzz has a female visitor, there's no need to be this desperate!"

"I didn't mean that b—"

She shrieked. " '*Go to funerals and pretend to know the deceased. There are lots of cute mourners.*' This is the most disgusting, pornographic—"

My cheeks were on fire, and not from mulled wine. I rummaged in my briefcase. "That wasn't the book I meant," I said. "My mother sent that one. I brought it along as a joke."

"Confess. You carry it with you at all times for inspiration and guidance." Then she looked at her watch and nearly jumped. "Have to rush," she said. "Company's coming in fifteen minutes."

"Mr. Anther Smut?"

"Dr. Anther Smut to you." She fluffed the sofa pillow she'd abandoned. "And nope. Not him. Somebody very un-Bluto. No pecs. No personality. A genuine business degree, like Jinx. Straight job. Even your mother would approve." She started fluffing sofa pillows while I was still on them, unsubtly indicating that I should head for the door.

I put the dating primer back in my briefcase and looked for my coat. "I need to be clear on something," I said. "The items you dropped off weren't all yours, then, were they?"

She picked up the ugly picture frame and looked a little sheepish. "Obviously not."

"There was a carton with your name. It was filled with

books. Do you remember where it came from?'' The question ached, like a verbal sore throat.

She interrupted her frenetic housekeeping to direct a peculiar look my way. ''I didn't filch any books.''

''I didn't say you did. I just need to know where the books came from.''

''But you do know. Remember?''

I was determined not to.

''Sure you do. I told you all about it. For my photo essay on greed, when I went to the baby birthday party? Those five-year-old buggers were terrific. Absolute monsters. Got unbelievable shots.''

I wished I had never asked.

''You look weird,'' she said. ''Are there books missing, too? Or do you think I illegally procured the carton for the sale?'' She laughed. ''Mom was right. One misstep and your reputation's ruined. I should never have touched that picture frame. But check it out yourself.'' She herded me toward the door. ''When your own sister tells you she gave me those books—''

Your own sister. Precisely what I'd been determined not to hear. My own sister.

''Ask her, ask Beth,'' Sasha said.

My degree of not wanting to hear, not wanting to know, was tenfold what it had been an hour ago. Outside Sasha's window the last light of day gasped and dissolved into the gritty sidewalk. The landscape inside her bright apartment felt just as bleak. So did the one inside my brain.

''Ask her,'' Sasha repeated with a tolerant, if patronizing smile for her friend the worrier. ''It'll set your mind at ease.''

I wished I could let her know how incredibly wrong she was.

Four

WHETHER IT WAS COWARDLY OR WISE, I WAS CONSTITUTIONALLY unable to rush to my sister. I went home instead.

I rationalized that it was too cold to drive my aerated car out to the suburbs, that I was sick and buzzed from mulled antihistamines, and that it would be stupid to approach Beth when her husband was home.

And mostly, I tried to tell myself the entire issue was a ridiculous mistake. It was inconceivable that Beth could be abused. Such monstrous acts could not be a part of the last Dick, Jane, Spot, and Baby family in America.

Except, according to the wretched book which I truly wished I'd never opened, they could.

Macavity the cat sat next to the small grocery bag I'd brought in. He yawned and pretended to be only casually interested in its contents. Then he sniffed disdainfully and stalked off as I extracted a can of chicken soup, vitamin C tablets, and a bottle of brandy—the combination either cures you or makes you not care that you're sick. I swallowed a capsule, poured a glassful, and put the Jewish penicillin on to heat. Then I took my briefcase to the sofa and spilled out its contents.

This was a night of daunting alternatives. Quizzes on dangling participles and an SAT vocabulary drill; two editorials about Senior Prom for the school paper, which I advised; a scary book on battering; a potentially battered sister; and my mother's annoying contribution, *A Million Ways to Meet Men*.

I picked up the last and least, and opened it at random. Its author delighted in men, capitals, and exclamation points.

TIP 24: READ A BOOK!!

That was a comfort. Actually, anybody reading that advice was already also following it, although perhaps this wasn't the sort of book the author had in mind. Saying, "Hi, I was just reading a book on how to meet you" lacked a certain subtlety.

> Guys love bright women, and being a person who has read a book makes a woman appear bright! "Read any good books lately?" is a tried and true winner of an opening line.

I tried—and failed—to imagine approaching somebody with that hackneyed phrase. Nonetheless, there was an illustration of a smiling woman and a beaming man holding cocktails, exchanging this badinage and presumably falling helplessly in love.

I felt a sudden almost irresistible urge to clean the house. This is always a sign that my options are becoming desperate.

"If you don't want to actually read a book," she burbled on, "then brush up on a book you've already read, perhaps in school."

What an argument for literacy. Books as sexual aids. Read a book today, get a date tomorrow. Of course, there was the problem of what happened when he discovered that the last book you read was part of your tenth grade syllabus. I threw the pathetic manual to the far end of the sofa, and seriously wondered about my mother's level of desperation. Was it really that terrifying having a thirty-year-old unmarried daughter?

One book down, but I still faced the unmarked papers and, most of all, the other book. I riffled through it again, trying to understand how devoid of hope a person would have to be to cry for help anonymously.

Macavity emitted a poignant meowl. He didn't point a paw at the clock or roll around clutching his stomach, but his message was clear. I apologized, put down the book and went into the kitchen, where I belatedly prepared his repast and listened to my answer machine.

I have some problems with delayed-action phone calls. If a phone rings in a forest and nobody hears it, it's not so bad, because nobody has to do anything about it. Why, then, do we connect it to a life-support machine and keep it artificially alive and unavoidable? Most of all, understanding that, why do I?

The can opener whirred as I checked in with my machine. All day long I am called by computers making sales pitches. I cannot bear thinking about telephone machines which are more sociable than I am, dialing each other in my absence to chat. The concept makes my fillings ache.

Mackenzie was not hostile toward machines. In his foggy twangy-drawl, he sent greetings and infuriatingly vague statements about being tied up for a while.

I imagined Jinx doing the tying, working him over with a rope. I wondered what other Southern perversities she'd cleared through Philadelphia customs. Macavity cocked an ear and purred at the sound of C.K.'s mutterings.

"You like the idea of being tied up?" I asked my boon companion. Then I remembered that game with the twine, cat's cradle, and realized that felines are kinkier than suspected.

Macavity stalked the can opener. These days food was his only passion.

Mackenzie said he'd get in touch. He didn't say when. Or with what.

The next voice was so determinedly chipper I knew she wasn't a friend because I wouldn't have one that perky. I listened to a cheery voice from Teller-Schmidt Learning Centers, a.k.a. TLC, remind me, the way my dentist does, that I had an appointment the following afternoon. I felt annoyed and patronized. The tutoring center had dealt with adolescents for too long.

Macavity emitted a plaintive plea. While the TLC voice chirruped, I absently plopped fishy kitty gorp on his plate, thinking about tutoring and incomc, the Mustang's broken rear window, and time on a warm beach.

I bet Jinx went on vacation whenever and wherever she liked.

Jinx. I couldn't fathom a mother's choosing a name that meant something that brings bad luck. Such a name must make its bearer grow up with serious feelings of unworthiness. I hoped.

Or maybe she spelled it Jinks. As in High. A madcap fun-and-games kind of gal.

All this flashed through my mind, like sun on bright water as Ms. TLC completed her merry spiel. She reminded me to bring recommendations and résumé, etc., etc. My only real reservation about the job concerned its moral ambiguity. The way I saw it, the less effective I made myself during school hours, the fewer students I actually taught, the more potential candidates for TLC emergency help I'd produce. Then I'd rack in bucks by miraculously becoming effective in the late afternoon, a pedagogic vampire coming to life as the sun sinks.

Macavity sniffed my offerings, checked that nothing better was available, and nibbled. I endured a whiny message from a senior who'd lost his contact lenses and whose parents refused to buy him a new set and who, therefore, could not possibly do his term paper. My thoughts veered to my own undone assignment, the book on the sofa. My sister.

I'd talk to Beth. I would. A little later. When I felt less afraid I'd be intruding, when—

I was so absorbed by my inner debate that I thought I was hallucinating, hearing her voice. But the senior had finished his lament and been replaced by my sister.

The book had indicated that violence often escalated during pregnancy. I couldn't remember if that line had been underlined or not.

"I have galloping postnatal cabin fever," Beth's tape-recorded voice said. "I know you have better things to do, but if you come visit, I'll do something nice for you. How 'bout I'll tell Mom you're engaged? Get her off your case. I'll make him splendid. A congressman, an, um, environmental activist or a movie producer. Wait—how about a venture capitalist? Your call."

She certainly didn't sound desperate, except for company.

"Come on out!" She sounded like a late-night used car salesman. "They don't call this neighborhood the *Main* Line for nothing."

Truth was, TLC's administrative office was a ten minute drive from Beth's house. I don't keep an eye out for omens, but this seemed a cosmic shove in my sister's direction.

I returned her call and she answered on the first ring, as if she'd been sitting with her hand poised over the receiver. My metabolism speeded up thinking of the book and Beth, and I grabbed for a last excuse not to do what I knew I had to do. "I have a head cold," I said. "I could be contagious."

"Alexander has no choice but to be hearty. His big sister is sniffling, as are all her friends. Don't worry. I'll keep him away from you. Even Sam's been feeling—"

My brother-in-law's name produced goose bumps. Good old Sam, a man whose only fault heretofore was intense blandness. "Come after school, spend some time," Beth said. "We'll have dinner, too. Sam's working late tomorrow."

I had no option but to do the right thing. "I have to stop at TLC first. I may tutor for them." I wasn't going to explain why, because Beth might remind me that I could vacation free of charge with our parents in Florida, a hop and jump from a certifiably warm beach. But the price was too high. Any woman who could send her daughter that book . . .

"That's Wynn Teller's place, isn't it?" Beth said. "Give him my regards, and Lydia, too, if she's there. She sometimes does office work for him." Beth knew at least three counties worth of volunteers. "I haven't seen her since the Valentine musicale. Gadzooks—that's a year!"

The innocuous conversation was bizarre, given my real concerns. Or maybe my concerns were bizarre.

"Alexander slept through the night," Beth said.

"Great. By the way—make him an oral surgeon."

"Alexander?"

"My fiancé. Your little joke? Don't you think Mom would find that more stable? Recession-proof."

"Ah, yes. I'd forgotten Mr. X."

"Bernard," I murmured, sipping brandy. "Yes. As in Saint."

"I'll be sure and tell her." I could almost hear the smile on Beth's face.

"Oh, you definitely must," I joked back. "That is just what the woman needs. You know, she sent me a book on how to snare men."

"Again?"

I sighed. "It tries so hard, it's kind of funny. I'll bring it over. But I might have to stay a long time. One of its big, capitalized rules is: 'Wherever you go, don't leave until you've met someone!' That of course means someone male."

"Does Alexander count?"

"Sure. The book also says: 'Don't be a numbers slave! Consider him, not his age!' No reason to think there's a bottom limit. Five weeks will do."

"Did you memorize the book, Mandy? Mama will be so proud."

Beth certainly sounded at ease, normal, even glowingly happy. My suspicions were ludicrous. Still, I double-checked. "Listen—you're okay, aren't you?" I asked.

"Okay? Me?" I could hear worry in her voice, and I knew it was for and about me and my questions. I felt even more uncomfortable.

"Yes, you. Aside from a need for grown-up company."

"Well, sure. Why, do I sound too dreadful? Are you worried about postpartum depression? Forget it. I'm fine. Tired, but fine."

And then Alexander howled and the conversation was over and I returned to the sofa, the tissues, the cat, and the book about wife-battering.

The more I read, the more upset I became. Even the historical sections that I'd skipped before were unnerving. "Our popular figure of speech, 'rule of thumb,' is derived from old English common law which decreed that the stick with which a man beat his wife could not be thicker than his thumb." Even formerly innocent language seemed corrupted now.

"Queen Elizabeth, in an effort to reduce after-hours noise, decreed that husbands could not beat their wives after ten P.M."

I felt increasingly overwhelmed and immobile, intensely aware of the frightening possibilities in being the so-called weaker sex.

"The view of women by the law is historically dismal. Not that long ago, law books still had footnotes saying, 'The above is not applicable to children, idiots, and married women.' "

Even so, the weight of semidistant history was nothing compared to the numbing current statistics and psychological data. I was completely caught up in—or trapped by—the text, blinking hard and feeling the sting of tears. I didn't even look up when I was interrupted by a ring.

Or when I heard a second ring. I kept reading. The machine would pick up.

It didn't. It couldn't. Machines don't pick up for doorbells. One slug of brandy and my brain disappears, so it took me a while to comprehend this. A long enough while that there was now knocking outside—and then the familiar scritch of a key.

Mackenzie walked in. Even though he had used our code of ringing, knocking, and, if there's no objection—verbal or via extra chains—coming in, I was still shocked to see him, and it must have shown.

"Said I'd be in touch," he said. "Haven't seen you in a while and I . . . gee, you look . . ."

"I think disgusting is the appropriate word."

Knowing he was spending excessive time with a former love had not brightened my outlook on life, but having him drop by—comparison shopping, perhaps?—when I looked like the *before* portion of a cold-remedy ad just about did me in. And then matters got worse.

"Jesus!" he shouted. "Your house's on fire!"

I turned and looked toward the sliver of kitchen. My eyes still stung, but I realized it might not be completely due to either the book I'd been reading or my cold. Dark smoke dripped off the kitchen fixtures, billowed over the counter.

"Extinguisher!" Mackenzie said. "Where is it?"

"There." I waved, but it was harder finding the fire, which seemed all smoke, no substance.

"How could you not notice?" he shouted.

I stood tall and kept silent. It is difficult to dignify the heartbreak of clogged nasal passageways. It is also difficult to smell anything in that condition.

Like the old saying doesn't bother to mention, an unwatched pot does indeed boil. First its contents do. Eventually, they evaporate. Then you have an unwatched pot of carbonized chicken noodle traces trying to boil itself. My pot was halfway to the molten state.

Mackenzie stood back—smugly, I thought—as I pulled the steaming, smoking mess off the range and opened the back window, thereby ensuring both humiliation and pneumonia.

I coughed and sneezed and blew my nose and felt like crying.

"Boy," he said, which was probably pretty innocuous, but it sounded like a devastating condemnation to me.

"I have a cold!" No sympathy whatsoever. Maybe colds got their name because of how chilly people are about them. Mackenzie could have commiserated, listened to my strained breathing, considered the dull ache between my ears. He could have provided tea and sympathy, but all he did was nod and say "Boy" again. He sat down on the sofa.

I sat down across from him, on my one comfortable chair. I was determined to sound normal, not like a sneezing frump who'd unwillingly fumigated her house. "So," I said. "How's everything?"

"Real good." He grinned. I wanted to slug him.

"Your . . . friend . . . she arrived, then?" I tried to sound casual, but I was enduring the irresistible tickle of a not-quite-here sneeze pinging through my sinus cavity, dancing up my nose, while I looked ever more stupid, my mouth half open, my tissue at the ready as I gasped—*ah-aaaaah*—and nothing happened.

Mackenzie paid no heed. "She's real stressed out. Y'know, her job's tough, and she's been through a rough divorce."

"But *I* have a cold!" Bud I hab a code. Stirring words, there.

He stared. Sighed. Shook his head. "Fix your car yet?"

I felt firmly put in my place. Still, if he actually expected me to sympathize with the emotional problems of his old flame who didn't have a head cold and who could afford plane tickets and intact convertible tops—if he thought I cared one whit about the well-being of his camellia, he was even more stupid than I was, which was saying a great deal today.

I tried to find a discreet way of asking what I wanted to know. I couldn't. "Where's she staying?" I blurted as subtly as a flare gun. I sounded precisely as jealous and hostile as I was. "I mean," I added, "I'm interested in what hotel you suggest to out-of-towners."

"Actually," he said.

I understood.

He looked uncomfortable, a tad uneasy.

"She's staying with you." Now I felt congested all the way down to my ankles.

"I wouldn' say *with*. But *in* my apartment, yes. There's that sofa bed contraption, you know. Besides, I'm out most of the time. Made sense to me. And to her."

I'll bet it did. It also made sense to me, only I didn't want to dwell on what it was I sensed.

"I came over to ask if you wanted to join us tonight. There's a trio down on Arch Street . . . but you look peaked. Maybe when you're feelin' better?"

I tried to remember the last time Mackenzie had taken me to hear a trio, a duet, or a solo. Instead, I remembered times he'd intended to do so, and crimes that prevented it. Maybe Philadelphia's dark side would prevail and Jinx would wind up with the late show, not Mackenzie. I felt a twinge of shame at more or less wishing for a homicide to detour the man, but a person can live with an occasional twinge.

Instinctively, Mackenzie examined his surroundings as if he were at a crime site, and naturally, despite all the alternative stimuli, he spotted the book containing a million methods of meeting males. He held it up, turned it over, opened it. "Assigned readin'?" he asked.

"By my mother."

Mackenzie nodded, then read out loud. What was it about

this book that forced readers to recite its contents? " 'Find a church without white-haired people and join up.' " He raised his eyebrows almost to his salt and pepper curly hair. "There's a certain religious spirit missin', don't you think?" He turned pages. " 'Choose a hobby men like. Buy or borrow somebody's collection so you seem credible.' My God! I thought you women were doin' your own thing now, bein' your own people. This sounds like the great white hunter in the jungle, catching critters and wearing camouflage!" He tossed the book back onto the sofa.

I felt as humiliated as if I'd written the rubbish myself.

"Your mom's gone baroque, don't you think?" He sounded mildly amused, but distracted, and then I saw he'd picked up the book my mother hadn't sent me.

"Why?" he asked. It upset me that he was more shocked by my having a book on battering than a disgusting date manual.

"It was in the stuff donated to the Not-a-Garage Sale."

"But why bring it home?"

"It's underlined."

"What are you, a fanatic? The English teacher tracks down the book defacer and gives him a detention?"

"Her. It belonged to a woman."

He fanned the pages, stopping to read, but his only reaction was a frown.

"See the notes in the margin?"

He nodded and slapped the book shut. "Why'd you bring it home?" he asked quietly.

"Some woman's in big trouble. Calling for help."

"Oh, Mandy." His voice was weighted with sorrow. "Don't. This is none of—"

"How can I ignore it? Could you?"

"Domestic violence is the worst. The most dangerous call. Stay out of it."

"But she says he'll kill her. There's a crime waiting to happen—happening!"

"There are always crimes waiting to happen. Stay away from them."

"Does a person have to be dead before you care? This woman's—"

"This woman's a stranger. You'll never find her. If she'd wanted to be found, she'd have written her name. She wanted to complain. Makes no sense to write an anonymous call for help. It's a game, like hide and seek. A prank. Maybe even somebody who knows you and knows you'll tool off on a wild goose chase. Or somebody writing a paper, underlining important—"

"The comments in the margin! How can you ignore them?"

Mackenzie is tall and lean and has a nice, slouchy Southern rhythm that often leaves me weak at the knees. But right now his posture and pronunciation both seemed infuriatingly casual. "Hey," he said mildly. "Ease up. I'm not the one hittin' on anybody. But assumin' she exists, why hasn't she gone to a shelter?"

"The book explains. I just read about it. It's called *learned helplessness*." I had to stop and find a tissue, but he waited, patiently unconcerned.

"They've done experiments," I said, eager to make him understand. "Dogs were given electrical shocks no matter what they did. After a while, the dogs caught on that nothing would help them escape the pain, so they did nothing. Even when the cage was opened, they stayed where they were and didn't avoid the shock. They'd given up, just the way that woman has."

He raised an eyebrow and looked unimpressed.

I tried harder. "They did it with rats, too—held them tight until they gave up trying to move, and after enough of that, when they were put in water, even though rats can swim, they didn't try. They drowned. They'd learned they were helpless, don't you see? That's exactly what happens to battered women."

He nodded—grudgingly, I thought. "It's awful, I understand, but that doesn't mean it has anything to do with you," he said. "Besides, this book could be old. These underlines could have been made any time." He kept his voice reasonable, which made me angrier.

"The copyright is last year."

"A year's a long time."

We had hunched and tilted our bodies and now stood

tensely, like duelists facing off before the count. It crossed my mind that Jinx, the sugarplum fairy, probably never, ever disagreed or behaved in this unladylike a manner.

"What do you want me to do?" I shouted, hoarsely. "Wait until he murders her?"

"Calm down," he said. There is nothing more infuriating than a man with nothing at stake telling a woman with a lot at stake to calm down. "You found a secondhand book that could have come from anywhere, could've been donated by one of a few hundred school families, or their friends, or somebody who left it in their beach house, or—"

"But what if you thought the person who donated it was—" I couldn't finish the sentence or admit the book had come from Beth's garage, but I wondered whether Mackenzie's interest level would change if I dared to say so, or whether his work had given him an incurable compassion disability.

"Was what?" he asked. "Was who?"

"A person you cared about."

He looked annoyed, as if I'd said something irrelevant.

My throat was tense, making it more acutely scratchy. "It doesn't matter who it is—except it's somebody in big trouble. Somebody who needs help."

"Mandy, I—"

"You're so damned smug!" It was useless. I couldn't budge him physically or emotionally. I felt diminished and powerless. Put me in a tub right now, I'd drown along with those rats.

"You'd better hurry," I said. "You'll miss your trio."

He leaned over and kissed me on the temple. "Feel better," he said.

I was glad to double-lock the door behind him and put all the chains across. Then I poured another brandy, chewed another vitamin C, and sat on the sofa staring straight ahead and holding the book on my lap. I felt exhausted, stupid, frightened, and helpless.

I felt a lot like the woman who had underlined the book, and I realized how easy it was to be made to feel like, even to become, her.

Unfortunately, it wasn't at all easy to save her.

Five

TUESDAY LIMPED ALONG THE WAY THE DAYS OF THIS SHORT nasty month were wont to do. On its second day, a few counties over, Punxsutawney Phil, the oracular groundhog, had seen his shadow, predicted a long, hard winter, and gone back into hibernation. Groundhogs knew how to handle February.

My ninth graders discussed Poe's "The Pit and the Pendulum," always fun, and definitely the literary high of the morning, the rest of which was devoted to oral book reports and still more SAT preparation. I spent my lunch hour in my classroom with an apple and a warm Coke. I had yogurt waiting down in the faculty lounge refrigerator, but I wanted to be alone. I wanted to read the book on battering again, hear her again.

And last period, Rita came through and led a discussion of attitudes about women as reflected in *Taming of the Shrew*. Of course, she wouldn't have phrased it that way, but I was nonetheless delighted. Even seeing WILLIE SHAKESPEARE IS A CHAUVINIST PIG scrawled on the board made me happy.

In fact, I felt altogether better today, more in control. I was going to handle the various crises of my life—money, sister, maybe even Mackenzie—in a reasonable order, and do what could be done. It all sounded sane and soothing, and even my cold had retreated to a dull occasional buzz in the ears and mind.

That's why it was particularly irritating to have Helga the Office Witch disrupt the debate—by now a heated discussion of women, men, and power—with an embarrassed messenger who informed me that I must read his missive to my class. Immediately. I cleared my throat and followed instructions.

" 'Three pounds (bulk) of processed American cheese are missing from the cafeteria.' "

Derisive laughter slowly, inaudibly, bubbled up from the floorboards, like lava boiling below the surface.

" 'Miss Hagenfuss, our Chief Dietician, is very concerned about this and further evidence of pilfering (details of which are not being released at this time) and we wish to remind the students of this school that stealing is never to be taken lightly. If you have any information concerning this or related crimes, please remember that it is part of your honor code and civic responsibility to notify the office.' "

"Ooooooeeee!" somebody whistled from the rear of the room.

I handed back the note and walked to the window. Sometimes it calms me down to look out at the small park below and think about its long history and all the lives that have crossed it since Penn's Greene Towne was first planned.

At the moment the square looked desolate. Old newspaper pages blew around empty benches. Lives were being lived elsewhere.

"Hey, kids, wanna know who the cheese thief is?" Joey Michaels's voice worked better than the long shadow of history. I turned around and laughed, and along with them, I faced the fuddled, puny ninth grade messenger and sang, "M-I-C, K-E-Y, M-O-U—" He left. We never did get all the way back to Willie Shakespeare's problems, but we were close when there was once again tapping on the classroom door.

"Yo! What's missing now? The macaroni to go with the cheese?"

But I opened the door on Neil Quigley, who looked likely

to drop if left unsupported. I closed the door behind me and took his elbow. "What is it?" I asked. "Angela? Has something happened?"

"Yes," he said. "I have to go. Yes. My class—could you cover . . . ?" I glanced at the clock. There were only four minutes left to the school day. His class would disperse before he was out of the building and before I could get to them. He obviously hadn't even noticed.

"Where is she? What's happened? Can I help?"

"She?"

"Angela!"

"No, I meant something happened. Not to her," he whispered. "It's my center. My tutoring center. It's gone."

The poor man had snapped. "Neil, buildings don't disappear. It was there yesterday and it's there today. Please, sit down, have a drink of water, rest a—"

"Burned to the ground. They just notified me. Happened three hours ago. Took this long for them to track me down. I—I—I'm ruined. Absolutely ruined. Everything's gone."

"No," I assured him, without any idea of what reality might be. "That's terrible, but it's insured, isn't it? TLC will rebuild. You aren't ruined."

"You don't understand. It's gone. Everything."

He was right, at least as far as my not understanding went.

The bell rang and Neil left, but first he turned around again and said, "Gone."

And I still didn't understand, but I was glad he was on his way home where, perhaps, he could simmer down in peace.

Shortly thereafter, I left for the mother of all TLCs, the office that administered all the franchises. I was accompanied by letters of recommendation, a copy of my college transcript, and my résumé. It had been a long time since I'd applied for a job, and I was nervous, but in a noncrucial way.

I fantasized the potential rewards of tutoring, beginning with the new convertible top and spinning far into lucrative mirages of trips to Europe and Tahiti—why not? Also an Oriental rug for the living room and even the jet-trimmed black silk evening suit in Bonwit's window and a place to wear it.

By the time I reached the center, the fertile fields of my mind, or the fertilizer in those fields, had turned tutoring into the ultimate game show, with everything I ever wanted behind Student Number Three.

The executive offices resembled a furnished desert. Only the clothing and flesh of two waiting people, one rubber plant, and random carpet stains broke the monochromatic beigeness. On one pale chair a man with rich walnut skin examined his cuticles. On a café au lait love seat, an angular matron in brown plaid and a snit flicked through a magazine so vigorously, she ripped three pages while I watched.

A cutout in the wall revealed, with a little effort, a receptionist, also color coordinated. She held up a finger, stared at her amber computer screen, and pushed a button that made a soft blip, the only noise in the room besides paper tearing and impatient sighs. I tried to understand what she was doing. I'd just suffered through a required faculty orientation for the school's new computer. Very little of it had penetrated.

Finally, the receptionist looked up, pushing back a lock of ash-blonde hair. When I told her my name, she nodded solemnly. "Mr. Teller's running late," she whispered, as if we were in a doctor's office. "We're so sorry. But you're next—the others are waiting for Mr. Schmidt—so it shouldn't be too long."

On the wall, next to the rubber tree, was a framed copy of the *Philadelphia Magazine* article that Edie Friedman had mentioned. It was headlined TLC TELLS THEM HOW TO LEARN AND THEY PAY FOR THE PRIVILEGE. Just as Edie had said, there was a flattering photo of Neil Quigley, typical happy professional franchisee. It seemed a horribly ironic choice, particularly today.

For lack of more interesting options, I read the article, one of those heartwarming all-American, upward and onward here-in-our-own-city epics. Poor but honest Wynn Teller had been bred in the Midwest, worked his way through state college, taught in various cities, then started the first Teller Learning Center, which multiplied and became a franchise. He was married to the former Lydia Ballantyre, only child of the late naturalist team of Lydia and Hubert Ballantyre. Lydia and Wynn were the parents of a son, Hugh.

His partner Schmidt's background had a similar triumphant trajectory. His only liability, as far as I could see, was his name. Cliff Schmidt sounded like a sneeze, or a German aircraft. In lieu of a wife with scientific credentials, he had a background Dickens would have loved. He was an authentic foundling. Pure Horatio Alger. Pure PR gold.

After the statistics, there was a great deal of philosophizing about TLC's ability to tailor education to the individual child, and about how gratifying it was to help both students and teacher-franchisers.

The article had the sound of a movie-of-the-week description. I was not thrilled, however, only bored. I saw the rest room down a short hallway and decided to follow Queen Victoria's advice and use a facility any time one had the opportunity. My interview might be long or harrowing.

Upon my return, I passed the partners' closed—camouflaged in beige—doors. The one with C. Schmidt on it failed to muffle agitated sounds like "cheated" and "damn it" and "screw you" and "criminal." Not quite the vocabulary or tone I'd expected in an educational haven.

I sank into a small dune of a settee. The magazines on the dun end table all dealt with parenting, the better to increase the guilt of anyone with an underperforming child. In desperation, I read a column on bed-wetting, skimmed a list of great vacation spots for kids—so I could avoid them—and was studying the six early warning signs of eye-hand coordination problems when the front door opened with a great blast of deep winter.

And suddenly there was Technicolor in the room in the shape of a short woman capped by a white fur hat and wrapped in a poison-green greatcoat that reached to her ankles. "Where's Wynn Teller?" she demanded of the room at large.

I happily discarded the magazine even though I had four warning signs left to go.

The receptionist stuck her head out into the room. "Excuse me? Do you have an appointment?"

The woman in the greatcoat laughed, a solid *hah!* like comic book characters make. "I don't need one," she said, waving her arms. One peacock, fingerless glove held a copy of *Philadelphia Magazine*, the other a green and blue lizard clutch purse.

"I'm sorry, ma'am, he's—"

Ma'am slipped off her coat and hung it on a tan peg on the wall. "Tell him Fay's here." Her voice was pure brass, constitutionally incapable of being soft. She waved to the three of us on our beige upholstery as if she were, indeed, a visiting celebrity. "Fay," she trumpeted again.

I put her at forty in years as well as chest, waist, and hip size. She was a sausage with cleavage and red-purple hair.

"Nonetheless, Miss Fay—" the receptionist began.

Fay rolled her eyes skyward. "*Mrs.*, honey. I served my time." She wore a layered black net skirt over a leopard body suit, a fashion statement generally made by rebellious girl-children twenty-five years and fifty pounds lighter. I snuggled into my seat with the same happy expectation I feel when a first act curtain goes up.

The receptionist was not as entertained as I. "If you'll leave a message, I'm sure—"

"I left enough messages yesterday and the day before, and I don't have forever. I'm only in town for the New Age festival." She turned and addressed us, her audience, directly. "I'm an aromatherapist." I felt she expected us to react by battering down Teller's door on her behalf. You don't keep an aromatherapist waiting.

"As I've said, he doesn't have time today for—"

"We'll see about that." She sat down next to me with a scratchy crunch of tulle netting. She adjusted the neckline of her leotard and centered a chain full of amethyst crystals so that pale purple cylinders filled her cleavage. She smoothed the magazine on her lap, then looked up and pointed at the article on the wall. "Hah!" she shouted, as if she'd made an important discovery. She swiveled toward me. "You read that?"

I nodded.

"Good idea, wasn't it?" She waved her copy of the magazine. It looked puckered with handling.

"Having the article? Great publicity for the—"

"I mean this place. TLC. This is the good idea. And by the way, you should wear rust and burnt oranges. You're an autumn, you know, with the auburn hair and green eyes. I did colors before I got into aromatherapy."

"Thanks." I wasn't sure if that was an autumnal response. I was sure, however, that orange was my least favorite color.

"Yeah," she said. "This place was a good idea. I thought so, too. When I thought of it."

"You thought of . . . ?"

The gentleman in tweed and the anxious matron in plaid were pretending not to hear her, which was ridiculous. People in North Jersey were catching these sound waves.

"I had no idea," Mrs. Fay continued. "I'm in this Unfoldment of the Spirit workshop and I see this magazine somebody left and there's his name on the cover and his face inside." She shook her hennaed curls, then leaned forward and waved in the direction of the receptionist. "Hey, you! Why don't you see what happens when you tell him Fay's here?"

"He's in a—"

"—pretty pickle. That's what he's in." Fay grinned.

"Really, miss." Cuticle man pursed his mouth, keeping his eyes on his fingernails. "We're waiting, too, you know. Show some patience and take your turn."

Fay raised her eyebrows. "A person can wait too long." She nodded, crimson curls bobbing. "I know this from experience." She stood up and tottered on stiletto heels over to the receptionist. I thought of all the times I'd lifted a ridiculous outfit off a rack and asked who on earth would wear such a thing. Now I never needed to ask again.

"I have a seminar on aromatic past-life regression in exactly one and one-half hours," she said.

I was so engrossed in her performance that I didn't immediately register the opening of Cliff Schmidt's office door. It was hard paying attention to anything except Fay, who, arms akimbo, ended her dickering with the receptionist by announcing, "Okay, honcy, forget Fay. Just tell Wynn Teller his wife's here."

Even the woman in plaid stopped flipping magazine pages and gaped.

"His wife my—!" The receptionist's skin became too florid for the color scheme. "Don't you think I know Mrs. Teller?" She swiveled out of sight, but I could still hear her. "This place," she said to somebody else inside the cubicle. "It used to be sane, but lately—"

Through which, Fay took diva-size deep breaths, visibly revving up again. I looked around and decided the other spectators were equally pleased that life had dropped the script and was improvising. Only then did I truly notice the open door to Schmidt's office, Schmidt himself, and my fellow voyeur. "Neil!" I said. "I thought you went home!"

"I didn't expect you here, either. I thought I said . . ."

I hadn't heeded his advice to stay away from the place, but he had given it without knowing about my Tahitian fantasies, or even about my convertible top.

Schmidt, a blocky beige fellow who blended into his surroundings like an iguana in sand, patted Neil's shoulder throughout Fay's outburst, soothing him, or trying to. It appeared to be futile making nice to a man whose business had just burned down.

By now, Schmidt wasn't giving Neil his complete attention. With all due modesty, I have to say he seemed very interested in me, giving me that full-forward, total sensory intake that men do—at the beginning. I felt flattered, then uncomfortable. "Neil and I work together," I said. He nodded. "He's told me a lot about the center." I smiled and seemed to embarrass him. He looked away.

"Wife," Fay blared. "Like I said. His first. His only. Mother of his children. You mean he forgot to mention us?" She laughed, not the comic book explosion now, but an angry bellow. "So did the guy who wrote the magazine story. Everybody forgot about us—except us!"

"Cliff," the receptionist said, "could you, er, lend a hand with this, um, matter?"

Maybe he could have, but just then the second pale door

opened and Wynn Teller, chuckling softly, ushered out a woman in mink. "You'll see how quickly his scores perk up, and—"

His good-looking face drained of color.

"Long time no see," Fay said. She lifted her copy of *Philadelphia Magazine* as a greeting or a warning.

Wynn looked from her to the furry matron on his arm. He patted his client's shoulder, then handed her a beige and white packet. "The receptionist will help you with the forms and any questions we forgot to cover." He took her around the corner and returned alone. "What do you want?" he asked Fay, softly.

"I'm in town for my convention," Fay blared, "and I see this magazine and I have no idea, absolutely no idea—"

"I think you'd better leave," Teller said.

"I think I'd better stay and *you'd* better talk to me. Alone." You could hear her strain to lower her voice, to address only him, but the room was small and her whisper was a battle cry.

"Now, miss," Clifford Schmidt suddenly said, putting a pale freckled hand on her shoulder.

"Mrs.!" she shouted. "Mrs. Wynn Teller!"

Mr. Wynn Teller looked tired. "I have nothing to say to you." His surface was calm, but I had a sense of inner organs trembling.

Her jaw dropped open so that her mouth formed a perfect fuchsia circle. "Nothing? What about stealing?"

Cliff and Neil both gaped. "What?" they said in chorus.

"What about lying?" Fay asked. She waved the magazine again. "What about—"

Teller took one of her leopard-patterned arms.

"Ow!" She jerked away. "Don't you dare touch me!" She clamped a hand on her hip in a Mae West pose. "Think you're so famous with stories in magazines that you can push me around? Think I don't have proof? I kept the letters, Wynn. I'll sue the bejesus out of—"

"Please," he said. "This is my office. These people aren't—"

"Think I care who hears? Think they don't believe in fairness?'' She turned to all of us, waving her arms for emphasis. ''Don't you believe in justice for all?''

Nobody appeared to, because we were all silent, perhaps sharing the embarrassment I felt for Wynn Teller. I stood up. ''I think I'll reschedule for another—'' I began.

Wynn Teller shook his head. ''Stay,'' he said. ''This is only—''

''I want my share!'' she shouted.

''Cliff,'' Teller said, ''could you . . . ?''

Schmidt seemed to read his mind, maneuvering Fay toward his office while she spluttered and protested.

''Hey! I'm next, Schmidt! No fair!'' The paper ripper was acutely unhappy. Nobody paid attention except the receptionist, who offered coffee all around.

Wynn Teller led me into his office, which was a shock to the system with its deep palate of non-neutral maroon and navy. There were even colorful abstract paintings on the wall. He apologized profusely for what he called the *unpleasantries*. He had the wholesome good but not handsome looks of the fellow who's always cast as the best pal of the romantic lead. ''Unfortunate woman,'' he said. ''Quite disturbed, but convincing nonetheless, because she believes her delusions. I feel sorry for her, and I hope you won't take any of her nonsense seriously.''

''You know her, then?''

''I know of her. Flipped-out Fay, they call her. She surfaces now and then, claiming credit for something successful. She tried this with the guy who first split his movie palace in two. That was her idea, too. As was the video arcade, when that was popular. Anything that gets publicity.'' He paused, closed his eyes, then nodded and his face relaxed, bit by bit. ''She'd sue the U.S. government, insist she invented democracy, if it got better press.''

And that was it for Crazy Fay. We settled down to business. TLC had standardized a teaching process and created workbooks, tests, and progress reports. Beyond that, it seemed a matter of time slots and paychecks.

Teller even outlined the mechanics of franchising. ''Of course,'' he said, ''I recognize that a teacher looking for a tutoring position isn't likely to have the necessary investment capital. That's why we created our slow-owner plan whereby we, in essence, loan you the money, rather like a bank finances your home with a mortgage. You pay it back over time, out of your earnings.''

I was impressed and intrigued. Only Neil Quigley's warnings stood in the way. ''I'm at Philly Prep,'' I said, easing into it.

''Yes,'' he said. ''I believe you once taught my son.''

I nodded. ''How is he?'' Teller's desk had a silver-framed photo of an elegant woman with a cameo face. His wife, I presumed. There was no picture of his moon-faced son.

''Ah,'' he said vaguely. ''It takes some of them longer than others to grow up, find their footing, as you well know.''

''He must be . . . sixteen?''

''Just turned eighteen.''

I was getting old, misjudging the passage of time. ''Is he in college?'' I asked. ''I was always so impressed by his singing, too. Is he doing anything with it?''

Teller looked surprised, and I suddenly remembered I wasn't supposed to be interviewing him, asking about his family. This was a job interview and I was muffing it. ''I'm sorry,'' I said. ''I didn't mean to—''

But now he was beaming, eyes crinkly and endearing. Further evidence of the tired truism that all the good ones are taken. ''What a caring, supportive teacher you are!'' he said. ''After all these years, to remember one little boy so well. You're exactly the breed we're looking for!''

Given that praise, and an irresistible desire to please him, I felt reluctant to raise a potentially unpleasant point. Nonetheless, I felt obliged to behave like an adult. ''I teach with Neil Quigley,'' I said.

''Poor man! To have something like that happen—and now, when so much of his life is in upheaval.'' He shook his head. ''Arson, the police are saying. Kids. Dropouts. A street gang. Just for the hell of it.'' He looked crushed.

''You can't save them all,'' I said softly.

He nodded and sighed. ''Of course, as far as Neil's concerned, we'll rebuild for him, refinance. And in the meantime, I know Cliff's working something out. We don't abandon our own."

Nice. Very nice. But still. "I gathered—before the fire—that Neil was having some problems. Financially, with the franchise."

Teller looked sad again. "Neil Quigley is an exceptional teacher but possibly not exactly a businessman. The system's designed for that—few number crunchers go into teaching, which is why we take care of that side. But Neil is, perhaps, even a little less . . . or, it could simply be all the pressures on him at this time. My point is, you mustn't generalize from one example. Speaking out of school"—he winked at me after his little wordplay—"we'll be working more closely with Neil from now on. He'll be fine."

He asked if I had any questions, but I couldn't think of any, so I was offered a packet of information to look over.

"What a day for your introduction to us!" he said. "A lunatic and a fire. I hope you understand things are generally more subdued." We thanked each other profusely. Not until I was outside, in my windy car, did I realize two things. One was that I'd never found out what had become of little Hughie Teller. And more important, I was still carrying my manila envelope of required material. I'd been so tense, I'd clutched it tight the entire interview.

I could understand my nervousness, but not Teller's. None of the obvious, basic questions had been asked. I wasn't even certain whether he knew what my subject area was. And yet interviewing candidates must have been second nature to him by now.

Unless, despite his serene exterior, despite his casual dismissal of the crazy lady's claims, she'd derailed him. And if so, why?

Six

BETH'S HOUSE HAS ALWAYS SEEMED AN OASIS OF CALM, sometimes annoyingly, phlegmatically so. It is dust- and anger-free, or so I always thought. It was nearly impossible to imagine its adult inhabitants raising their voices, let alone fists.

But I didn't spend all that much time with my sister, because our lives don't have a lot of crossover points. To some extent, Beth is a living museum, the Fifties *before* photo contrasted with today's woman. She wears aprons and bakes cakes from scratch and performs unpaid good deeds for family, friends, and community.

The truly happy homemaker.

At least I always thought so.

But maybe I was only invited over during what the book identified as Phase Three—the loving, repentant final third of the violence cycle. Maybe when the tension built again, Beth stopped calling and we all looked the other way, like Sasha's bruised family skeleton.

I INSPECTED BETH DURING THE LONG-DISTANCE, GERM-FREE kissing and cooing over baby Alexander, still curled in his prenatal position, but outside his mother nowadays, in a sling she wore on her belly.

"Don't stare," she said. "I know I'm still a tank. If he'd

weighed forty-five pounds, I'd be as svelte as you, but he was thirty-eight pounds short."

The house denied the idea of cold or winter or night. Firelight flickered over low, full bookshelves, comfortably upholstered furniture, and a teapot covered by a cozy. Ella Fitzgerald was singing "Just One of Those Things." My niece Karen raced in, hugged, jumped up and down, made note of how silly-looking her baby brother was, then bounded off toward the sounds of "Sesame Street" floating in from the family room. The baby slept close to his mother's heart and we could have been on the set of a prime-time special called "Home Sweet Home." I hoped it wasn't as much a facade as that would be.

Impossible. Beyond this point may lie monsters—but not this particular point. Sometimes, in this setting, I feel the Pauper to Beth's Princess and I yearn to get to the part where our roles are reversed when Beth tackles the singles' jungle, unpaid bills, maladjusted kids, and men in not much better shape. Let me cope with polishing silver and kissing scrapes.

But only sometimes, and only fleetingly, and definitely not tonight.

Beth asked how the interview had gone, and I regaled her with the doings at the Learning Center. "Poor Wynn," she murmured. "Kooks seem the price of fame, don't they?"

"Things were so crazy, I forgot to send your regards to him or his wife," I admitted.

"No matter. I'll see her soon. She missed the last meeting—she has some condition, something that started in Africa when she was a child, and she—" Beth stopped and wrinkled her brow. "Wait a minute—*I* was the one who missed the meeting." She slapped her palm to her forehead. "Sam says my brain's become baby-mush."

She smiled. It wasn't serious. Or was it? Did he secretly criticize her? I remember that from the book, the impossible and desperate attempts to be good enough, to *be* enough. Was it a lack of confidence that drove her to be so devoted and intense a housekeeper? I certainly couldn't fathom any other motive.

She poured me a cup of herbal tea. She was nursing and

avoiding drinker-unfriendly stimulants and substances. "Sam won't be home until late," she said. "Business dinner." She looked distinctly uncomfortable. "So, um, look, I feel funny about this, but . . ." She took a deep, steadying breath.

Now, I thought. She's going to say something before I have to. A shiver ran from my hair follicles to my toenails.

"Karen's feeling displaced," she said while I told my follicles to relax. "The new baby blues. Anyway, she's been begging for pizza at Fireman Dan's, and Sam absolutely refuses, so would you consider—"

"No problem." Karen would be happy, the baby would be asleep, and Beth and I would talk. "Actually, I'm starving." An apple and a Coke last only so long.

Beth drove because her Volvo had car seats and no hole in its hood. "Fireman Dan's!" Karen repeated loudly all the way there.

We saw neither hide nor hair of Dan, but perhaps he'd been trampled by children rushing to push joysticks or climb the firetruck in the middle of the room or cheer the animated cartoons on the walls. Or perhaps he had wandered off, dazed and deafened by screams and clangs, by high-pitched electronic shrieks and zings and Hollywood special effects. My impulse was to follow him, wherever he had gone, as long as it was out of here.

Karen, however, was in a state of bliss. She could play with mutant turtles, and Alexander the dummy couldn't. She could eat pizza, and Alexander the baby didn't even have teeth. "And I can climb the firetruck, and you're too little," she told his sleeping head before she ran off.

"What's happening with Mackenzie?" Beth asked before I had swallowed my first bite of pizza. She's my mother's daughter and possibly her clone. If my mother hadn't mailed me the tome on how to meet men in my spare time for fun and profit, Beth would have. I told her about the visiting Jinx.

"Uh-uh," she said, shaking her head. "I don't like it. Not at all. Asking for trouble."

"Trouble is her name," I said mournfully. But I appreciated the fact that old-fashioned Beth didn't raise the issue of whether men and women could truly be friends. She didn't turn Gertrude Stein-y and remind me that a sofa bed was a sofa bed. She didn't mention that I was supposed to trust Mackenzie, who was, in fact, being open and straightforward about this business.

No. In her archaic, old-fashioned, knee-jerk, thoroughly appreciated way, she simply disapproved, irrevocably, clipping out stern-jawed dictums about decency and respect, terms that usually signal a sibling dispute. Tonight, I had no quarrel with them. Men were rats. I finished the piece of pizza with gusto and debated another one.

"He's abusing your trust!" she said.

Maybe we were pushing it a bit far. He had told me, after all. Maybe I was abusing his trust. And suddenly I was tired of indignation, righteous or not. And without it, only the word *abuse* remained, echoing.

No matter the ridiculous surroundings. When we'd be home again, it would be time for baths and bedtimes and, very possibly, Sam's return. Now or never, despite a background that sounded like a disaster movie. I pushed away the pizza. "Beth," I said, "my school's having something we call a Not-a-Garage Sale this weekend."

"I know." Her eyes dropped to her baby. I couldn't tell if it was a case of adoration of him or of avoidance of me.

"Yesterday, I was sorting books." I paused and waited for a reaction.

Beth raised her eyebrows with polite, but dim, interest.

"The thing is, somebody donated . . ." Donated was too genteel a word. "Somebody put in a book that had . . ."

"Umm?" Eyes still on Alexander. Was this standard obsessive new-mother behavior, or terror?

"I think it had a message. *Was* a message. A call for help."

"Somebody left a note in a book?" she murmured, touching her lips to the baby's hair fuzz.

"Notes in a book. On the pages." My voice was too harsh, fighting the sounds of bedlam and Beth's charade of noninvolvement. "Underlined passages."

"Remember Miss Ardmore and that business about a book's being a holy temple, never to be defaced?" She giggled.

"I'm not talking about that kind of thing. I'm talking about a woman leaving a message in a book that she's being—"

Beth's brow wrinkled. She was listening now.

"That a man is . . ." I remembered the night she tiptoed in and woke me up and showed me her engagement ring. "Hurting her, Beth. Beating her up."

Her eyes narrowed. "Awful," she said. "Who wrote it?"

"Don't you know?"

"Me? How could I?" She rocked Alexander back and forth. He would someday spend time in analysis working through a preconscious Fireman Dan trauma.

She seemed capable of playing Let's Pretend indefinitely. I wasn't. I leaned close. "Beth—it was your book."

"Why on earth are you saying that?"

"Please. Don't be embarrassed or sorry that you broke the silence. You don't have to pretend anymore. No more coverups."

"I have to be honest, Amanda."

"Good."

"You sound insane."

Insane. How had I managed to forget that the woman in the book had been thought schizophrenic because of her lies and coverups? Beth had never been institutionalized.

"Mom! Aunt Mandy! I nearly won! I nearly won! Can I have more quarters?"

Broke or not, with moral reservations or not, beginning to feel creepy and embarrassed or not, I gave the child two dollars to be turned into change by one machine and swallowed by another.

Beth waited until her daughter was gone. Her face was a reserved mask. "Why would you think *I* wrote in your book?"

"Because, well, Sasha told me you gave it to her the day of Karen's birthday party. Remember?"

"No. A book? Karen turned five two weeks after Alexander was born. All I remember was hoping he'd sleep until after they left, and that I'd have the energy to pick up the cake the kids were throwing and squashing." Her expression darkened, features contorting into something close to anger. *Beth* anger, which was scary. "How could you for one minute think Sam—*my Sam* . . . ?'' She sat back in her chair, as if getting as far from me as she could.

''The book,'' I said, feeling lame. ''The book said you couldn't tell. That those men aren't monsters—or not visibly so. They're ordinary men. Doctors, lawyers—''

''Sam wouldn't even whap the dog when we were house-training him. Oh, Mandy, how *could* you?'' She looked ready to cry.

I picked pepperoni off the remaining slice of pizza. ''I guess I can't, really. I'm sorry. But then who could it be? Who is it?''

''I don't have any way of knowing. I haven't *dusted* our books, let alone sorted through them, and I never owned a book about wife-beating.''

''Sorry,'' I said again.

She sighed. ''Sasha confused me with somebody else. That girl can be a flake, you know.'' I could see how tired she was, and I volunteered to wean Karen from the machines.

We returned to the calm and glowing stone house and I endured and somewhat enjoyed supervising and unwillingly sharing some of Karen's bath, but all the while, internal voices reminded me that although Beth was not a victim, somebody still was. If the underliner wasn't my biological sister, did that mean I could ignore her call for help and not even try to extricate her from the hell she lived in?

Except, of course, I no longer had a clue as to how to find her.

''He's asleep,'' Beth said, entering the bathroom. ''But I finally woke up. Or at least caught on. When Sasha was here, I was grumbling about how tired I was and how many projects I'd left undone before Alexander, let alone since.''

Karen, scrubbed and shiny and looking like a pink bunny in footed pajamas, stopped brushing her teeth. ''Alexander, Schmalexander,'' she muttered.

Beth sat down on the edge of the tub and yawned. ''So,'' she said slowly, ''I must have mentioned the garage, which was an absolute mess. I was the drop-off house for Main Line Charities, but they didn't want everything for the silent auction—and the leftovers plus our normal clutter was so bad I couldn't park my car inside. Sasha offered to take a few cartons with her. For your sale. I'm embarrassed to say I still haven't cleaned the garage, so I don't know what she took; but it could have been books." She yawned again. "I'm beat," she said. Then she opened her eyes, stood up and put her hand on my shoulder. "That means I'm *tired*, not wounded, understand?"

"Who donated the books?" I asked.

She shrugged.

Karen lathered her teeth then turned and drooled toothpaste foam. I smiled at her and spoke carefully to her mother. This was not a fitting bedtime story. "You understand," I said, "it isn't over for the underliner. I hope."

Beth stood up heavily, like a woman twice her age. "Somebody probably picked it up at a bus stop. The sort of people we know, the kind of women involved in Main Line Charities. . . ." She shook her head. "They're *nice* people. I don't care what your book says—I mean truly nice people."

"Is that code for people who aren't poor? People who aren't the stereotype?"

"Don't get huffy and self-righteous. Hurry up, Karen!"

"Why won't you say who dropped those books off?"

"Oh, Mandy, I was four years pregnant at that point and not paying much attention. Besides, I won't let you humiliate any of those wonderful people, including yourself. There is no way on earth that Mar—that—"

"Mar? Who?"

"Nobody. Slip of the tongue. There's no way that book has anything to do with anybody I know. Even I, Mandy—it *hurt* having you think I—Sam—could be—"

"Sometimes sisters don't know what's really going on," I whispered. "It's terrible, but it happens."

She shook her head. "You're too fond of playing detective, although I know you mean well. Maybe sometimes it's worth it, but why now? Your boyfriend's off with an old flame and maybe you need some excitement in your life, but not this way!"

Karen padded out to choose her bedtime story. I turned and faced my sister. "I'd stake my life that those messages are genuine. That's a real woman in there. Isn't it worth a little embarrassment to save a life?"

After I'd read a chapter of *The Wind in the Willows* to Karen, I found Beth at the foot of the stairs holding out her address book. "I give up," she said with a half smile. "My error. You'd only root around until you found this and then you'd check out everyone I know whose name begins with *mar*—the Margies and Marnies and Margarets and Marlenes. Which would be even more humiliating. I think Martha Thornton dropped it all off."

I copied Martha Thornton's whereabouts and put on my coat, leaving Beth in peace, at least from me.

"I'll tell you this, though," she said at the door. "Martha didn't donate the books. She doesn't read. That's why she didn't join our book group. You're on an absolute fool's mission, but go ahead. You'll enjoy her." She looked at her watch. "I told her you'd be there by seven forty-five. You have twenty minutes."

"You what?"

"Well, why shouldn't I warn a person that my lunatic sister is on her trail? Even *criminals* get read their rights." And then she leaned back against the foyer wall and issued a profound, world-weary sigh. "Please," she said softly. "Be careful."

"I'm fine," I said. "Just a little deaf from Fireman Dan's."

"I'm serious. I hope you never find her. The real her."

"She's the one in danger. Not me."

"Not yet. Not until you're part of the equation. Things tend to explode when you add an outsider to people's private lives."

I blew her a germ-free kiss. "There's nothing to worry about."

I remember saying that.

"I'm not doing anything dangerous," I added.

I remember saying and believing that part, too.

Seven

I PULLED UP IN FRONT OF A GRAY STONE HOUSE SET WELL back from the road. To my surprise and immediate discomfort, it nestled next to a matching gray stone church.

I hoped Martha was the rectory's cleaning woman or cook. I was ashamed of my class assumptions, but the truth was it would be easier to have the wife beater be anyone but the minister of this serene suburban house of God.

I detoured to the announcement board that informed me the Senior Study Group was meeting there this night and, as my spirits sank, also made note that one Right Reverend Oliver Thornton was their spiritual leader.

I was tempted to drop the quest, slink back to my floppy roofed car and take off. I hadn't counted on this level of complication. In my fantasies, I'd moved with the ease of an androgynous superhero who saw a problem, swooped down, and solved it. End of scene, tremendous applause, over and out. Eat your heart out, Wonder Woman.

I hadn't reckoned on ministers and prestigious congregations.

When the door opened, I realized I hadn't reckoned on Martha Thornton, either.

She was apple-cheeked and white-haired and slightly out of breath. The Pillsbury Dough Grandma wore a purple top hat, tap pants, and matching patent leather pumps. The blouse was white with full, loose sleeves. She held a glittery cane in one hand.

"Me and My Shadow" filtered out of a room farther down the long entry hallway. She tossed the cane up, caught it midway down its shaft, and began to strut her stuff. Or tap it, feet moving double-time back down the hallway, then forward again, heel-toe, side-together, whatever. Her legs weren't at all bad and her timing was impeccable.

"Greetings!" She stopped to lean in time-honored tilted style, both hands on the cane handle. "Tuesdays are for tapping and I wouldn't normally answer the door, but your sister said it was important, dear heart. She also said you were very discreet, so I trust this passion of mine will remain our secret, yes?"

I nodded. "You're very good," I said.

"It's not easy being a minister's wife. Many people confuse devotion with dullness." She closed the door behind me and tapped down the hallway. We stopped near the opening of what would have to be called a front parlor. It was filled with dark upholstery outlined with carved wooden frames, and had the look of having been there for generations, lovingly maintained.

Shuffle-shuffle, tap-tap-tap. Martha Thornton took my coat, slinging it over her shoulder like Gene Kelly in a saucy mood, and tapped it farther down, to a closet.

"Aerobic, you know," she said as she shut the closet door. "Three times a week. Hate jogging and rowing and oh, the righteous slowness of the church walking club." She shuffled off to the parlor, turned off the record player, and returned. "And fun, although my grandchildren think it's disgraceful. You don't, do you?"

"Me? Not at all."

"Good. Now there's coffee brewing in the kitchen. Come along."

I trailed behind her clicking shiny feet. "Wanted to be a Busby Berkeley girl," she said. "Not a star, mind you, but I knew I'd die happy if I was one time part of an overwhelmingly choreographed extravaganza."

We had reached a kitchen that looked out of an ancient

Good Housekeeping. I wondered if it was deliberately kept a relic of Americana, or if the parishioners wouldn't shell out for renovations. In any case, it had a flour bin, enamel drainboards, iron skillets, and not a laminate, microwave, or food processor in shouting distance.

Martha opened the short, round-edged refrigerator and poured milk into a small jug. Cups, napkins, and spoons were on the oak kitchen table. "But I met Oliver," she sighed. "Handsome as a movie star, and dramatic as all get-out. I assumed he was an actor and that we'd take Hollywood by storm. Only he turned out to be a seminarian, and worse, irresistible. Forty years later, here I am. My life with Oliver turned out to be my extravaganza."

She didn't look at all sorry about her choice as she retrieved the coffee canister and poured two cups. "It's unleaded." She shook her head. "Getting old is annoying." She filled a plate with star-shaped cookies covered with pastel sprinkles, then sat down across from me. "Now we have some sort of problem to work through. Is that it?" The tap dancer was gone, and in her place, a good solid standard-issue minister's wife. "I'm so fond of your sister. How is that brand new baby? Adorable, I'm certain. But what's troubling you, love?"

"Maybe Beth's told you that I'm an English teacher at Philly Prep," I began.

Martha raised her brows. "No, she certainly didn't! And what a frightening profession!"

"The kids I teach aren't really all that bad."

She shook her head. "I meant, who talks to you? Surely everybody's as afraid to speak to an English teacher as . . . as I? As me? No, of course not—oh, heavens, do you see what I mean? So intimidating." She put two spoons of sugar in her coffee and frowned as she stirred it.

I doubted I could cure her grammatical insecurities quickly, so I plunged right into the issue. "The school's having a flea market," I said, "and we've gotten donations from everywhere."

"People are sweet, aren't they? Even in hard times. Always try to give myself, although, of course, there's only so much to begin with, and I'm afraid at the moment I'm quite depleted. Of course, I could bake, if you're having a cookie sale."

"I'm not soliciting donations."

"No? Then what on earth?"

"I'm trying to find somebody who donated a particular book."

"Oh, my," she murmured. "A book." Martha Thornton's crepey skin appeared untouched by anything but time. It was difficult envisioning a tap-dancing battered grandmother in the first place.

I felt a twinge, like the first hint of a toothache. Maybe I was a fool, imagining things, stupidly rushing off hither and yon. Maybe all of this was compensation for Mackenzie's being otherwise occupied. Maybe I was even trying to usurp his role as detective. Maybe I was the one who needed help.

Martha interrupted my silent pop psychology session. "How could I possibly assist you with this book that was donated to your school?" she asked softly, patiently.

I swallowed hard. "I thought perhaps it was yours."

"Oh, dear heart, I'm sure Philly Prep is a fine school, but we try to donate to our own Main Line Charities, the local Red Cross, you know—and of course, even then, only when the church can't use the items for a fund-raiser."

I nodded. "This carton had been intended for Main Line Charities, not us."

She pulled back. Only a fraction of an inch, but sharply and immediately.

"I gather your group held a silent auction this time and didn't want the used books," I said.

The skin between her eyebrows puckered.

"My sister said you'd dropped off the carton a while ago—for Main Line Charities—but because they didn't want it, she donated it to us."

Martha Thornton had gone rigid, back straight as the chair spokes. "Your sister is mistaken. Perhaps the strain of having the baby?"

"You didn't drop off the carton?"

She made a mild half-shrug. "I don't think so. Of course,

one is always dropping off and picking up things. But I didn't donate books. A soup tureen, I think." She nodded. "Yes. A chip on the base, but quite lovely. Not books." She folded her hands on the table, like a good student. "Books are our friends," she said. "Isn't that what English teachers say? I like to keep my friends." She laughed sociably.

She was lying, which was odd, but it was irrelevant, because she was not behaving like a woman who'd put out a call for help.

So that was that. I was at the end of the road, and my mission of mercy had been aborted. I wasn't sure if the sensation in my stomach was disappointment or relief.

Martha looked toward the punched-tin kitchen ceiling. "But if you say I dropped that carton off, maybe I could think real hard about when it was and whose books they might have been, and perhaps . . ." She stood up. I had forgotten the purple satin shorts. She walked into the hallway. "Why don't I check with Patsy?" She took a receiver off a small telephone table and leaned over to dial. The legs were amazing for a woman her age.

"Quite a reader, Patsy," Martha said. "Buys by mail, of course. Such a shame, cooped up like that."

My antennae, which had gone floppy, popped back up.

Patsy must have been cooped directly next to the telephone because it hardly had time to ring before Martha was questioning and nodding. "I thought so!" she said with delight. "Well, there's this dear child here—do you know Beth Wyman, Patsy? No, well, what a shame. She's lovely, and she seems to have found a book in your carton that—I know the entire carton wasn't yours, darling. Of course your mother would be upset if you were giving books away at that rate—but do you know whose else they were? You think maybe Ardis? Really? I've had trouble getting her to donate anything. It must be your special charm."

All the wrong feedback. Why mention the woman's mother? And who was Ardis? I was suddenly weary of the whole affair, including the tantalizing, infuriating sort of woman who'd leave anonymous notes in a book.

Martha half danced, half walked back to the kitchen table.

"I'm afraid that wasn't too helpful," she said. "Although Patsy said you could come talk to her, of course. And I'm sure Ardis will agree, too—if it isn't one of her sick-headache days. And there might be others."

One woman was cooped in, the other had sick-headache days. Either could be hiding bruises, recovering in secret. Maybe it wasn't so crazy, then.

"I remember now," Martha said. "I picked up bags of books from Patsy. You have to do that sort of thing for her. Her mother's in a wheelchair; can't expect her to do a lot of hauling. And Ardis left books, too. Must have been three, four bags altogether. Ardis is never home days and doesn't answer the bell after dark, so she left hers on Patsy's porch."

I nodded, eager to cut to the chase.

"I don't mean to probe, dear heart," Martha said, leaning toward me over the table, "but what sort of book would provoke such a search? If you can say, of course."

"Well, it's rather personal. Writings . . ."

"Oh!" she said. "Not an ordinary book at all. A diary, perhaps." She cocked her head. "Can't think what secrets either of those girls would have. I mean the one hasn't left her house in thirteen years, and the other only ventures out for work and church. Never have even seen Ardis at a movie, let alone on a vacation. Don't know when she buys clothing. And for that matter, when does Patsy?" The furrows returned between her eyes. "I suppose Patsy's mother takes care of that, too," she said. "Does everything else—and it's all so odd. She's the one in a wheelchair, but she gets about, even drives."

"And her daughter?" I asked. "Patsy?"

Martha shook her head. "Gets weak and can't breathe soon as she goes near the door. Thank goodness she has her mother right there, don't you think?"

An agoraphobe. "Is Patsy married?"

"How could she be?" Martha lowered her voice. "Never had a date. Been inside that house since day after high school graduation. Thirteen years ago. And the oddest thing is, all she does is read about explorers and watch those educational specials on the far corners of the world."

I remembered sorting books about camping the South Pole and trekking Borneo. I'd imagined a rugged outdoorsy traveler. I felt sorry for Patsy, but doubtful that a husbandless, housebound agoraphobe living with a wheelchair-bound mother was my woman. "And Ardis?" I asked apprehensively.

"Oh, her." Martha sounded almost snappish. "I know they don't use the term anymore, and I don't mean to sound uncharitable, but Ardis is an old maid. Certainly not a bachelor woman or a swinging single or whatever they call them now. Ardis doesn't like anybody—not men, not women. Told me she was one of ten children, and has wanted to be all by herself ever since."

So Ardis could be the underliner only if she were a schizophrenic beating herself, and I wasn't ready to tackle that.

"You look sad, child."

"I don't think the woman I'm looking for is Patsy or Ardis. Somebody else is in trouble."

"Trouble, eh?" Martha raised her eyebrows. "Is it a matter for the police?" She sounded halfhearted.

I thought of Mackenzie's reaction to the story of the book and turned it into concentrated police-force strength disdain. "It's not their kind of thing."

She folded her hands and looked extremely depressed, but she brightened when I requested a last soft-shoe demonstration before I made my farewells. I drove home slowly, sad to have failed so thoroughly, but also, definitely, unburdened. There is a certain dry joy in running out of resources and being unable to do anything.

THAT NOT UNPLEASANT MIX OF EMOTIONS LASTED UNTIL I was home, belatedly reading the morning's *Inquirer*. First the comics, then hard news. My city was in even worse economic shape than I, being temporarily bailed out by the public school teachers' pension fund. You knew a government was in trouble when it had to borrow from its most underpaid workers.

Pages later, among the lesser stories, I stumbled over a familiar headline: MAN KILLS WIFE AND SELF. Usually, I skim accounts like that, but tonight I gentled Macavity off that part of the paper and read.

". . . a history of domestic violence, according to neighbors . . ."

I felt breathless, as if I'd been running for a long time.

". . . many calls to the police . . ."

Philip and Caroline Abbott were their names. He was a pastry chef. She was a kindergarten aide. They lived in Cherry Hill, New Jersey.

Caroline Abbott was not the woman who'd written in my book. That didn't make me feel markedly better.

I tried to concentrate on other articles. The advantage of reading stale news is that you realize how little of it actually matters. There will be new stories in a few hours.

Mrs. Abbott's last domestic argument was a one-day wonder.

Except that somebody in editorial had decided that Caroline Abbott deserved remembering. There was an earnest condemnation of violence against women.

Nice words. Yatata, yatata. Platitudes and tsk-tsks. Except for a statistic he included. "Every day four women in the United States of America are beaten to death by their husbands or boyfriends."

I stared at the line until it was imbedded on my lenses. There'd been three other dead Mrs. Abbotts today. There'd be a new quartet of battered corpses tomorrow. I wouldn't save a one of them. No longer did I feel the slightest relief at having lost the lady in the book, even less so acknowledging that there was nothing to be done about it.

Eight

"BEEN READING THIS BOOK I GOT FOR THE TERM PAPER. So Colleen's with Ronny, like always, and says some nothing thing, and he goes watch it bitch, you're out of line. And he like pinches her, you know? Hard. And she goes 'ouch!' and he tells her she has a big mouth and somebody better teach her a lesson, but soon.

"So I go, chill out, Ronny, you're an *abuser*. And he looks like I'm talking some foreign language. So I say listen up, creep. You don't hurt women. Period. Got it? And he did, if you want to know the truth. He looked ashamed.

"And the best thing is, next time he starts up, Colleen goes, 'Lay a hand on me again and you're history.' *Way to go Colleen!* " The housefly on Rita's cheek and her black lipstick kept her from appearing as jubilant as she obviously was. The nose ring was also a deterrent.

She had remained after class to share the moment with me, and I concentrated on the message and not the medium. Hearing I'd been successful somewhere on the brutality front was particularly heartening today.

"You know what I read?" Rita continued. She erased the side board as she spoke. We had bonded. "That in England, long time ago, villagers used to clang pots and pans to shame a violent man. They called it *rough music*. It's a shame we don't do it no more. Nobody does nothing. So I decided that I will. I *am*."

Me, too, I wished I could say. We walked down the broad staircase together.

"Do you think it's maybe the same with men like with dogs?" she asked.

"I don't understand."

"We have a Doberman, you know? And like when we got it, the trainer goes the first time that mother growls at you, smash him with a chair. Honest! He said just once and he'll never do it again."

I didn't ask if they'd smashed the Doberman. I merely said that I thought there were differences between dogs and men.

"Yeah, but I bet Ronny doesn't push Colleen around so much anymore," Rita said. "You have to stand up for your rights, you know?"

I agreed, completely. "You have to with any bully, and men who pick on women are bullies. But maybe not with a chair." Then I watched Rita rush off to locate and terrorize other potential abusers. I wondered if Shakespeare would be proud of what he'd wrought or if he'd consider the newly sensitized Rita a shrew.

And what would he say about her creative use of language? Now if I could convert her to standard English as well . . .

I stopped at the office. Halfway through the semester, we were required to light a little dynamite under our most resistant students. "Failure warning forms," I told Helga, the office witch. "Please."

"How many?"

"Seven." Helga is a dictator with a frustratingly small power base. She is mistress of red pencils, chalk, the key to the copy machine, and our principal's ear. She makes the most of it. And she makes the faculty miserable.

As now. "Seven," she scowled. Her chin pushed out, her brow lowered until she looked like somebody trying to taste her own forehead. "Seven," she repeated, waiting for me to tug my forelock and grovel. I couldn't tell whether she considered seven goof-offs too many or too few. With heavy, reluctant steps she went to the appropriate stack and counted forms as if I might embezzle and sell extras on the failure-warning black market.

There was a brand new and expensive state of the art computer on her desk, gift of a parent in the business. One of his stipulations had been that faculty also have access to it. Hence the recent tutorials. Knowing how difficult it was to extract failure notices from Helga, I wondered what teacher would ever dare to request time at the woman's machine.

She presented me with my forms and a While You Were Out memo.

I hadn't been out. I'd been upstairs teaching when Martha Thornton called, two hours earlier. The message was simply the one word *important*. "Helga, you interrupted my class yesterday about missing *cheese*! Why didn't you—" My agitation was giving her pleasure. I settled for what I hoped was a seething glare and flounced out. The phones in the main office were in the Helga zone, so teachers tended to buy privacy at the pay phone meant for student use.

At the moment, it was occupied by Neil Quigley, looking pasty and agitated. If it hadn't seemed crucial to find out the reason for Martha's call, I would have left the tortured man in peace, but he hung up right then, and I thought it was as good a time as any to ease his worries about my involvement with TLC.

"Neil," I said. "Wait a second. I have to make a call, but I want to talk to you about TLC."

He looked startled, although I'd been standing two feet away. He also looked as ready to cry as an unweepy man is likely to.

"Please," I said. "I'll be a second."

He nodded, like a lost child deciding to trust the helpful stranger.

I went into the booth and dialed, fingers crossed once they weren't pushing buttons, hoping she was still at home.

She was. As soon as I identified myself, she whispered, "Dearest? I feel dreadful. Ashamed of myself, as well I might because, oh my . . . I lied."

"About what?" I asked softly, although of course, there was only one topic available for lying.

"About your question. You know."

Euphemism heaven was where I had landed. Why couldn't any of us say what this was about? I thought of Sasha's bruised relative and the silence surrounding her, the bad taste of mentioning reality, and decided that not much had changed. We spoke in code, averting our eyes. "I'm listening," I prompted.

"Not now," she whispered. "Oliver's in his study and I'm here in the hallway. It's so complicated and humiliating. Please, could we meet? Somewhere else?"

"You did donate a book, didn't you?" I said.

"Yes," she whispered. "I did."

We made a date for an hour later. A strictly kosher deli that didn't seem a likely haunt of her fellow congregants. I hung up, so absorbed by the happy tap-dancing grandmother's dark secrets that I almost forgot Neil, still waiting, still looking agonized, outside the booth.

"What's wrong?" I asked. "Has something else happened?"

"What else could?" he asked. Our voices echoed off the marble floor and staircase into the acute emptiness of a studentless school. And into Helga's waiting ears. I guided him past the office, into a room that was probably where bad servants had been sent back when this building was a private mansion. Now the cell was, ironically or not, the faculty lounge, although stretching, let alone lounging, was hardly possible in it.

Neil behaved as if my fingers on his elbow were a tugboat pulling him. He seemed to have no motor of his own. I suspected that if I hadn't led him, he'd have stood in the foyer until students trampled him next morning.

"Ruined," he said. "I'll have a baby and debts and nothing else. Nothing. What am I going to do?"

He was still in shock about the fire, I realized. "Neil," I reminded him, "they're insured. They'll rebuild the center and find a place for you meanwhile."

"You don't understand."

I was getting sick and tired of people saying that to me.

"They can't rebuild burned records. My proof."

"Of what?"

"And Schmidt still insists I owed them money! It's a scam. Tutoring legitimizes it, that's all. They're loan sharks. The whole thing is to get us to slow-own—that's their word—a center. You ever look at your mortgage?"

"I rent," I whispered. I thought he had gone mad, or was definitely about to.

"In the end, you pay two, three times what the house costs. Same goes for the center. Plus advertising and promotion and initial consultations and God knows what else, and try and find a profit when you're doing that. Rebuilding makes it all okay for them, but not for me!"

"Why don't you sit down?"

He looked around, took a while to notice the ragged sofa—a piece rejected by shoppers at a previous Not-a-Garage Sale—and then he more or less crumpled into its sprung coils.

"I'm sure—" I corked the reflex it'll-be-okay noises ready to pour out. The man had problems. A sick wife with a difficult, high risk pregnancy, and money worries that put mine to shame. Situations did not automatically improve. It could be pretty dark indeed just before it became pitch-black.

Instead, I poured him a cup of faculty brew, chewable caffeine. There was a typed message above the machine, warning us, in Helga-language, that leaving the coffee machine on endangered the physical plant. Somebody had added an *e*, so that Mr. Coffee now endangered the planet. I flicked off the switch and took a cup of tar to Neil, who sat straighter, his jaw clenched.

"I'm not taking it," he said.

"No problem. It is pretty sludgy," I admitted.

"Not sitting down like this." He made his point by standing up, and I grasped that he was not discussing my offering. "They think they have me with the fire, but I'll show them." He had the revelatory glaze of a fanatic.

"Neil? Neil, who are you talking about? The fire was arson. Neighborhood kids. Terrible, but—"

"You're naive. But someday you'll understand. I'll see to that." His voice lowered. "I'm going to get him, Mandy."

With a few long strides he was at the door. "Trust me. Wynn Teller will never, ever, pull tricks on teachers again. Whatever it costs, I'm doing it. After all, what do I have to lose?"

The coffee sloshed over my hand as I ran after him, reminding him what he had to lose, like his wife and baby. But he was gone. I stood holding the cup until I accepted the idea that it was too late to stop Neil. I checked my watch. If I didn't hurry, it'd be too late to meet Martha Thornton, too.

I HAD NEVER BEFORE REALIZED THE TRYSTING POSSIBILITIES of Sammy's Deli. Not only was eau de pickle an instant aphrodisiac, but the brown booths' high wooden backs provided privacy as well. I had to search for Martha, who had arrived early and claimed the booth farthest from the door.

She sat over a soda, looking like any suburban granny. No makeup, no purple tap pants, no—it seemed—personality. When I sat down, she smiled nervously while she fiddled with a plate of sour tomatoes and pickles.

I suddenly panicked, wondering what I would do when she looked me in the eye and said, "He's going to kill me. Help me." Up until now, I had thought in macro-terms. I would save the woman in the book, period. I left the details of *how* to on-the-spot inspiration, and a hotline number I'd copied down.

Martha fiddled with the pickle plate, then with her straw, and finally with the napkin dispenser, while I ordered half a chopped liver sandwich and simultaneously took a vow of future diet atonement. I would eat no more this day, and tomorrow I would eat the yogurt and apple in the school refrigerator, instead of succumbing to the chili dog and chips lunch menu, as I had today.

Deferring virtue always relaxes me. Martha and I made talk so small it was infinitesimal. That was okay. She had called the meeting. She could set the agenda.

Then my order arrived and, as if chopped liver were the secret word, Martha switched gears. "A minister's wife is something of a public figure, dear girl," she said abruptly. "One's private life . . . well, there's a reason they call it that, don't you agree?" She didn't check whether I concurred, but concentrated on folding and refolding a paper napkin until it was a stubby square.

A tingle, like a mild electric shock, raced through me. This was it. I felt as if I'd been looking for her forever, although it was only forty-eight hours since I'd found the book. But now, like one of those people who search for water with a stick, I was shaking in the presence of my goal.

"One is," Martha said, now unfolding the square, "perchance rightly, perchance not, less than eager for people to know everything about oneself."

The more she approached her secret, the more archaic her expressions. I had to intervene before we were back to Chaucerian English or caveman grunts. "Maybe," I suggested, "if people knew, people could help."

She arched her eyebrows, then lowered them into a frown. "You already know, don't you?" she whispered.

"I believe so."

Martha's expression was bleak. "I was afraid you did."

I rehearsed my speech about how she had to stop feeling ashamed, that this wasn't her fault, but *his*. I was ready to commiserate about how scary it must be to dare to change after all these years. I would assure her that she had lots of happy, tap-dancing nights left.

"I suppose you were horrified." Her voice was no more than a whisper.

"I was shocked, and upset, of course. Anybody with a shred of decency would be," I said.

"Oh, dear, oh, dear!" A sparkle of tears filmed her eyes. "But how could I have known? Main Line Charities seemed so anonymous and safe. I would have never—if I'd known an *English* teacher!"

"Excuse me?"

She took a deep breath and pushed the wrinkled napkin aside. "At my age, one worries. Disaster strikes without warning. Strokes, broken hips, heart attacks." She leaned closer. "I couldn't sleep, worrying what would happen if my children or grandchildren had to come care for me and they found out. And Oliver worried, too."

I tilted my head, hoping to catch the sound waves I was

obviously missing. "Oliver?" She nodded. Was she saying that she'd underlined a confession of battering, but had donated it to charity only so that her grandchildren never found out? That she and the batterer colluded on this? "Mrs. Thornton," I said. "I don't understand." I reviewed the entire conversation in my head, to see where I might have misunderstood, or whether we were burying ourselves in euphemisms again. Something about this discussion felt like a rerun. I'd had this misunderstanding before.

"Isn't it understandable that Oliver would worry even more than I did?" Martha asked. "He's a man of the cloth. People would talk."

"But . . . but so what? Isn't worrying about something like that hypocritical?"

She turned her head away as sharply as if I'd smacked her. "Try to understand, even though it must be hard for you. It's shameful, but once it's started, where do you stop?" She shook her head. "It's been going on since we first married, and I'm as much a party to it as he is."

"Mrs. Thornton, please. Stop assuming responsibility for a situation your husband created. It isn't your fault."

She waved away my words. "Please, dearest." She finally looked me in the eye. "I beg you, even if you are shocked, even if you can't understand or approve—please, get rid of them and don't tell anyone."

"Them?"

"I would never have put them in a collection box for a *school.*" She looked up through the pickled air to heaven. "I should have burned them or thrown them in the compost heap."

Them. I repeated the word to myself a few times.

"But," she leaned across the table, "the terrible truth is, I thought somebody else could, um, enjoy them the way we did."

I added the word enjoy. Enjoy them. What the hell were we talking about?

"I never dreamed an English teacher! Why, ever since Miss Letterbelt and *God's Little Acre*. About how smut corrupted you, poison through the eyes, she said. About how she had to take a *bath* after reading it.'' Martha Thornton was talking to herself, her eyes focused inward. ''My own fault, of course. I should never have brought it to school, but I promised a friend, and it fell on the classroom floor. In front of her, and I knew she could see right through me, could see into my corrupted brain and know that I'd read others just as bad. But to send me home—in front of everybody. To have *Mother* know and—''

''Those books?'' Confessions of an Anonymous Barmaid, Peyton Place, Jackie Collins. That's where I'd had this conversation before. With Sasha and the picture frame. Just switch a few euphemisms and vague allusions. Damn us all for our false and dangerous tact. ''You're talking about sexy books?''

She flushed. ''Never intended for the eyes of an English teacher!''

''But I—''

''The fact is, Oliver didn't—doesn't think they're wrong.''

''Honestly, Mrs. Thornton, I—''

''Please. I would never have admitted to it, never have come here today, but I was afraid you'd decide to ask Patsy and Ardis after all, and then they'd know, too. Patsy's mother, God love her, has a mouth.''

''But—''

''I beg you to destroy them. And keep my secret. Don't tell anybody. I am—we are—at your mercy, dearest.''

''Listen, I'm not Miss Letterbelt.'' Maybe we needed an antidefamation league for English teachers. ''Mrs. Thornton, can you keep a secret?''

''Dear child, isn't it painfully obvious that I can, and have?''

''I took *Fanny Hill* and *My Secret Life* home with me. Your copies. And I'm enjoying them a great deal.'' That wasn't completely true. I hadn't yet retrieved my cache from backstage, but she needed all I could give her. There were forms of abuse other than spousal, and Miss Letterbelt had been expert at one of them.

Only then, when they doubled in size, did I notice that

Martha's eyes were aquamarine. "Can you keep another secret?" she asked.

I nodded.

"I didn't give all of them away." And then she giggled.

"Here's a plan," I said. "Whenever you're not reading them, put them in a box labeled 'Confiscated material. Please save for Sunday School report.' Then, you don't have to worry if your grandchildren ever do find them."

"That's what you do, eh?"

"That's what awful Miss Letterbelt did, too. All those prudes—think about it. Was it absolutely necessary for her to read all the way through something that disgusted her? Couldn't a reasonably intelligent person tell by page ten? And in the bathtub, of all places!"

Recognition blossomed on Martha's face. "Miss Letterbelt?" she whispered with amazement. Sixty years old at the least, and still convinced English teachers were born without sex organs. She giggled so hard, white-silver ringlets bounced on her head. "Well, well," she said. "So that's that. And now, no more of your search for the, um, *diaries*." Her smile brought out her dimples. "Dear heart, what is it?" she asked. "You suddenly look so unhappy!"

"You don't understand. I really was looking for a woman who left a message in a book. She underlined passages and wrote notes. A woman afraid that her husband was going to kill her."

"And you thought it was me? That Oliver would, or could . . . ? Why on earth?"

"The book was in that carton. The one meant for Main Line Charities. The one you dropped off at my sister's house."

"But I didn't, dearest. That part was true. I was a collection point. I picked up donations from Patsy and Ardis—actually, Ardis left hers at Patsy's house—but I didn't take them anywhere."

I reached across and put my hand on hers. "Please," I said. "Who did?"

"Who picked them up?" She wrinkled her brow. "My memory isn't so . . . we joke and say that's why we have to read those sexy books." Then she brightened. "Oh! I remember. But it's too silly, because Lydia Teller wouldn't deface a book. And beyond that, of course, she's not in any danger. It's too ridiculous to mention."

"Why did she pick it up from you?" I needed to make sure Lydia Teller wasn't another false lead, another single step in Main Line Charities' endless chain of volunteers.

"She was area captain. The Learning Centers have a large van, and it's easier on the person whose garage we're using, like your sister, if only one drop-off is made, not dozens."

"Let me get this clear. Nobody except Lydia was involved with that carton between your house and my sister's house. Am I right?"

Martha hardened, moved behind a gloss of proper matronhood. "It isn't Lydia you're seeking, the poor woman. Sickly, you know, and absolutely adored. I've seen how tender and caring that man is toward her. He sends her flowers, beautiful gifts for no reason. He protects her, is with her constantly. Comes home for every meal, they say. They're members of our church. Good people. The best. I've seen how it is with my own eyes."

No. She'd seen how it was with the public's eye. Lydia Teller had let me see how it really was. Let Martha think Wynn gifted his wife for no reason. His wife had shown me his reasons.

It made sense. The little I had so far all fit. "Please don't think I'm nosy, or out of line," I said, "but has Lydia ever gotten help for . . . emotional problems?"

"And what if she has? Do you know about that son of hers? A slap in the face to his father, if you ask me. I mean here's Wynn, saying any child can succeed, and Hugh goes out of his way to prove he won't. He's Lydia's emotional problems, far as I'm concerned. And she'd already had enough trouble in her life. Both parents dying in that crash, no family. Things pile up. Really, Miss Pepper, I thought prejudice about psychiatric help was over. You aren't going to upset her with this lunacy, are you? I'll be sorry I ever talked to you if that's the case."

"The last thing on earth I want to do is add to her problems."

"Good."

"Where does she live?"

Martha's aquamarine eyes turned arctic. "You can't think I'd help you do something cruel like that."

"I think she's in trouble."

She shook her head and opened her wallet.

"No," I said. "My treat."

And that was that, once again. Martha left, but I sat a while longer. I pushed the untouched sandwich out of sight, because I was sick to my stomach.

I thought of pudgy Hugh Teller and what horror he must have lived through. The faraway boarding school became comprehensible as protection. She'd underlined the part about hurting the children. The child.

His problems and acting-out. The *slap in the face to his father*, as Martha had put it, was less metaphorical than she suspected, and very understandable.

But, oh, I felt ill. I liked theoretical villains. Categories, types, behavior patterns, not a man who'd charmed me. I'd liked him, been attracted to him. Given other circumstances, he was a man I would have dated.

Then it could have happened to me. I was no smarter, no more magically protected from becoming a victim or recognizing danger than the terrified woman in the book.

I wanted out. Everybody was right. I was an English teacher, not a lawman. If I hadn't, by chance, opened a book two days ago, I'd have no idea this was going on, and my main concern would be getting kids to use semicolons. A potential murder was none of my business, and I was involved only by happenstance.

Why me?

And then I wondered how often and for how many years Lydia Teller had asked herself that same question.

Nine

TODAY, THEN, I WAS GOING TO FIND HER. THE ANTICIPATION nearly paralyzed me. I took deep breaths and thought of the underliner. I could at least be as brave as she was, couldn't I?

It was still afternoon. Wynn Teller would not likely be home. Lydia might well be. Which meant it was time to turn my words into action, even though my limbs felt heavy as sandbags.

I went to the back of the deli where the rest rooms and telephones were. I intended to use both, but couldn't. No W. or L. Teller listed. Of course not. How could I have believed it would be that easy, ever?

I had no dimes, so I deposited a quarter and a computerized voice informed me that I had a five cent credit with the phone company. They failed to tell me how to collect it.

"Beth, I need Lydia Teller's address," I said after minimal pleasantries.

"Why on earth?"

"She's the lady in the book."

"What book?" Beth asked. Then she answered herself. "Oh, for heaven's sake! That's ridiculous! Laughable, if you weren't so grim about it."

On and on she went. She didn't get to speak to adults often enough during daylight hours. I wondered if the phone company would remember my credit and allow me an extra five cents' worth of sisterly monologue.

"If you knew the Tellers, you'd know they aren't that sort at all!" she said.

"There is no *sort*!" Now that my stereotypes had been thoroughly disabused, I could be high and mighty about the less informed.

"Well, whatever sort they don't have to be, they aren't!" Beth's grammar was confusing, but her message wasn't. "They're famous for their perfect marriage. I mean really, Mandy—first you thought I was the one, then Martha, now Lydia. You have a serious problem." I hadn't paid much attention to her wise older sister routine since I was twelve, when Beth at least had interesting facts of life to demystify.

I counted to ten. "One question. What would you do if you found a note from a woman who thought she'd be killed soon and the police wouldn't be interested in doing anything about it?"

"I certainly wouldn't create problems where there aren't any."

"Wouldn't it be better to risk making a mistake than to risk somebody's life?"

"You might as well know right now," Beth said. "I don't have Lydia's address or phone number."

If she weren't a nursing mother and I hadn't been in a public restaurant, I might have shouted ungentle words. Instead, I clung to logic by my fingernails. "You're her friend. You worked with her."

"Not a close friend, and I never went there. I saw her at meetings, events. She's very reserved and private. Some people think she's chilly, actually, but I don't."

"I don't, either. Maybe not even reserved or private. Just scared that if somebody got close, she'd visit at the wrong time, ask the wrong questions. Find out what really goes on in that house."

Alexander conveniently had a fit, and the conversation ended. When I hung up the phone, my cold, which had been in retreat, thumped back on the field. My head ached and my eyes felt like Red Cross flags.

I stomped through the deli to the cashier's stand and paid the bill, ready to throw in the towel, or the book, and go home and huddle under the covers. Catch up on some of those million ways to snag guys. I was pretty sure that gratuitous sleuthing was not on the list.

My exit was halted by a sound that further disoriented me. "Mandy! Hey—over here!"

The call of my sort-of-beloved, peeking out of one of the trysting booths, where he didn't belong. I didn't need to go to detective school to deduce who occupied the other side of that brown wooden nook.

I considered bolting, but by the time the concept reached my muscles, Mackenzie was at my side.

"Come meet Jinx." He guided me to their booth, as if I couldn't find it myself. He'd been infected with acute southernness by his houseguest. "Went to the Barnes," he said.

Mackenzie, while a man of many talents, had never seemed such a fanatic art lover that he'd take a day off from work to view an art collection, no matter how spectacular.

"Interestin' place."

"How? On a weekday." Even dead, Albert Barnes remains one of the city's eccentric codgers. In the 1920s, critics sneered at his collection of Impressionist art—Renoir, Cezanne, Monet, and Gaugin. They said paintings by Picasso, Matisse, and Modigliani were figments of diseased minds. Instead of having the last laugh, or letting anybody else do so, Barnes set his huff in concrete. Only personally selected art students were allowed a peek during his lifetime, and although a posthumous lawsuit somewhat modified his dictates, it was still necessary either to petition the museum for special admission or to line up on weekends and wait to be one of the one hundred unreserved admittants. I always meant to write and reserve a time. I always also meant to lose five pounds, jog, and read Proust in the original.

"Jinx took care of it from down home." Mackenzie looked proud of the little lady's accomplishments, which didn't enhance my nonpleasure in meeting her. Nor did seeing her.

She didn't look any of the ways I'd imagined. She wasn't exceptionally anything, except, perhaps, predictable. Predictably shiny blonde hair, predictably blonde face. Predictably pert. I couldn't fathom the attraction.

I also couldn't compete on the pertness scale with my scratchy eyes, stuffed nose, and depression. I therefore detested everything about her, from her neat, inoffensive jacket and sweater to her cultural awareness and her pragmatic professional choice and the fact that she'd heard of the elusive, reclusive Barnes Collection while she was down in the Bayou.

"Saw such *wonderful* paintin's!" she said after we'd made our introductions.

"Umm," I murmured, over-aware that Mackenzie had seated himself next to her.

"This city's really *fun*!" She squeezed Mackenzie's upper arm for emphasis. "No wonder there's that famous sayin', 'I'd rather be in Philadelphia.' "

"W. C. Fields," I muttered. "And not much of a compliment."

"Pardon?"

"W. C. Fields, the comedian, supposedly has 'On the whole, I'd rather be in Philadelphia,' carved on his tombstone."

She stared blankly, a worried but well-meaning smile trembling on her lips. "Tombstone," she echoed. I wondered whether her MBA was mail-order. "Oh," she said, her mouth working in slow motion. "I get it. It's a joke."

"And what are you doing in the hinterlands?" Mackenzie asked after we'd made our introductions. "Visitin' your sister?"

That made me sound as dull and sexless as a missionary. Or, I suppose, as a spinster schoolmarm.

I shrugged, meaning to suggest trysts, luxurious suburban indulgences, anything to stir envy in Mackenzie's heart and Jinx's pert eyes. Unworthy motives, but I was prepared to lie as much as necessary. Then something possessed me. Something remarkably akin to a desire to tell the truth, the whole truth, and nothing but. I hadn't done that in days. Also, I wasn't averse to Mackenzie's seeing how clever I'd been identifying Lydia. And he could help. No sweat for cops to find somebody's address. So out it came. Everything.

Jinx said "Oh, my!" every third word, and "My goodness!" in between. She was attentive, even goggle-eyed, laughing when I got to the—anonymous—story of the grandma and the porno. The impressing-the-hell-out-of-her part of my mission seemed accomplished, until I realized her reactions might be nothing more than reflex Southern good manners.

And during this time, Mackenzie's nostrils flared and he drummed the table. "Finished?" he said the instant my mouth stopped.

Jinx looked startled. I was sure that north or south of the Mason-Dixon line, nobody had spoken to her that curtly.

"Of course not. Not now that you know she's not imaginary. Nor is this a prank the way you said. Her name is Lydia Teller. Wynn Teller's wife. I'm sure you've seen his ads on TV and in the paper." What did I expect? That Mackenzie would catch her name like a football and run with it? Come along, as a civilian, and help me get her out of the house and into safety?

"Mandy," Mackenzie said, "if teachin' doesn't keep you busy enough, maybe you should switch careers." The fact that the edges of his syllables were soft did not lessen their sting.

"You won't help me?"

"I am helpin' you. I'm askin' you to give this up. You're obsessed. Sick with it."

I stood up. "How many dead ladies in the headlines will it take to convince you people about what's going on?"

Across the aisle a boothful of diners ignored their blintzes in favor of watching me. But they didn't answer my question. Nobody did. I took as deep a breath as my clogged system allowed and flounced off.

Then I remembered, and turned back. "Very nice to have met you," I told Jinx. I didn't want her to think Yankees lacked manners.

I COULDN'T BELIEVE IT WAS STILL DAYLIGHT. STILL AFTERNOON. Several years had passed since the teaching day ended, and I wondered if we had skipped to summer's deliciously late sunsets in the interim. But the temperature was miserable, and the light was grudging, so I knew we were still stuck in February.

And I was still searching for Lydia Teller.

I had crossed the street en route to my car before I realized I didn't know where to go once I entered it. In my frustration, I kicked the side of a bus stop bench. And then stood staring at its back, emblazoned as it was with a TLC ad.

A genuine, irrefutable sign, by gum.

The beige receptionist didn't blend in as well today. She was wearing a patriotic sweater in a red, white, and blue flag print, having undoubtedly gotten special dispensation for color deviance. At the moment, the back of the sweater was toward me and she was complaining to a brown-haired girl at another computer. "I mean how much more is he supposed to take? I worry about him. You see him this morning? Or yesterday?"

Clifford Schmidt appeared from down the hall. He stood at his office door, looking almost ready to say something to me, which would have ruined my plan, but happily, he changed his mind and sequestered himself.

The brown-haired girl eyed me and pointed silently, until the receptionist swiveled around.

"Hi," I said. "I'm an English teacher and—"

She smiled expectantly, blankly. I had really made a big impression on her yesterday. "Applying for a tutoring position?"

"No, I—"

My sound waves crossed others blasting out of Teller's office door. It sounded as if he had a crowd in there—high pitches and low, male and female. Good. If it was still business as usual, then Lydia Teller must still be alive.

The receptionist smiled even more brightly.

"I was wondering. I taught Mr. Teller's son, and he called and asked for a recommendation. I gather he's in a bit of a hurry—late college application, most likely—and since I was coming out this way, I said I'd pick up the form in person. But I just this second realized I left his address and phone number home, and my cat is no good giving me information over the phone." I laughed, weakly, horrified that this oafish routine came to me so naturally.

"Mr. Teller's son?"

"Yes, and what a relief to realize I was near here, where you'd have it, and I wouldn't seem like such a dope."

She bit her bottom lip.

I smiled hard. "I'm in something of a hurry," I said. "Well, I mean *he* is. Needs to have it in the mail today. Overnight mail, actually. You know how rigid college deadlines are."

The phone buzzed and she raised a finger to put me on hold while she answered it. Her face grew stony and she closed her eyes in exasperation. "I've given him the last five messages and he will respond as soon as he can."

She listened again, holding the receiver out from her ear. "His schedule is already full, that's why. Sorry, he's already coming back here after dinner. Through nine, and I'm not to schedule beyond that." Again the receiver was held away from her head and I could hear a furious male voice. "Of course I know how to spell your name, Mr. Quigley," she snapped.

I shuddered.

True to her receptionist code of honor, she filled out a pink telephone message form and added it to a small stack. "Look," she said when she realized I was still there, outside the cutout square, "this is a really bad time."

"Oh, my, I can see that. So if you'll simply pass over the Rolodex, I'll take a peek and be on my way."

"I'd have to check first," she said without interest. "You'll have to wait."

My smile muscles ached. "I could understand if I were selling anything. Or if I looked like a terrorist. But I'm an English teacher, trying to help a kid." I wondered if saying *kid* had hurt my chances.

"I certainly don't know why he told you to go to his house when he was coming here." Her smooth voice had a tendency to squeak now and then, as if she had sanded it down but missed spots.

"Here?" I thought he was among the missing and had been for years.

"Already is, so whyn't you take a seat?" She returned to her computer screen, which blinked with various heights of orange columns. "Take a seat," she said. "He'll be out any second."

"He told me to pick it up at his house, so maybe he left it there, and . . ." I sounded unbearably feeble, but I was plumb out of ideas.

"Young people are unpredictable, if you know what I mean. Why don't you leave the material if you don't want to wait?"

"No, no. He was leaving something for me." The lie had outlived its usefulness, and so had this place. "Okay," I said. "I'll give Hugh a call later." I hoped that saved face. "We'll work it out."

"Please don't bother phoning me again," she said in clipped, exasperated tones. "I cannot provide the requested information."

"Not you. Hugh."

She stared.

"Hugh," I repeated, treating the first syllable like a hurricane. "Hhhugh. The name. With an *h*. Hugh Teller."

"Who?"

"Hugh!" I cleared my throat and took a deep breath. "His son. The person you just said was in the office with him."

"I never!" We might have gone on forever playing Hugh's on First, but Teller's office door opened and Wynn Teller, tall and solid, held the door for a young man and woman who shared his height, blocky build, and fair coloring. Their large, definite features were similar—especially their unhappy cast.

"This woman wants to see you," Glenda said.

"No, no." This young man was nothing like Hugh—too old, too fair, wrong-featured.

"Miss Pepper," Wynn Teller said. "I'm surprised and delighted to have you return so quickly. Does this mean you're going to join TLC's staff soon, I sincerely hope?"

"Miss Pepper says she was Adam's English teacher. She's

here about his college applications?'' Glenda sounded suspicious and ingratiating, as if the king would reward her for unearthing my duplicity.

''No I didn't,'' I said.

The fair young man looked down at me. ''I'm Adam Teller.'' He smiled hopefully.

''And I'm Eve Wholeperson,'' the young woman snapped. ''Adam's sister. We're twins.'' She was what the kids at school called an *organic*: unornamented and dressed in layers of wrinkled dun, as if both color and irons were politically incorrect. She was aesthetically out of synch with her twin, who wore penny loafers and a blue blazer. ''Bad enough living in a phallocentric society,'' she said. ''I won't tolerate a patronymic as well.''

I didn't have time for fem-babble, so I smiled as unencouragingly as I could.

''I'm afraid I don't remember you,'' Adam said, ignoring his sister. ''Although I'll bet it was tenth grade, right?''

''There's some confusion,'' I said. ''I didn't mean . . . look, I'll be toddling along.''

''But what was it you wanted?'' Wynn Teller could have posed for the spirit of honest, compassionate concern.

What I wanted was to pull his lapel jackets and tell him I knew the bully who lived below the smart tailoring. I settled instead for not arousing suspicion because what I also wanted was to get Lydia to a shelter without alerting him. I didn't want Wynn terrorizing me, or even suspecting a linkage.

''A phone call from Hugh, she said.'' Glenda implied that she was too smart a cookie to believe that. Actually, she was.

''I wish I could meet Hugh,'' Eve Wholeperson said. ''It's unnatural to have this half brother you never ever saw. I mean it's weird meeting my father for the first time, too. It's all been weird since Mom called, actually.''

''Oh,'' I said softly. Now it all jelled. The crazy lady. Fay, who said she was the mother of Wynn Teller's children. But Wynn had so successfully dismissed her as a crank, I hadn't stored her words carefully.

Intriguing, but this portion of the family was not, however, my problem.

''Hugh called you?'' Wynn asked. ''Why? When? About what?''

I wasn't sure how I'd gotten mired in so many levels of untruth. ''Today. A message,'' I finally said. ''On my phone machine. About applications for school. About a recommendation. I was surprised to hear from him. But—maybe I misunderstood. I must have.''

Teller raised his eyebrows, held them there, then lowered them. ''But he—he left town last weekend.''

I caught myself before I admitted surprise that he'd been around at all.

For a moment, Teller sagged, his face aging, going slack. He looked almost afraid. Or defeated. And then, so quickly I thought I'd imagined that there'd been any change at all, he was back, everything in place and smooth. ''Of course, he's a hard one to track. Once they leave the nest, you know. Maybe we should band them, like they do with birds.''

''Sorry for the confusion,'' I said.

''So he's considering college after all, is he?'' Wynn Teller wore the sour look of one who'd won a victory, but who possibly preferred the defeat.

''Guess so.'' I felt as if I was betraying Hugh's rebellion. I extended my hand. ''Very nice to have met you,'' I told the twins. This was certainly my day for saying it was nice to have met people it wasn't particularly nice to have met.

This was also my day for not getting what I came for.

I reentered my mobile wind tunnel, sneezed, and decided that perhaps humans were too much trouble. There was a lot to be said for inanimate objects. They couldn't lie or have scruples or say you were crazy or unwise.

I therefore directed myself toward the most inanimate of objects, Philly Prep. The fortress of learning was locked and battened against the night, but not against me or pilfering for a good cause.

I was going to find Lydia Teller. And I was going to find her today.

Ten

ONE OF THE FEW WAYS IN WHICH PHILLY PREP TREATS FACulty as professionals is in granting whoever might need one a key to the side door. The sports and drama coaches have them, and so do I. As faculty sponsor of the school paper, I have an unfortunately frequent need to use mine. Not that a monthly high school paper is besieged with late-breaking scoops, but our reporters write their stories with the same urgency they bring to their academic work. Brenda Starr didn't go to Philly Prep. Which is to say that every month, for too much of the month, I stay after school to goad and coerce.

But I am never alone at these sessions, and I never enter a locked and silent building.

The side door had probably once been where tradesmen entered or trash was put out. It was at the end of a long, dark passageway between the school and the residential apartment building that butted up to it. It had never looked as formidable or lengthy.

Something skittered, claws scraping cement as I approached the door. I didn't look down to check what it was.

I am saving somebody's life, I reminded myself. The end justifies the fear. My hand fumbled with the key. Besides, I could be coming back for papers I forgot. Or a book. Innocent, plausible motives.

I finally opened the door, then closed it behind me. The side door brings you in downstairs, near the science rooms, locked and hazy in the antiburglary lights casting long shadows along the corridor. The staircase loomed, all unfamiliar angles. I tiptoed up, holding my breath, although I couldn't hear a sound.

Schools at night are unnatural, like postapocalyptic visions. During the day, they burst at the seams with raw life. But vacated and silent, the books and desks and lockers seem artifacts of a lost civilization, remembered only through the indelible aroma of adolescence, tennis shoes, and chalk dust.

I checked the auditorium, but Wednesday's Not-a-Garage Sale team had gone home, leaving tagged doodads behind. The gym was silent. Our basketball team was playing in Chester County. The game was supposed to be a romp.

I felt intrusive and a little lost, and I touched my purse, reassured by the book inside it. My talisman, my admission ticket to Lydia, my press pass, my credentials.

I walked to the office and again used the key, thanking whatever frugal or thoughtful soul had decided that both doors could logically have the same lock.

And then I was inside, the door clicking shut behind me as I headed for the files that covered the back wall of the main room. Current Enrollment: A–D, E–H, etc. I moved to the right, past the W–Z file to the previous year, then the year before it, and on until Hugh's year.

Only then did I notice, or allow myself to notice, the keyholes that topped each bank of files. Small and round, they had nothing to do with the nice key that opened the side door and the office.

Permanent records were legal documents needing protection. I should have realized that. I probably did.

I wanted to yowl with frustration.

I sat down, guiltily, on the Office Witch's chair. Think, I advised. Think, I cajoled. Think, I demanded, but I was as unresponsive as my students generally are. The files sat behind my back, their treasures locked tight.

I put my head down on Helga's desk, or tried to, but it landed on a thick book. I recognized its logo from the staff computer training workshop. That was about all I remembered. That and the fact that you had to turn the thing on and that it didn't have a carriage return to slam with your palm. It appeared that Helga wasn't very far ahead of me. Her user's manual had stickums strategically placed. MOVING THE CURSOR one said in her crabbed handwriting. MOVING FILE BLOCKS. BACKUP FILES. Gibberish.

Useless manual pushed aside, I put down my head in despair and saw, behind my eyes, a face like a cameo, contorted with fear. Still, I couldn't think of what to do. Perhaps in the morning I could figure an excuse for requesting Hugh Teller's old records, or I could wedge something into the file cabinet while Helga was around and it was unlocked, then retrieve the file later. Kind of a Watergate-inspired break-in.

But what if Hugh's records were gone? He hadn't completed even one school year with us. He was history, gone and forgotten. Don't call me, I'll call you.

Don't . . . something nagged, tickling inside my brain where I couldn't scratch. Don't call . . .

Of course. Hugh might have left, but even if he was forgotten, his parents never would be. Not only diamonds were forever. So were private school requests for contributions. No stay at our school, no matter how brief, was too insignificant to put a parent on the permanent hit list.

"Yes!" I shouted. It was difficult calming down, because I was sure that now I had it.

I had listened to that lecture enough to know that lists and labels were the computer's justification for existence. I just hadn't listened long enough to figure out how to extract them. "Open Sesame," I whispered, but that didn't do it, so, with a sigh, I approached Helga's operation manual. Part of my computerphobia is caused by the manuals theoretically explaining them, the only printed material that gives me hives.

I flipped the toggle that said *Power* and felt insanely proud as the machine whipped open like a flasher and showed its contents.

Or something. It took a while to translate *physplt* and *mhpercor* into *physical plant* and *Maurice Havermeyer's personal correspondence*, but once I had a handle on the code, the list seemed more like a game of hangman or that TV show where you fill in the blanks. I wondered if this meant I was now computer literate. I scanned the list for something called *sukrlist*, but Helga wasn't that obliging or obvious. I reached the end without finding anything, and panicked until I saw a funny little key with an arrow pointing toward me. I was reluctant to admit that there might be some logic attached to computers, but I pushed it, and the file miraculously lowered its eyebeam and showed me more of itself.

Computers were a cinch.

And so were Helga's peculiar headings. *Facevals* made me think of noses and eyes for only a moment, and then it became *faculty evaluations*. I was tempted to sneak a look, but it was probably only blank forms Havermeyer and department heads had to fill out.

Computerwise, I had peaked. I stared without comprehension at *tchrec, reqsupp, nxtclndr, misccorr, mhtrvl, mlnglst, subac, flrwrngs*, and my favorite, *ogzmic*. That last item produced a great deal of speculation and wasted time. By the time I optimistically pushed the little arrow and got nothing but *end*, I resumed full-fledged despair. Or *flflgd despr*, as Helga might have had it.

Take them one by one. The Twelve-Step computer program, one imponderable at a time.

With effort, some unraveled into sense. *Tch* was obviously teacher; *clndr*, calendar; and all *mh*'s, Dr. Havermeyer's. I wondered whose initials were *ml*.

No use. I wasn't Mata Hari, even with a stupid Helga-designed code. I'd never find *patsies* or *bleedmdri* or whatever the woman called her damned mailing list.

And then I looked again at *mlnglst* and laughed out loud.

Now there remained the problem of getting into it. I wished I had paid more attention to that lesson, but I'd been preoccupied wondering in what century I could afford a computer, and whether by then, I'd have figured out why I needed one.

But what I did remember was that the answers, garbled and barely intelligible though they be, were inside the bulging, daunting user's manual. I took a deep breath and opened it up.

For once, luck was on my side. Or maybe it was stupidity, or ignorance. In any case, this book was dedicated to rarefied processes—desktop publishing and mass mailings and footnoting and indexing and I don't want to know what else, but my problem—how to look at what was in a file—was so primitive it was answered on page one, in the "How to Start, Idiot" section.

And in I went, pushing my trusting *down* arrow through the alphabet until I got to the T's, and then, to Wynn and Lydia Teller.

Columbus couldn't have been more excited than I was, discovering my own new world of mechanical wizardry.

A squeak somewhere outside the office ended the elation. My pulse rate doubled as I strained to hear, and my hand trembled as I pulled a sheet off a pad embossed with FROM THE DESK OF HELGA PUTNAM. Another squeak. Closer. Did buildings still settle after one and a half centuries?

My hand shook even more as the noise changed. Feet scuffed on the marble foyer now. Just outside.

I scribbled the address in a handwriting I'd never seen before. The writing of a trapped woman.

A shadow darkened half of the closed, frosted glass door to the hallway. I shoved the paper into my bag, then stared at the computer screen, mind as blank as I wished it would become. I was about to be caught illegally using Helga's computer. I was about to be fired. Soon, Macavity and I would be living in the car, sleeping under the ripped convertible top, hoping for a dry spring.

I glanced at the manual as the shadow inserted a key, turned it, and shook the door in vain.

I'd left it unlocked and the shadow had just locked it. Which gave me maybe ten seconds.

No time to find out how to exit gracefully. The instructor had said something about saving, about not destroying disks, but it was too late for niceties.

"Sorry," I told the machine, hearing bits and bytes scream in agony as I eradicated them by simply switching the power off.

I stood up and tried to activate my innocent *who, me?*

facial muscles. But they didn't hold when the door actually opened. "Why—what are you doing here?" I asked, one millisecond after it was asked of me.

Neil Quigley looked terrified. His gangly body gangled more than usual. "I . . . I . . . I forgot my roll book. Failure warnings due, and I couldn't . . . well, I couldn't come sooner, you see, because, um, because I couldn't." He tried for a laugh, but missed by a mile. "It was a shock seeing you here."

Our mutual terror agreed upon, we left. A needle-sharp, icy rain threatened sleet, and when I got into my damp car, I sighed and hoped that I was projecting and that Neil was not as crazed and frightening as he'd looked to me tonight.

THE PILFERED ADDRESS LED ME TO A PLEASANT TWO-STORY house not far from my sister's. Philadelphia and environs are a medley of brick: weathered and new, rose, yellow, tomato, rust, brown, wine, and pink. Even wet, and in the dark, the Tellers' house was on the rosy end of the spectrum. It was two stories and square, with a peaked roof and chimney, its green front lawn split by a walkway to the front door. It looked like a child's drawing of home. A separate garage, to the left and rear, was a miniature peaked-roof replica.

Carefully laid-out flower beds lined the walk and foundation of the house. They were mostly empty now, except for bushes carved and coerced into unnatural egg shapes and oblongs. The topiary, plant abuse if there was such a thing, confirmed all my suspicions.

It was eight o'clock. Dinner should be over by now, and if Glenda had been honest on the phone, Wynn was back at the office.

I walked the path between the frozen bushes, rehearsing my spiel. I had the hotline number of the shelter. I could get her there, and they could get her to a safe house. By the time her husband returned, she'd have disappeared without a trace.

A chill crept through my bone marrow, and it had nothing to do with the freezing rain.

It had nothing to do with the house, either, glowing at every window against the wet night. I heard music in its recesses, and I faltered, suddenly draggy, exhausted, and full of doubts. Everything—except the topiary, but my view of it is not widely shared—indicated the sort of ideal family Beth and Martha and *Philadelphia Magazine* suggested. Time, perhaps, to beat a hasty retreat from this radiant shelter. Everybody's incredulity now became rational.

But so did doing something about that book. I promised myself that if this were another dead end, I'd give up the search. But meanwhile, I'd consider the glow proof only of being wired for electricity, not of connubial bliss. I pressed the bell and waited. Then waited some more.

The music was very loud. I heard a rousing chorus. Something familiar, Broadway, upbeat. The least depressing of songs, but its decibel level jarred and didn't fit my mental image of how the cameo woman would fill her time.

Plus, it meant she couldn't hear me.

I followed the foundation plantings around the house, looking through the ground level windows, hoping—and fearing—finding her, but getting musical, not human, cues. I finally identified the song. "People Will Say We're in Love," from *Oklahoma!* I listened at the window of a living room that matched my mental image of Lydia—understated, elegant, and painfully correct. Nothing looked used. The plush carpet still showed vacuum tracks. There were no personal touches, no idiosyncratic chances taken. It was as carefully safe, designed for the public, and as desperate not to offend, as she had to be. I moved on, imagining Lydia curled deep in a more comfortable, private part of the house, afghan over her knees, letting Rodgers and Hammerstein take her far away to sunny fields of corn.

I wouldn't have minded a quick trip there myself. My legs were wet to the knees, and I had to stop for a sneezing fit as I reached the back of the house. There was a small covered porch, and I ran toward it.

I took the three steps quickly, eager for the shelter of the overhanging roof. The music was even louder here, a different song now, slow and dolorous.

I raised my hand to knock before it registered that the top

half of the Dutch door was open, swinging in the gusts of wet wind, and then I shook almost as wildly as the half door.

"Mrs. Teller?" I called, standing back, away, hand held rigid. My voice quavered like a ninety-year-old woman's. *Bam!* The half door slammed into the frame. The dirge played on.

I backed up a step. Gone, my vision of quiet rooms and afghans. Something was seriously wrong. Too wrong.

I was too late and I was sick with the futility of good intentions and what was that song, that low, rumbling, funereal sorrow? What had happened to the happy music?

Bam! Another gust of wind, another smash of wood on wood.

"Mrs. Teller!" I screamed over and over, voice drowning in the wet chorus of winter storm and mournful song. I gathered strength to come closer, to look through the open half of the Dutch door.

When I finally did, I grew silent.

Sometimes it's too scary to scream, and too late, and too useless.

I recognized the song then, too. Back in fictional Oklahoma, the villainous Jud was six feet under.

But there, in the Tellers' blue and white kitchen, things were more on the surface—ruby splatters on the refrigerator, a crimson splash on a white counter, and a bloody handprint on a cabinet door.

"I'm sorry, I'm sorry," I whispered, "I wanted to save you, but I'm too late, too late."

I finally forced myself to lean over the open edge of the Dutch door and look down below the cabinets and the counters. I gasped in shock, surprise, horror, confusion—I don't know which. There on the blue and white tiles, in a scarlet puddle, lay the inert and disfigured remains of Wynn Teller. What was left of his face looked as disbelieving of his condition as I did.

Poor Jud was dead.

Eleven

I BACKED AWAY FROM THE GORY REMAINS OF WYNN TELLER.

Down the three steps, out into the rain, where I breathed deeply—once, twice, a dozen times. It didn't make much of a difference. I held on to an oak tree, the wet ground beneath me shining in the deceptively warm and homey kitchen light.

There were procedures you were supposed to observe. Tell somebody. Notify somebody, but don't disturb the crime scene. As if I'd dare go in that house. I released the tree and backed off. After two days of obsessively searching, insisting time was running out, it had. There was no need for urgency.

I had to fight a powerful desire to rush home and bury my head under my comforter. The house to the right of the Tellers' was dark, so I ran to the left and pushed the bell. "Help!" I shouted. I was soaked and scared and toppling toward hysteria. "Help!"

Nobody did. I wheeled around and checked the other side of the street, or what I could see of it in the downpour. A picture window directly across was brightly lit, so I ran, slipping in the middle of the road, soaking through my coat all the way to my underwear.

"Thank God you're home!" I said when the door opened, even though I couldn't see anyone.

"Why wouldn't I be?" I thought for a moment she was a dwarf, because her head poked forward halfway down the door. Then I made out the edge of a wheelchair. "No door to door allowed in this neighborhood," she snapped. "It's a law. No soliciting. I saw you—I saw you over there, and now you're here." She shook her head so vigorously her glasses slid down her nose. They were steel-rimmed, as was she. From her iron-gray hair to her gun-metal wool dress to the chair itself, she was of a piece, and that piece was pure unyielding metal. "Well?" she said.

I was dripping and shivering at her half-open front door. Poor frightened wheelchair-bound woman, but poor me, too. "May I use your phone?" I asked. "It's an emergency."

"Car won't start? No wonder. That maroon number across the street, isn't it? You're too old for that kind of thing. Teenagers drive cars like that." Then she sighed, slowly and deeply, as if pneumatically lifting the weight of her considerable chest. "Tell me the number and I'll dial it for you."

I knew that was good sense. I do it myself when strangers want to use my phone, and this woman was especially vulnerable to crazies; but I was nonetheless shaking and soaking wet and as threatening as a dying flounder. "The police," I said through chattering teeth. "Call them. They're needed at the Tellers'."

"Oh, my Lord!" Her iron ore melted slightly. "Used to be a safe neighborhood. I have nightmares thinking what happens these days."

My nervous system was shot and my core temperature sinking too quickly for nonessential empathy. To be precise, I couldn't give a damn about her bad dreams. "Please," I said.

"Wait a minute," she interrupted, eyes squinting, "why are you calling if they were robbed? Who are you, anyway?"

"Mother," a gentle voice said. Its owner was a younger, upright version of the wheelchair-bound woman, with the minerals leached out. "I'll call," she said. "But please, what division needs to be alerted?"

"Division?" Her mother coughed a hard-edged laugh. "What are we talking about here? A war?"

"Homicide." It is difficult to say that word gently.

The daughter looked stricken and suddenly much older

than her childish voice and gestures had made me think. She turned and ran deep into the house to phone.

"Tell them I'm waiting in my car," I called after her. Damp seats would be more hospitable than these front steps. "The Mustang." Tell 'em to look for a lady in a car that's too young for her.

"Oh, no. Wait. Wait a second," the young woman said. It took longer than that, but not much, for her to return. "They'll be right here, or rather, right there," her daughter said. "I'm Patsy Benson, and why don't you come in out of the rain?"

"Patsy!" her mother hissed.

Patsy waved me in.

"Well," her mother said. "Don't blame me if we wind up dead, too." She shook her head. "Just don't drip all over my clean floors, you understand? I'll make tea so you don't get sick and sue me. I know how people are these days." She swiveled around and wheeled off.

"Please don't mind Mother," Patsy said. "When she's nervous, she's gruff, and she's nervous a lot. Runs in the family, I guess." She took my dripping raincoat and waved me toward a sofa. I tried to remember where I'd heard her name before.

Patsy headed for a weathered wing chair that faced the front window. She turned it so that it more or less aimed toward me. "I'll keep an eye out," she said. It seemed obvious that her eye was constantly out, although what there was to watch on a dull suburban street escaped me.

Making conversation under these circumstances is not easy. I smiled to be sociable, but couldn't think of anything except Wynn Teller's destroyed face, my own pathetic rescue fantasies, and the terrible way Lydia Teller had solved her dilemma herself.

"Who is it?" Patsy whispered after a long silence.

"Mr. Teller."

The brown eyes behind her round glasses widened. "I was hoping it was one of their guests. Nobody I know. Oh, why is it always the good ones? He devoted his life to helping children." She pulled off the glasses and wiped at her eyes.

"Always kept it so pretty over there, too, shaping those shrubs so beautifully. I'll miss his flower beds . . . he'd always wave to me."

She stood up and clasped her hands, then sat back down. "Poor Lydia, too! What will she do? They were so close—a perfect marriage, everybody said. He even came home for lunch every day." Then she pulled back, looking even more alarmed. "Oh, heavens, I didn't even think—is she all right? Lydia?"

"She wasn't there." Actually, I didn't know for certain whether that was so. What was I assuming—that if she were still there, having heard me call, she'd have stepped over the corpse with a cheery "Can I help you? I've just murdered my husband and it's a bit of a mess, but give me a sec."

Was Lydia alive, or had I just seen half of another MAN KILLS WIFE AND SELF headline? "What guests did you mean?" I asked. "Were the Tellers entertaining?"

"I thought they might be."

"Who was there?" Hordes, I wanted her to say. All carrying guns.

Patsy put her glasses back on. "People. I only saw their backs, and the rain, you know. Coats, umbrellas." She shrugged.

"But a lot of them?"

"Half a dozen, give or take. One or two at a time."

Her mother wheeled in. "Tea's ready. Come into the kitchen, and don't listen to Patsy. How could you see anything, daughter, while you were washing dishes back in the kitchen?"

"Before then, Mama." Her voice and attitude lost two decades when she talked to her mother. "And after. You know."

"Don't I ever," her mother muttered.

I placed them. The adventure reader who never left home, and her mother. I controlled an urge to tell Patsy there were phobia programs that could help her. From now on I intended to keep a lid on all do-good urges. I stood to follow the two women into the kitchen, but lights flashed silently outside. The police were not using their sirens. "I'd better go over," I said.

"You'll catch your death!" Mrs. Benson snapped.

An ill-chosen idiom given the circumstances, but I acknowledged her kindness and took my leave. The best thing I could do for my health, both mental and physical, was get this over with.

There is an amazing similarity between policemen. Like springer spaniels, or guppies, they are a breed with only minor variegations and distinguishing marks. The species specific trait I detected for genus suburbia was that they seemed rather more shocked by the fact of murder than the exhausted and jaded city police have become. It endeared them to me. And then it made me wonder, and worry, whether they might have reacted differently than Mackenzie had if I'd brought them the book.

A plump and businesslike policeperson looked as reluctant to let me in from the rain as Patsy's mother had been, but she eventually took me to a covered patio and through its sliding glass doors into the edge of a family room, where we huddled in relative dryness and warmth. We couldn't speak for the teeth chattering and for the deafening refrain of "Everything's Up to Date in Kansas City." I saw the phonograph player, its arm up so that a record would repeat through eternity. I also saw more disarray and upheaval than I would have believed possible of the woman who cared for the pristine living room I'd glimpsed earlier.

My policeperson told me to stay right there and shouted some questions and suggestions to a cohort who came in from the center of activity in the kitchen and turned off the record player. "Okay, now," she said. "From the beginning."

"I was looking for Lydia Teller," I said. "Is she okay? She's not, she wasn't also . . . was she?"

The policewoman shook her head. "You're her friend, then?"

"More an acquaintance." I wasn't going to incriminate Lydia with talk of the underlined book.

"Do you know her present whereabouts?"

"No. I was looking for her here."

I retold each step of my arrival and discovery. Take away the book and the dreadful pressure it had produced, my arrival wasn't much of a story when you got right down to it.

No, I said, I hadn't seen, let alone removed, a murder weapon.

The questions continued, but they were not the ones I wanted answered. Like where was Lydia, and who were the people Patsy'd seen coming and going tonight?

My mind backed up and bumped into Neil Quigley, wild-eyed in the office, stumbling through an unnecessary explanation of why he couldn't have picked up his materials earlier, forcing it on me, although I wouldn't have even wondered if I hadn't had such a guilty conscience and if he had simply kept quiet. That same Neil who, earlier in the day, had sworn he'd *get* Teller.

I had more secrets than I could handle, so I said only what I absolutely knew, which was nothing. And I said it several more times. Yes, I had met Dr. Teller twice, but only in a professional capacity. I'd applied for a tutoring position.

Soon as I said that, I realized that the death of the man who'd interviewed me probably meant I could kiss my island fantasy good-bye. My sad sigh seemed to convince the law that I was not a warped killer who'd stayed to call the cops.

"You didn't see anybody leaving?" the policewoman asked again.

I shook my head. "They must have left before I got here. It's obvious some outsider was here," I said.

The room was the *before* picture of the living room. Similarly comfortable furnishings, but neither cool nor fastidious. There were family photos—I recognized several of Hugh, and another of Lydia's cameo face above a high-necked Victorian blouse. I wondered if she'd adopted a covered-up style because she liked it or because she needed it. There were bookshelves with ornaments and photo albums along with the encyclopedia and assorted volumes.

But the lived-in ambience had been pushed a bit far. Record albums littered the sofa cushions, photos were strewn around, books tossed helter-skelter on tables, chairs, and the floor, drawers open, papers mussed on a desk in the corner.

I have a certain expertise with slovenliness. Enough, at least, to know that Lydia didn't qualify, even from where I stood at the back edge of the room. "It's not what a messy person would do," I said. "No glasses making rings on furniture, no dishes with food remnants, no discarded shoes or clothing. None of the typical droppings that . . ." That I have been known to leave around, but I didn't say so.

"Right!" she said, with visible relief. I recognized another guilt-ridden woman who didn't always hang towels back up or wash dishes immediately. "Although, of course, she could have done it herself, tidily, like it is, trying to make it look like a break-in."

"Why would she do that?"

The policewoman squinted at me, as if I'd gone out of focus.

"No," I said. "A cover-up? I can't imagine Lydia Teller doing that." And as I said it, I realized how peculiar it was, because what I had truly imagined was Lydia Teller herself. The only things I hadn't made up were an underlined book, a few photos, and random comments by her acquaintances. I suddenly felt frightened and wanted to go home.

"Can you think where'd she go? Who'd take her?" The policewoman's expression was cryptic.

"Take her? Why?"

"There are two cars in the garage. Hers and his, unless they had more than one apiece. Doesn't seem a night for a long wander on foot, does it? We'll check the cab companies, of course, but I thought maybe you'd have an idea."

I shook my head. I'd done that so often tonight, I felt like one of those plastic dolls with springs for necks.

Shortly thereafter, I was dismissed, leaving behind my phone number, address, and employer's name.

There have not been many nights in my life when home seemed more appealing. I nearly dived into my car. I wanted out, and away, and done with it. I had to work hard not to floor it, but I wanted no further business with the police.

My bed and comforter beckoned. If my luck changed,

there'd even be a clunker on the late show, a movie whose plot hinged on a quaint old-fashioned defunct morality. Where whether Rock Hudson or Sinatra would seduce an innocent rather than marry her was the single burning issue—and a wedding was the happy ending. Where not even the concept of wife-beating existed. Give me undistilled, one-hundred-percent-proof genuine make-believe, please.

I drove carefully, letting my muscles untwist and unknot one by one. And then, directly behind my right ear, so close I felt its breath and heat, a voice said, "Don't scream."

I did anyway.

Twelve

Some of my students claim I have eyes in the back of my head. Right then, I wished I did.

I careened wildly, jerked hither and yon, all the while shrieking and babbling and wondering who or what could have hidden itself in the stingy space behind me.

"Please!" I heard.

Another wild carom and scream. What kind of kinky villain said please?

"Hush, now. Calm down."

Hush? I once again tried to oxygenate my lungs, then pulled the car over to the first free curbside. Now all was silence behind me; so slowly, one ligament at a time, hand on the door handle, ready to bolt, I turned around.

"I'm sorry," she said. "I didn't know what else to do. I couldn't take my car. The police would find me, and besides, I don't know where to go. I saw you through the window. I heard you calling me. You seemed almost familiar. I don't know. Safe, maybe. A second sense I had, so when I saw you go across the street, to Patsy, and I was sure you were calling the police—it was all I could think of as a place to hide."

Lydia Teller's face in the streetlight was frightening, the skin mottled and broken, one eye swollen almost closed.

She had moved the plastic container. There wasn't room

for it and a person in the back. It was raining on her. I told her to come up front, and she did, docilely. She was a woman too accustomed to being told what to do.

"Why were you looking for me?" she asked.

"I found your book."

She wrinkled her forehead, as much as she could with her puffs and bruises.

"The book you underlined."

Still nothing, and then a gasp, a searching look. "That book? But that was a while ago."

"I just found it." My voice was as low as hers, raised only to cover the sound of passing cars and honking horns. "Two days ago. I've been searching for you ever since."

She shook with long, hard sobs.

"Let me take you to the shelter people," I said.

She shook her head. "I can't. They'll be looking for me now, won't they? The police? Wouldn't they have to turn me in?"

I didn't know how far the shelter's vow of secrecy went, but I suspected it stopped at homicide investigations. "Mrs. Teller, I want you to know I don't blame you. When I read that book, I was sick at what you've been put through."

"Don't blame me for what?"

"Everybody has a breaking point."

She pushed her body against the side window, away from me. "You think I did it."

"Well, I—you didn't?"

She shook her head.

"Then who did?"

She shook her head again.

"How could you not know? You just said you were in the house when it happened, didn't you?"

She looked up at my scaly convertible top and blinked hard. "You see? That's just how the police would be, but I don't know who did it. I don't!"

"Where were you, then?"

"Upstairs, in the bathroom. Locked." She put her hands up, as if to cover her bashed face. "Hurt me. I ran up. Locked the door. He pounded and swore and said he'd be back, but

I waited and waited, then I thought he'd gone to sleep, passed out like sometimes, and I came out and there he was. On the floor.''

''You didn't hear anything? A quarrel, a gunshot?''

She shook her head. ''I was upstairs, in the bathroom, locked.''

I couldn't tell if she was in shock or repeating a rehearsed alibi.

''I put on the record,'' she said. ''I wanted to listen to it forever, then you rang the bell. I couldn't answer. Couldn't. I made the music so loud I wouldn't hear. My son's a singer. Every school he went to, he starred in their show. In *Oklahoma!* he was Curly.''

''Hugh was in my class at Philly Prep.'' I introduced myself, although it felt a peculiar time and situation for the formalities.

''That's why you seemed familiar,'' she said. ''That's why I felt that way about you. He liked you. That's where he did *South Pacific*, Lieutenant Cable. Oh, yes. 'Younger than Springtime,' remember? I have that album, too. I have them all.''

I nearly wept for the image of her sitting in her family-less room, summoning and knowing her son only by other people's renditions of his musical comedy roles. ''How is Hugh?'' I asked.

She held her head high, almost defiantly, and then she winced, and slumped. ''He's a good boy,'' she said softly. ''Being a student isn't everything. There are lots of talents. Wynn's too hard on him, so I barely ever see my son—his son—he never can—he—'' And she remembered, and stopped talking.

''Come home with me.'' The idea set off alarms from my stomach to my brain, but I couldn't think of any other place to safely deposit her. I couldn't believe she was capable of violence, and even if she had murdered her husband, it would have been to save her own life. I was sure I had nothing to fear from Lydia Teller, only from hiding her, but I saw no other option. ''All right?'' I asked her.

She nodded like a prisoner being moved to a different holding pen.

"We'll think of something," I said as I drove. "They'll find whoever did it and then you'll be free."

She didn't seem particularly cheered, but how jolly could a woman with a murdered husband, a messed-up son, and injuries to her face and psyche be?

Her vulnerable gray eyes, old-fashioned face, and waiting silence made me want to protect her, and I couldn't comprehend how anybody—let alone anybody who theoretically loved her—could bear to hurt her.

"Do you know if anybody else was there tonight?" I asked, trying not to further upset her.

"Of course," she said. "The person who shot Wynn."

I nodded. "Patsy Benson said several people—"

Her sigh was enormous, enough to stop me. "Patsy knows everything that goes on in our house," she said. "Except what really goes on."

"She said lots of people came and went."

"I was upstairs, in the bathroom. I'm sorry."

We reached the end of that conversational alley almost precisely at the moment we reached our destination.

"Home," I said, pulling up. I hustled her inside. "Your room's upstairs. The top floor. It's tiny, with only a fold-up bed. I'm sorry. The bathroom's on the second floor." Definitely not four stars, but I did have emergency first aid supplies, which I left with her while I removed my car from my preinternal-combustion-engine street and walked home from my parking lot double-time. I didn't even bother with an umbrella, since I was already sopping wet and beyond help. I stopped at the drugstore for a toothbrush for Lydia, wondering whether civilization could be reduced to that one essential.

When I was home again, while water boiled for tea, I filled two brandy snifters—without asking Lydia whether or not she needed it. If she didn't, I'd drink hers, too.

She didn't give me the chance. With shaky hands around the snifter, she downed hers like medicine while I explained my working hours and the rather obvious requirement that she not answer the phone or make any calls. I showed her where my small stock of food was located and promised to buy more. I warned her not to feed Macavity every time he feigned starvation. Showed her the idiosyncracies of the toaster oven and TV, and then I was done, too poor to afford any more quirky appliances.

Lydia gave my house tour the attention due something much more complex. A weak smile flickered across her face. I could see how exquisite the once-upon-a-time-happy Lydia must have been. She had an old-fashioned face, oval with a small pointed chin and heavy-lidded almond eyes. At least, she had that beneath the swellings and discolorations. She was small-boned and would have looked fragile even without evidence of abuse. She should have been cherished.

"Thank you," she said. "You make me feel safe." And then she inhaled so sharply, it sounded like a swallowed sob.

I hugged her, gently, so as not to press on her injuries. She was definitely no longer a creature of my imagination. The kettle whistled, and I busied myself fixing a tray while she sniffled and blew her nose. She stood near the room divider and lifted, of all things, the zillion ways to get a guy tome. She flipped through it, and as much as it is possible for a wry smile to play over swollen and livid lips, one did.

"We work so hard to win their affection," she said softly. "Pervert ourselves, deny ourselves. Look at this telling you to take up a hobby you don't like, join a club or a church without personal meaning—read magazines you couldn't care less about—" She pushed it aside. "Men complete the job, but we start it. Don't," she said. "Look at me and don't."

I promised I wouldn't. I didn't even explain the stupid book's origins. We settled down in the living room. I pulled the curtains in an attack of paranoia, as if a Lydia-hunting posse were likely to charge down my little street.

The geometric completeness of baroque music is as effective as tranquilizers, at least for me, so I put on a Bach three-part invention, and after a long, almost comforting silence, Lydia spoke.

"I grew up in Africa," she said. "My parents were naturalists. For what seemed half my life, they studied wildebeests. Gnus, by other names. The wildebeest has an odd disease. It starts to run in circles and can't stop. The circles get smaller and tighter, and on they go till they're more or less spinning. And then they drop. That's what my whole life feels like.

"I tried so hard, but nothing was enough. Nothing was right. A speck of dirt, or dinner a minute late, or overcooked, I talked too much or not enough, I was too dumb, or too loud, or laughing too much or not enough, or Hugh, poor dear, was . . . anything. Just was. Angry at him from the day he was born."

For once, Macavity was not perverse. He studied Lydia, saw a need and filled it with little cat feet gentling their way onto her lap, and then an audible purr. For that, cat, pâté tomorrow; I promised. Lydia smiled with the parts of her face that still could. "Wynn wouldn't allow pets," she said. "They're messy, like people."

She spoke without animation, almost as if she were reading a text that she still found confusing. I wanted to cry, to rush back in history and unmake it, to do something, but she'd said she felt safe, and she sounded as if she believed it, and I was afraid of disrupting whatever peace she had hold of.

"My parents died in a plane crash when I was sixteen," she said at one point. "I came back to the States and my grandmother took me in, but when she died two years later, that was it for family. And then Wynn appeared . . ." She was silent again for a long while. "He wasn't that way then. He was strong, you know. Had high standards and all, but not cruel. I don't know what happened. I had never seen men shout at women that way, let alone hit them. I thought it must be my fault. I told a counselor that my husband got mad a lot. She said I had to try harder. She knew Wynn, said what a nice man he was. I knew nobody would believe me. Thought I was crazy. Depressed all the time and lying about why I couldn't be where I should be because how could I say my lip's split, I can't breathe, he strangled me, my shoulder's dislocated. Half the time I didn't even believe it myself. He told me I had fallen against the stove, tripped into the wall, and I wanted to believe him even though the more he drank, the clumsier I got.

"And then he'd be so loving, take care of the hurts, give me gifts, and it seemed over. Forever." She sighed and drank tea. "I loved him so much," she said. "He was my hero. And he loved me, too, like in the movies. He did, you know. Couldn't live without me, he said."

"The thing is," I said, "nobody knows what kind of man your husband was, am I right?"

"He's the Chamber of Commerce's Man of the Year. Was."

"Then why would anybody suspect you? For all they're concerned, you had a perfect marriage. That article in *Philadelphia Magazine* said so. Patsy said so. Maybe your safest bet is facing the police, explaining that you're innocent."

"How would I explain where I've been?"

"How about a walk? A long walk. You were sad and needed time alone."

"Why? It's so cold and rainy tonight."

"Because of . . . because of Hugh."

"*Hugh?* Why drag him into this?" Her voice was shrill with a lifetime of protecting her child.

"Because . . . he's so far away and you never get to see him."

"But even Patsy knows he was here Sunday."

Right. I remembered Wynn's reaction to my lie about Hugh needing a recommendation. He'd been surprised, said he'd thought Hugh had left town this weekend. "Say it was a sad visit," I improvised.

"It was. Very. But I won't involve Hugh."

"You've had a rough time with him. People would accept the idea of your being upset."

Her face darkened, making her bruises even more prominent. "I've had a rough time with Wynn! Hugh tried to protect me. Since he was a baby, he tried. But Wynn would brush him away. Until he was bigger, and then . . ." She shook her head.

"Your husband hurt him, too."

She nodded. "So I put him in boarding school, away, safe, and he'd get crazy and run home. To save me, he said."

"Why didn't you leave?"

She looked down at her clasped hands as if they might hold the answer. "For so long, I thought it was my fault. I made him angry. If I tried harder, I could be a better wife. Wynn was so patient with students and teachers. Everybody thought he was wonderful. Besides, I didn't have anyplace to go, or any way to make a living or support Hugh. And then, as if he suspected what was happening in my mind, Wynn said that if I left, he'd find me and kill us both. That he couldn't live without me. I believed him."

"But when you read that book, didn't you see it wasn't your fault? That there were things you could do? Didn't it change how you felt?"

She nodded. "It was like finding a friend. Somebody to talk to, as foolish as that sounds. I didn't feel so alone. I wanted to keep it, but I couldn't, not where he might find it, so I tossed it in the book box when I drove that time. I could have put it in the trash, but some part of me wanted somebody, somewhere, to know."

"And still you stayed. You thought he'd kill you, but you stayed."

"Not forever, no. I decided to leave, but Hugh had finished high school and he was on his own, somewhere. I couldn't leave without his knowing where to find me or we'd never see each other again. I had to wait till he showed up, and he did, this weekend. I thought there'd be some time, a plan, but it was terrible between them and Wynn threw him out, told him to never come back. And he went." Her eyes welled up again.

I stood up, to get some distance from the mare's nest of the Teller family. I straightened a picture on the wall, went into the kitchen, sponged off the counter, and finally broke through the thick silence. "Let's get back to what to do now. I still think you should go to the police. Let's be honest. Nobody would ever think of you shooting somebody."

She looked at me, then up at the ceiling. "I grew up with guns," she said calmly. "It literally was a jungle out there, you know. I can shoot anything, pretty much." She looked sad. "The odd thing is, I lived in the wilds, places people think of as scary, but I always felt safe, until I married Wynn Teller."

"Do you—was there—in the house, do you own a gun?"

She nodded. "Several. They're a legacy. Great-great-grandfather worked for Mr. Deringer here in Philadelphia. When President Lincoln was killed with a Deringer pistol, Great-great-grandfather was so fearful that it was one he'd crafted that he became morose and never spoke again. His pistols were the beginning of a collection. Philadelphia Deringers and Colts, mostly. Some are quite ornate. Silver chasing and carved mother-of-pearl." She yawned.

Please, I implored the god of ballistics, don't make the murder weapon be an old and unusual gun. I thought I heard a snicker or two from above, and I looked despairingly at Lydia Teller, a woman with the best of motives for murder, plus the skill and the opportunity, and minus an alibi.

Maybe the same series of thoughts crossed her mind. "If it's all right with you," she said, "I'm a little dizzy. I'd like to go upstairs and lie down for a second."

Which is what she did. I thought of settling in for the night, too, but although it felt as if enough time had elapsed to put us in the next calendar year, it was not even late enough for the movie I'd promised myself. Besides, somebody with no consideration of the kind of day I'd had, programmed an Annette Funicello beach movie, an Elvis musical, and *Tora! Tora! Tora!* I felt personally betrayed.

What I definitely did not want to do was think about Lydia Teller's future anymore tonight, which left only the failure warnings as diversion. They weren't a major project, merely tiresome. They didn't make students improve scholastically, but they did provoke endless debates of why the warning was incorrect and/or unfair.

Name, grade, section. Then came the part I resent, where I have to explain the warning. I'm always tempted to write something like *Are you kidding?,* but I have to find stern euphemisms for the girl who appears lobotomized (*little class participation*) and the boy whose textbook has never been out of his locker, its virgin pages uncut (*not working to potential*)—

My head jerked at a knock at the door. And then one at the front window. There was a largc silhouette on the closed curtains. I pressed back into the sofa, but then the silhouette put its thumbs in its ears and wiggled its fingers.

"Sasha," I said, opening the door. "What are you doing here at this hour?"

"Saw the light on. I was around the corner. At a movie." She pulled off a Sherlock Holmes raincoat and a shiny broad-brimmed black hat meant for either rainstorms or a wet garden party. Sasha stood in front of the coffee table, looking down at two each of brandy snifters, cups and saucers. "Dick Tracy's here?" she asked. She looked spiffy in a rose peplum number from the early Fifties.

I shook my head.

"Left early, did he?" She slumped into my worn suede chair, legs stuck straight out in front of her. "I tell you, Mandy, I've *had* it with men!"

"Everybody knows that." I poured her some brandy.

She tapped a long fingernail on the side of her snifter. "I was stood up! Me! Can you believe it? Can you?"

I could probably believe almost anything about her. "You want to talk about it?"

"I waited and waited at the damn restaurant—he had to pick a fancy one, right? Where the maître d' eyed me like I was a hooker."

"Anybody I know?"

She shook her head. "Nobody I want to know anymore, either. Creep. I wore shoes that hurt for him, too! Waited an entire hour. Cost me twenty-seven dollars for an appetizer and a glass of wine. And then I said to hell with him and went to the movies where I didn't see a damn thing except red. He didn't even have the courtesy of calling the restaurant, a message."

"Maybe there's one at home for you."

She shook her head even more vigorously. A silver-trimmed comb fell out and she jabbed it back in place. "I checked my machine ten minutes ago. *Men!* They're all scum.

I'm finished with the lot of them. From now on, I'm concentrating on my work and my friends and clean, healthy living."

"I've heard this song before." Maybe a thousand times.

"Ought to sing it yourself. I mean nameless is not exactly ideal, rushing back to Evangeline." She nodded toward the extra snifter and cup. "Trust me, the entire species is defective."

Misery loves company, especially man-hating misery. I wasn't worried that Mackenzie was scum, but I was concerned about what I would do about Lydia when and if C.K. shook Scarlett loose. This house is very small.

"Women can at least hope to understand each other," Sasha was saying. "But add testosterone to the mix, and the animal becomes unintelligible, unbearable, un—"

"Would you do me a favor?" My voice was low, but perhaps my anxiety was audible, because Sasha stopped.

"Why not? You're not a man."

"Could somebody stay at your apartment? Until . . ." I had no idea for how long. Until the police caught and locked up a killer? "Until a while?"

"Very secretive," she said. "Maybe subversive. Who is it?"

I shook my head. "Think of her as Madame X."

"Madame," Sasha said, and despite her anti-male ranting, she looked disappointed, as I'd known she would. "Not the mint julep, is it?"

I shook my head. "This woman's in big trouble. I can't really say much more."

Sasha's eyes twinkled. "She can't stay here because Hercule Poirot might find her, am I right?" She'd avenge being stood up by one man by duping another. This is the way serious pathology begins, but we'd handle that later. "Fine, sure, when? She isn't dangerous, is she?"

"Now and no."

"She's here? What did you do while he was over?" She looked at the duplicate coffee cup again, then at me, squinting. "Oh. He wasn't here at all, was he? The creep! So where are you stashing her?"

I took the stairs double-time. I felt brilliant at having thought of this, and lucky to have a friend like Sasha. Nobody would ever find Lydia now.

She must have collapsed on the cot, and there she still lay, fully clothed, uncovered, sleeping so deeply it would have been sadistic to wake her, not to mention difficult. I watched her even breaths, remembering her smile at finally feeling safe, and I knew I'd give her this night.

I slipped off her shoes, tucked a blanket around her, and turned out the light.

"I'll bring her over after school tomorrow," I said when I was back downstairs.

Sasha glanced toward the stairs as she pulled on lined leather gloves. "Long as a woman sleeps alone, nothing much bad can happen to her."

We were smug and self-satisfied at outwitting the universe. And we were wrong.

Thirteen

NEXT MORNING, ALL WAS STILL SILENCE ON THE THIRD floor, even after my radio burst into high-decibel rock 'n' roll. I try to avoid the alarm itself, which sounds like warning of a nuclear attack, but music that's loud enough to jolt me awake isn't much better.

I washed and dressed quietly, although if "Great Balls of Fire" hadn't penetrated Lydia's sleep, the sounds of stockings slipping on certainly wouldn't.

I tiptoed, shoes in hand, wondering if my stairs had always been that squeaky, and made myself coffee. Instant, and I pulled the kettle off the range before it began its train-whistle scream.

Harboring a fugitive, even a potential one, felt peculiar, but I was on the side of good, at one with the families who manned the Underground Railroad, or the people who hid Anne Frank.

I took out a large piece of paper. I'M AT SCHOOL, I wrote in letters big enough to catch her attention. I'LL BE BACK 3:30. MAKE YOURSELF AT HOME. DON'T— I had a long list of warnings, most of them obvious. Don't answer the door or phone, don't open the drapes, don't go outside. Don't panic, don't lose faith, don't play loud music, don't be afraid. Don't get caught.

Don't treat her like an idiot, I told myself. I would simply tell her not to worry. I got as far as wo when I heard a scritch, familiar but upsetting. The scritch of my erstwhile beloved's key in my doorway.

Now? After ignoring me all week?

I corrected my own irate mind. The week wasn't over yet. We were up to Thursday morning and I'd seen him Monday evening and yesterday afternoon. The fact that both sightings were brief, impersonal, and unpleasant didn't matter. Still, was this the time to come calling?

The front door opened. "It's dawn," I said. "You scared me."

"Not as much as you're scaring me."

And instead of wasting time figuring out what the devil he meant, I asked the only relevant question. "Does this mean Jinx left?"

"What?" One of his shoulders shrugged. "Not till Sunday, you know that."

Oh, yes. Airline rates improved if you stayed over Saturday. My temper did not.

"Listen, if you thought I was upset on that message—"

I looked down and for the first time noticed the blinking answer machine light.

He raised his arms in disgust or despair and turned his back, then swiveled. "Not surprisin'. L'il things like checking messages slip the mind after a busy evening."

I didn't know what was eating him, but I hoped it was the aftermath of a vicious quarrel with Jinx. On the other hand, I wasn't willing to take the brunt of his clashes with the Confederate chickadee.

"Well," he said, slouching his tall, lean way around my living room, "if you ever do give a listen, you'll hear me try to talk some sense into you, call you off your quest."

"Thanks." I wished he'd put the idea of saving me on hold until such time as I needed it. At the moment, it seemed too much like meddling, or downright oppression. I'd have to think about this sometime.

"On the other hand," he said, "no point botherin' with it now, is there?"

"What are you talking about?"

He looked up at my ceiling and I panicked, afraid he knew about my secret guest, but then I realized he was merely seeking divine guidance, or patience. "You tellin' me," he said slowly, "you don't think it's a tad late to try and call you off?"

"Off . . . what?"

"Off the sad Tellers." His mush count was on the rise. When suffering stress, Mackenzie reverts to the language of a childhood spent in a bayou where humidity apparently rusts intelligibility the way it does iron. His words flake, disintegrate into powder, and I have to strain to hear him criticize me, which doesn't seem fair. "I happen to think it's too late because I watched TV this mornin'. An' read the paper." He looked like a curly-haired avenging angel.

"Why would I be in the paper?" I asked.

"Why wouldn't you?" He'd told me that I should point it out when he became incomprehensible so he could work on his pronunciation, but this wasn't the time to mention that he'd compressed all of *wouldn't* into a sound like being punched in the stomach might produce. I added *whunt* to the book of Mackenzie-speak and moved on.

"My name would not be in the paper because I haven't won any awards or had an affair with a famous person."

"Concernin' the Tellers."

"Come on, Mackenzie. There weren't any reporters there, and I didn't speak to anybody except the police."

"Damn! I was right. I knew it was you! Damn! Paper said an unnamed woman found Wynn Teller's body and called the police. My stomach cramps told me who that mysterious female had to be."

I couldn't tell if he was furious at not being listened to, or furious because he cared about me and somehow thought I was in danger.

"Do me a favor?" he said. "Explain how you knew exactly the worst possible moment to go there, precisely in time for a murder."

"After a murder, which makes it less precise."

He made a strangled sound, something between a moan and a yowl. "How do you get involved in these situations?"

Then he sighed heavily, shook his head, opened his arms and looked up again, frightening me anew until I realized he was doing the *Fiddler on the Roof* bit with God one more time. "What'd they say when you told them?"

"Told them what?"

Another hand throw and heavenward glance.

"Tevye didn't come from Louisiana," I said. "Use your own ethnic gestures, would you?"

"What did they say when you told them about Lydia Teller?" His voice was overcalm. The tone you use with people whose eyes are spinning. "About Wynn Teller's habits? About the book?"

"You said it was foolishness. Why would I bother *other* police professionals about it?" I hoped that zing to his expertise stung.

"And it was, wasn't it?" he said. "Because he didn't kill her after all. She killed him. And what a great alibi or defense she's provided herself through that book. Through you."

No. Impossible. Too convoluted and improbable that the timing should be so exact. Ridiculous. Too much was out of her control, including her life and ability to plan. All the same, given the people I'd alerted who could have then alerted Lydia, a case—false but convincing—could be made by a determined prosecutor.

"What's this?" He picked up the large printed note. I'M AT SCHOOL.

"A little joke," I said, somewhat frantically. "For Macavity." The beast stopped tapping the kitty food cupboard for a moment. "You know how we spinsters treat our kitties like people."

"But writin' to him? 'Make yourself at home'? This is the mos' interestin' document I've come across in an age."

A little stomach jet spouted pure acid. Mackenzie's dumb-Southerner act is donned to play to our prejudices while he hides what and how quickly he's thinking. " 'Don't wo'?" he said.

"It's—it's a mistake. It needs another O."

"Don't woo?"

"Hey, there's a reason they call philanderers tomcats."

"Amazin'. An' I thought he never left the house. Never even wants to when I'm here."

"Well, mostly, but—" I looked at my watch. "I should be—"

"Her car was in the garage, but she wasn't there." He'd dropped his good but not too smart ol' boy voice.

My blood felt aerated, like seltzer. It was not a comfortable sensation. "I really, truly, have to be on my way." I kept my voice low, trying to sound like my normally subdued and grumpy morning self.

He looked at his watch and raised one eyebrow. Many happier mornings we had calibrated precisely how much time remained before I had to leave. He knew it wasn't yet.

"I care about you," he said softly. I listed in his direction. I could do with a bit of caring about.

And then I heard, faintly, a creak. I coughed, trying to cover it. "Cold won't go away," I muttered. Stop, Lydia, I thought with all my power, hoping there was something to mental telepathy. Sit down on that step and wait. Think about God. Think about Anne Frank.

But she was thinking about a bathroom. There was a brief pause, then another creak.

Mackenzie took a deep breath. "Don't wo," he told me. A pretty feeble joke.

I wondered how I could have avoided this. Oiled the stairs? Given her a chamber pot? Thrown Mackenzie out? The creaks stopped. Perhaps she'd reached the second floor bathroom. Please, Lydia, I telegraphed, no hygiene. Don't flush and don't wash your hands after, no matter what Mama taught you.

"How come you have nothin' to say about the Tellers this mornin'?" Mackenzie lounged against the newel post and smiled a big, bad grin.

He had changed for the worse these last few days. Jinx had contaminated him. I busied myself around the room, loudly putting dirty cups in the sink, opening the closet for my raincoat. Anything that made noise and covered upstairs noise. But I understood the futility of my actions because I understood Mackenzie's relaxed stance. There was no way out of the house except past him. He could afford to be casual about it.

"By the way," I said in as bright a voice as I can manage on a single shot of caffeine. "I was wondering about you yesterday."

"Me?" The eyebrow went up again, endearingly.

"I was wondering if perhaps your C. and your K. stood for Carl-with-a-C and Karl-with-a-K? Perhaps your parents were really, truly, enthusiastic about that name?"

"You're not even close, and how come you didn't tell the police about the book?"

"The other twofer that occurred to me was Constantine Konstantine. Could that be it?" I was so sure that wasn't it that I didn't need to hear his answer, which was one reason I asked it. My ears were already sticking up and out like Bugs Bunny's as I again heard the tentative squeak of a floorboard. So much for telepathy. I kept my eyes on my feet because they wanted so much to look up, see what was happening. Philadelphia realtors think these authentic, wide plank floors that predate the house's indoor plumbing are a selling point. They might be, but they are also geriatric cases that moan and groan about everything.

"It *is* Constantine!" I squealed, doing my best floorboard imitation. "And don't old houses make a lot of noise?" I squeaked. I believed in complete honesty between partners, but not, perhaps, absolutely all of the time. Certainly not now.

"I'm still not clear why you didn't tell the police." A great chunk of his attention was aimed up the stairs.

"What would I have said? I don't know who shot Wynn Teller." I spoke loudly, hoping Lydia was listening.

That got his focus back on me. And his disapproval. His mouth turned down, like a have-a-rotten-day button might, and he took a deep breath. "You were eager enough to tell everybody about the book. Why not the police?" His voice was low and still, in deliberate, smug contrast to mine, which now rose still higher.

"I had nothing to tell them! Lydia Teller didn't kill her husband!" I was nearly shouting now.

"Your cold's left you a little deaf." Slowly, lips exaggeratedly forming each word for hard of hearing me, he recited a variation of my own list, much to my increasing depression. "She's missing now, but was there to make him dinner. And . . ." I knew he was going to say what I didn't want to know. "And it appears, according to this morning's news, that the late Wynn Teller was shot with an unusual, old-fashioned caliber, and, by incredible coincidence, Mrs. Wynn Teller happens to own antique pistols and revolvers." He folded his hands across himself. Case closed.

"I know it sounds bad, but—" I blared, but then I stopped because my Klaxon voice hadn't covered a wooden squeal that was unmistakably the sound of a human foot on a quaint Colonial staircase. And there it was, encased in a shoe and topped by a leg.

"And you'd be Lydia Teller, wouldn't you?" Mackenzie spoke with great gentleness.

"Leave her alone!" I said. "This isn't your business and it didn't happen in your city or your turf and she's been bullied enough!"

C.K. looked startled. "What'd I do?"

Lydia stood straight. "I was listening." Her voice was low and composed, a dignified contrast to her livid bruises. "This is something I'm doing of my own free will. Me. For once in my life, I'm doing exactly what I want to."

"What does that mean? What are you saying? What are you doing?" Knowing the situation was completely out of my hands and knowing also that I had at least partially created it, I was filled with terrible, directionless energy. I understood the insane movement of trapped birds.

"I'm turning myself in," she said, as I knew she was going to. "There's no point hiding out this way, putting you in danger."

"I'm not in any—"

"I was thinking upstairs. Even before this . . . gentleman arrived. I've been lying and hiding for half my life. I don't want to do it anymore. I want to stand up for myself publicly. I want to tell what my life was. I'm tired of keeping secrets and being ashamed. If other women can read about it in the papers, maybe they'll be smarter and stronger and quicker than I was. And all those people who would never listen would finally have to. Maybe I was too ashamed to say it loudly enough. Now I will."

I protested, pleaded, told her she was the prime suspect and this was going to make it worse. "I know," she said with infinite calm.

"I have to warn you, ma'am," Mackenzie said. "Even though it's not my jurisdiction, I may be obliged to come forward with evidence. This is a capital crime."

"What's this? Are you reading her her rights?" I couldn't believe any of this.

"So mind what you say in front of me," he continued. Then he looked at me. "I'm not arrestin' her."

"I don't like hiding," Lydia said. "I don't want any more bad secrets. I'm going of my own free will."

"I'll be glad to drive you there," Mackenzie said softly.

"I'm sick of feeling guilty."

"There's no reason to! She didn't do it, Mackenzie! You didn't do it, Lydia!"

She looked puzzled by my outburst. "I know that. That's what I feel most guilty about."

Fourteen

I GATHERED UP MY FAILURE WARNINGS. I WAS THE ONE WHO deserved one. And not a warning, either. A notice of failure.

If I'd never opened the book, never determined to find the underliner, never drummed Lydia Teller's name into Mackenzie, a suburban murder would have been of peripheral or no interest to him. If I hadn't popped up on the Teller doorstep immediately after her husband was shot, Lydia would have had time to think things through, even to escape—and not into my car and not into my arms or those of my conscientious policeman-caller. Without me, she would have had a chance.

With not much of a stretch, one could say I had set her up and directed suspicion her way, and intensified whatever troubles she had. And so I said it. Over and over, walking to my parking lot and driving the brief stretch to school, until a clear message was etched on the crevices of my brain.

You created this mess. What are you going to do about it?

Somehow, I had still managed to arrive at school early enough to retrieve my daily ration of stupid reminders. Today's had to do with failure warnings, of course, and with misuse of the copy machine. Plus one notice that said a Miss Glenda Carter of TLC had called—yesterday afternoon, I noticed, possibly around the time I'd been chatting her up in person—to say I'd forgotten to leave my recommendations and résumé and would I please drop them off at my earliest convenience? She still wanted them. The business was, after all, a partnership. Teller-Schmidt Learning Centers. Mr. Schmidt was presumably still alive. Perhaps tutoring, like showbiz, goes on.

Helga watched me with her witchy scowl. I watched her back. I knew things about her now. I knew about the *ogzmic* file.

There was sufficient time left to repeat my miserable mantra.

You created this mess. What are you going to do about it?

I thought of something I could do. A start. I ducked into the entryway's pay phone and called my brother-in-law.

Sam isn't a criminal lawyer, but with his mild variety of annoyance, he reluctantly agreed to find out what could be done.

I headed for the teachers' lounge, exchanging weather pleasantries en route with the ever-smiling Latin instructor, Caroline Finney. Season in, season out, Caroline and I establish that we like each other and are civilized by speaking of the weather. We also establish our differing personalities through this code. I complain about meteorological imperfections and Caroline finds something heartening about whatever is given to her—hail, blistering heat, floods, or blizzards. Today, I said it was nice to be finished with rain, but it was a little too windy for me.

Caroline replied, "*Nihil est ab omni parte beatum.*"

"What did you say?"

"That nothing is an unmixed blessing. And Horace actually said it two thousand years ago."

Once inside the lounge, I decided that Neil Quigley could have taken a few sparkle plenty lessons from Caroline. Every day, he looked more like Norman Bates, thin and tightly strung as a high C piano wire.

"Morning," I said.

His hand trembled as he gulped coffee, holding his cup as if it contained a magic elixir that might save him. "Neil," I said quietly, "last night—"

He twitched. "What about it?"

Edie Friedman entered, looking tremulous and expectant, as if her One True Love might be lurking in the lounge. I wanted to shake her. The last few days had made what happened or didn't between men and women incomprehensible. I didn't know what to make of the evidence. Cruel marriages, like Wynn and Lydia's; and plagued marriages, like Neil's; and delusions of romance conquering all, suffered by Edie and whoever wrote the dating book; Sasha and her schizophrenic social life; and even me. And C.K. And Jinx.

Edie looked a little tired. *Love Story* had been on cable last night, she explained, looking acutely wistful. She poured herself coffee and left for hockey tryouts.

"My cup." The words were not said, but delivered by Potter Standish, *Doctor* Potter Standish as he often reminds us, who leaned back on his heels, studying the pegboard where we put our cups. His hands were behind his back in a scholarly stance, and his lips scrunched as if sipping something bitter. Finally, he put out his right hand and retrieved his somber black mug from the bottom left side. "Who moved my cup?" It was a rhetorical question, as he didn't look toward us or seem to care, and certainly nobody else gave a damn. "Shouldn't have." His words always seemed flat and printed in caps, like moving headlines that electronically revolve around buildings.

Potter taught chemistry poorly and by rote during the day and drank enthusiastically by night. There were rumors that he had something on Havermeyer and was blackmailing him. I couldn't imagine what my principal could have done that would be that juicy and worrisome, but I also couldn't figure out why else a school with no tenure would keep this man.

Potter downed his coffee while we watched. He then squared his shoulders, rinsed his cup, and hung it up again, but on *his* peg, near the top right. "Shouldn't touch a personal possession." And he left the room.

"What about last night?" Neil asked as soon as the door closed behind Potter. He sat in one of the degenerate armchairs, but so tensely, he seemed to levitate an inch above its cushions. "Is coming back for a roll book a federal offense?"

I backed off a pace and bumped into the refrigerator handle. "I was talking about Teller, not . . . us. Did you hear?"

He squinted, lifted his chin almost pugnaciously. "What now? What was I supposed to hear?" He stood up, thrumming with tension. "I didn't have time to hear, even to think about him. Angela went into a false labor that lasted all night. Why?" His eyes squinched into fleshy slits. He was obviously, and with cause, exhausted.

"When—when did that happen? The false labor, I mean."

"When?" He shook his head. "I don't know. After dinner. Why?"

Because he hadn't mentioned it when we bumped into each other last night, and it would have made sense to, wouldn't it? "Just wondering if she's okay," I said.

He nodded impatiently. "What was I supposed to hear about Teller, Amanda?" He leaned against an archaic mimeograph. Helga thought we should use it instead of the copy machine. Its dust filmed Neil's blue blazer, but he had more on his mind than good grooming.

"Teller's dead."

Neil paled. Pulled away from the machine, opened his mouth and made a breathy sound, then closed his lips again.

It was, I felt, overdone. A bad actor's concept of how to simulate shock.

The bell rang—shrilled, really. Voices and calls flooded the hallway outside. I gathered my coat and briefcase. "I know it's a shock. Even for me, I—"

"The bastard's dead," he said.

We left the lounge and joined the student crush. He hadn't even asked what had ended Teller's life. "He was murdered," I said, out in the hall. "Somebody killed him last night."

Neil navigated through the students. We climbed the stairs toward our rooms and reached a little island of clear floor. Only then did he stop and study me. The tic near his eye pulsed the seconds away. "You think I did it, don't you?" he said.

"Of course not! Why on earth would I?"

His sad eyes looked at me levelly. "Because you're intelligent. He did me harm and meant to do more. He was killing me. That's why people kill other people. It's all about self-defense." And, looking weary, he lifted his hand in a sad farewell and crossed the wide hallway to his room, there to transmit the lessons of history.

Not Neil, I told the gods. Not Lydia. But who, then?

The students seemed unnaturally, disgustingly rowdy for the early hour, and I made my way through them as invisibly as possible. This is no big feat, as there is nothing they enjoy more than ignoring faculty. Still, there seemed an inordinate amount of hilarity, but then, they were teens.

I was involved with a graphic designer my first, shell-shocked year of teaching, during which my every educational illusion detonated, along with the relationship. I take full blame. I was obsessed with my professional loss of innocence, the fear that I didn't have a calling, but a sentence.

The graphic designer had style. As a parting gift, he created what looked like an illuminated manuscript page, but what really was a quote from Shakespeare's *Richard III*. "Each hour's joy wracked with a week of teen" it said. Act IV, Scene 1. It was comforting—cold comfort is better than none at all—to discover that *teen* meant annoying and vexful even before the idea of adolescence was invented. The poster hung in my classroom, as ignored as anything else Shakespeare ever said, until m'lord Havermeyer, checking his fiefdom before Parent's Night, actually read it.

My first-period ninth graders were midway through a unit on Poe, always a happy time with his grisly, compulsive stories and resonating rhymes. We had fun with "The Cask of Amontillado" today.

Second period was still doing oral book reports, another comfort, for me, if not for them. Oral book reports are required by the curriculum. Ivory-tower educators believe the process teaches communication skills and reduces fear of public speaking. This is a pleasant concept, and completely fallacious. After decades of oral book reports, nationwide polls still show that the majority of the populace would rather face a firing squad than an audience.

Besides being ineffective, oral book reports are excruciatingly boring. One by one, students, eyes riveted to three-by-five prompts, rehash Cliff Notes or movies, while their classmates listen only to how many *uh*s or *and*s they say. Nonetheless, it was a time during which I could both listen and, I hoped, do some serious thinking.

Nonnie Waters was the fifteenth tenth grader to read Steinbeck's *The Pearl*, inspired less by its bitter wisdom than by its slenderness. "It's, um, about these divers, see, for pearls, and they, um, have a baby, and, um, so like they find this pearl and it's really valuable and I forgot to say they're like poor, I mean really poor, and they can't even get medicine for their baby, who has this weird name, which is something I didn't like about the book, but anyway . . ."

Eventually Nonnie reached her critical summation. *The Pearl* was kind of boring, but okay, too. Too many *um*s, the class decided.

Next up, Dwight was so surprised that *Shane* was good that he had absolutely nothing else to say about it, including even the barest rudiments of the plot. Allison, bespectacled and shy, broke my heart by compounding her geeky reputation by confessing that she'd read *Jane Eyre* because I'd recommended it. And last for this morning, Didi Donato admitted that an Ursula LeGuin fantasy had been good. "Well," she said, flinching as if she expected a violent reaction, "actually, I thought it was as good as a movie. No," she insisted, as if she'd heard a chorus of disbelief. "It actually was."

A normal morning. I found that awkward. Things were too skewed in the universe for us to be involved in ordinary pursuits. I kept contrasting Lydia Teller's day with mine and obsessively walking the road to hell I'd paved with good intentions. If Sam got her out on bail, where would she go? To that place that couldn't feel like home with its ugly memories and a gory kitchen off limits as the scene of a crime? She had no family, and her only child had been driven off by the husband she was now accused of murdering. I sighed so loudly that the class stopped counting how many *and*s Didi used. Instead, they pointed blank faces in my direction.

Who? I repeatedly asked myself. Who had been there last

night while Lydia was locked in the bathroom? Who killed Wynn Teller?

My eleventh graders were having a vocabulary quiz, gunning up for next autumn's SATs. Every word I randomly picked from the list seemed ominously weighted with new meaning. "Fiasco," I said. Noun. That which my good intentions helped create.

Chicanery. Vindictive. Cadaver. I scanned the list for less grisly words and found a section based on *mono, bi,* and *tri.*

"Monotheism," I said, breathing more easily. What a nice, respectable, noncriminal word. "Monologue." A student groaned, as if she'd been dreading the word instead of learning what it meant.

"Bigamy."

Bigamy! Of course. How could I have forgotten the woman dressed like an indigestion nightmare who'd insisted she was Wynn Teller's wife, the mother of his children, the creator of the idea of TLC? Plus those hulking, unhappy children of hers. There were two abused wives, a slew of motives.

"That's only seven!" a student said. I blinked and looked around.

"Is that all?" the child asked.

"All what?"

She rolled her eyes so far up they were nearly all white and definitely disgusting. "All of the spelling quiz," a redheaded boy near me said, his voice embarrassed on my behalf. I was grateful for his concern.

I cleared my throat. "Trio," I said.

Fay and Adam and Eve. One cheated of her idea, income, and husband, the others of their father and perhaps their share of the business. Could they have? Did the police know about them?

"Ahem!" It was a sound out of a comic book. Nobody except my students actually said it, but it did bring my attention back where it belonged, the vocabulary list.

"Misogyny," I read, and I sighed. All words led to Wynn Teller.

"Frustration."

All words.

Fifteen

THE FACULTY LOUNGE IS THE ONLY IN-SCHOOL ALTERNATIVE to the student dining room with its chaos, food fights, and, most appalling aspect of all, students. The lounge, ugly and cramped as it is, is therefore popular by default. Its atmosphere is also generally much more pleasant than its decor. But this particular noon, it was nearly as distressing as the other dining option. Not food, but daggers hurtled through the air.

"You could have *asked*," Commercial Art snapped at Biology.

"About what? I told you I didn't take your schnecken."

"My *mother's* schnecken. I was going to give you one, anyway. Didn't I yesterday?"

"I didn't take your mother's—"

"What's going on?" I whispered to Edie.

"She's sure he swiped the goodies she had stashed on top of the refrigerator. There was a tin—with her name on it, as she keeps reminding us. I said write it off to the Philly Prep Phantom, but she won't quit."

"Not one left!" the art teacher keened.

Edie unwrapped a fragrant assemblage of cholesterol and preservatives on rye. "Want some?" she asked. My mouth watered, my heart shouted assent, but I shook my head.

"I brought in tons of yogurt Monday and I've been cheating every day since." I needed a shot of self-righteousness anyway.

However, I wasn't going to find virtue in yogurt, because I wasn't able to find yogurt, for starters. My entire supply was gone. I felt my lips pucker with annoyance and I suddenly shared the art teacher's fury. What were we becoming that we pilfered each other's lunches?

"My yogurt's gone," I answered. "Anybody see it? Blueberry. Not premixed." Next I'd issue an APB and have its photos put on milk cartons. Three inches high. Blue and white. Have you seen this yogurt?

"Maybe the janitorial service takes things," someone suggested.

"They're only here Fridays," I reminded them.

"We should padlock the refrigerator," Gladys the computer skills teacher said.

Edie Friedman brushed crumbs off her skirt. "What good would that do? We'd all need separate locks, and then what? Forty keys to use every time we opened it?"

"And that wouldn't help my schnecken," the art teacher whined. "Cookies don't get refrigerated!"

I tried to look sympathetic, but schnecken weren't going to do it for me on this particular day. Instead, I retrieved my coat and decided to go to the deli around the corner where, I promised myself, I would purchase only leafy green foodstuff.

"By the way," Edie said with a private wink, "that lamp better work."

The kids in the classroom had been astoundingly, abnormally normal, but the faculty had obviously been replaced by oddballs from outer space. Neil twitched, the art teacher fumed about schnecken, and Edie shared hopes about a lighting fixture. "Are you okay?" I asked.

"I'm great," she said. "Except for hockey tryouts. But the lamp—the boudoir lamp, remember? For seductions? I took it home. I *know* I shouldn't have, but I had to—and I don't know, it just makes me believe things are going to change for the better."

How could she actually believe that better automatically

included a man? Still, I tried to look pleased and optimistic for her. "And thanks for reminding me. I put things away and forgot to take them." I just about backed out of the lounge. They were all crazy. Maybe it was something in the school heating system, a psychological Legionnaire's Disease.

It was blustery outside. A great day for catching cinders in one's eyes. I was grateful for the warmth of my down coat, and for all the shivering geese who had sacrificed their feathers for me. The streets were nearly empty except for a handful of hard-core students braving the out of doors. Anything, even frostbite, for the sake of a few minutes out of school.

It was a day that justified the great indoors. A day for comfort food. I stood at a corner of the square, rethinking the necessity of that leafy and unsatisfying lunch.

My train of thought, idling between thick sandwiches and thicker soups, was suddenly derailed as I felt myself grabbed from both sides and nearly lifted off the ground.

"Hey!" I shouted. "Let go!" They—whoever they were—carried me by my edges, as if I were a large canvas on its way to being hung. I turned my head, but my slouch hat twisted along with me and blocked my vision. "Help!" I screamed.

An incredibly short osteoporosis victim crossing the park looked my way, then hustled in the opposite direction. I really hadn't expected her to save me.

"We won't bother you. We just want to talk, okay?" The voice was male, unbright, and on my left.

"Then let me go!"

And he did. So did the other pair of hands. I adjusted my hat and looked up at the oversize, alleged spawn of the late Wynn Teller. "Don't touch me again, you understand?" I said.

Adam looked cowed, but Eve put her hands on her solid hips. "I ask your help in the name of sisterhood," she said.

"Where are you from?"

"Buffalo, why?"

"Because in the outer forty-nine, people don't talk that way anymore, okay? Enough that you're saying you're Teller's daughter. Don't get it all confused by saying you're my sister, too.''

''It's not meant the same—''

''Listen, I'm a teacher. I get a forty-five minute lunch break and nearly half of that is gone. Talk fast and follow me.''

''You were there. You could testify.''

We passed a sadistic nanny forcing a little boy in a snowsuit to play despite the wind-chill factor. The game he chose was called kick the nanny.

''I don't know what you're talking about,'' I said.

''Our father,'' Adam said. I thought he was praying. ''He's dead,'' he continued.

''My condolences, of course.''

''No, you don't get it. How are we going to prove he's our father now? But you were there, in the office, a witness. Remember?''

I did, but so what, and how the devil did they remember me? I asked all of that while we hustled along.

''We went back this morning, asked Glenda, the receptionist, and she had your name in the appointment book, and then there was the record from when you interviewed of where you worked and everything.''

''They're open? Today? Business as usual?''

''Maybe not as usual,'' Eve said. ''But yes, open. What does that have to do with anything?''

I didn't think she'd be interested in my need to deliver my résumé and references, which I'd now do right after school. ''Look here,'' I said, ''the truth is, I don't remember much about what was or wasn't said. Certainly nothing that would stand up in court.'' We entered the aroma zone of a deli. They followed me in and stood sniffing, Eve with less obvious pleasure than Adam. I suspected she only ate third world foods, like yak butter, but her political correctness seemed peripheral when she thought she was in line for Daddy's bucks. Scummies, I'd heard the genus called. Socially Conscious Unless Money Is Involved.

While I was ordering, she poked me in the shoulder. ''You

teach literature, right? I'll bet you only read the standard dead white men."

I shook my head and ordered a container of vegetable soup and a pastrami sandwich. "Hardly," I told her with my sparklingest, sisterhoodiest smile. "You'll be glad to know that I've dropped Hawthorne and Twain so we'd have time to do the entire Barbara Cartland canon. Every book she wrote."

When we left, Adam and I had matching takeout bags. Eve already had heartburn from her own raging anger.

"Come on." She grabbed my arm again.

"I warned you!" I looked around for a patrolman. I didn't see one, but Eve let go anyway. I still wished I'd seen a patrolman.

"I never had your advantages," she said in a shrill voice that made me less than upset about her sufferings, real or imagined. "I never went to college to become an English teacher."

"I had a scholarship." I stupidly defended myself when I didn't have to.

"My mother had to scrub floors," Eve shouted, "and—"

"She never scrubbed floors," Adam said. "Our floors were always a mess."

"It's a metaphor! Give me a break, you pig! Bad enough I had to share a womb with you!"

Maybe it wasn't the heating system at Philly Prep. Maybe everybody's brains were being sucked out the holes in the ozone layer, even up in Buffalo. I vowed never to use an aerosol again.

"Look, Miss—" Adam began.

"Miss! How many times do I have to tell you not to identify women by their married condition!" Eve sighed histrionically.

I always think of myself as a nonviolent person, so I'm shocked by how often I have the urge to slug somebody. Like now. In the name of sisterhood. Even though I do prefer *Ms*. Nonviolently.

"The thing is, there were letters," Adam said.

"You don't have to tell her everything!"

"But we couldn't find them. I mean, we have the ones he

wrote our mother, but they're vague, you know? Like they say *idea* instead of spelling it out. Like: *Your idea sounds very interesting*. But the ones she wrote him, they said it, like let's have tutoring centers. We need those letters. For proof, you know?"

What I knew was that Adam Teller couldn't walk and talk at the same time. Every time he had to do so much as think, he stopped in his tracks and placed himself so that he blocked me. I considered an end run, but then looked at his formidable sister and held off. "It was her idea, you know," he said. "He said it had gone belly-up. He lied."

"Men!" Eve snarled. It was amazing how much subtext that teensy word could contain, and how often I'd heard that subtext lately.

"Whatever the letters might say, why on earth would he have kept them all these years?" I asked, moving us along.

Adam stopped again. "Because she said he did that."

"Be quiet, would you?" Eve said.

"Stop bossing me! She thinks she can do that because she's seven minutes older than me," he said. That thought stopped our progression again. "Mom says he keeps everything, that's why, and a leopard doesn't change its spots, Mom says."

"Did you . . ." I wasn't sure how to phrase the question. "How do you know the letters are missing?"

Eve slitted her eyes and clamped her mouth shut.

Adam, open-eyed, didn't even have to stop walking for this one. "Because they weren't there!"

"At the house, you mean?" I asked softly.

Adam nodded. Of course. The looted family room. I wondered if they'd done a number at the center, too.

"So the only avenue left is to have witnesses testify that he identified us as his children," Eve said.

"What does that have to do with your mother's having originated the centers?"

This was a long pause, an enormous pause during which I considered the size of the two of them. A quarterback must feel this way now and then, I decided.

I was not without fear. We were at the far corner of the

square, out of sight of the school, and anything was possible. They wanted something, anything—recompense for whatever ails life had dumped on them up in Buffalo. Somehow I'd become the magic provider of it.

They had not found what they wanted last night, and Wynn Teller was dead now. It was possible that was cause and effect.

If I couldn't save them, or if they thought I wouldn't, they could toss me in a dumpster and nobody would ever know what had happened.

"Mom's not so sure she can find the marriage certificate," Adam said. "She's not so sure that their wedding was, like . . . completely official. By the court's standards, that is. And you can write any name on a birth certificate, so . . ."

"Why? Why are you telling her all this?" Eve screeched.

"Because she could tell them!"

"Who?"

"Her! She could tell the judge she heard him say we were his children! She could get us to inherit. Don't you understand?"

They were squaring off, readying themselves to do battle, expressions as dense as their muscles. I decided I preferred the milder craziness inside the schoolhouse walls, and I bolted.

But not fast enough. His legs were longer, his arms like Plastic Man's, and he grabbed and held me.

"Let me go!" I screamed.

"You have to!" he shouted. "You have to tell them!"

"You're hurting me!" As if he cared. He clamped both my arms behind me. My soup and sandwich dropped. It was not a pretty sight, carrot cubes and cooked peas splatted on the sidewalk. "Let me go!" I screamed again.

And then, out of the sagebrush, or really, from behind the triangle of dormant hedge, a favorite spot for smoking, came the thundering troops to the rescue. Truly.

"Yo!" A voice shouted. "Lay off!"

I turned, using Adam's moment of stupefaction—he couldn't be stupefied and grasp at the same time, either—to pull free.

"Don't you be abusin' my teacher!" Rita screamed, full force. "Don't you be abusin' anybody, you hear, scumbag?"

And behind her, Colleen, her less thundering echo. "Yeah," Colleen said. "Yeah."

And behind Colleen, a body-builder type, so proud of his pecs he barely covered them even now, in arctic weather. The infamous Ronny Spingle, I was sure—*bad news* stamped on him like U.S. Prime Beef on a steak. But not now. Right now, suitably intimidated by Rita and Colleen, he, too, strutted forward, fists clenched. "Yeah," he said. "Lay off, pea-brain."

I loved Rita, loved Colleen, felt kindly to Ronny Spingle and his pecs, loved fly tattoos and weird hairdos and running with them away from the scary duo, laughing, then stopping at the doorway, out of breath and kissing them all.

"I learned good, huh, Teach?" Rita said.

I didn't dream of correcting her grammar. She was right. She had learned good.

Sixteen

THIS TIME, THE THIRD AFTERNOON IN A ROW I'D STOOD OUTside her cutout window, Glenda Carter squinted at me as if just maybe she had seen me somewhere before. The outer office was empty except for me and the potted plant. Someone had removed the framed magazine story with the glowing photograph of Wynn Teller. That was probably tactful and correct, but I nonetheless shivered at the speed with which people disappear, trace by trace.

I was about to hand Glenda my packet and be on my way when Mr. Schmidt emerged from his office. "Miss Pepper, isn't it?" he said, coming close. "Neil Quigley's friend and associate. You've been a regular visitor lately, haven't you?"

"I forgot to leave my résumé when I interviewed." I felt shy, as if he were the principal and I had committed some offense.

He smiled and took my credentials packet and waved toward his office.

"I was already interviewed," I said.

"I know, but in the light of what's happened . . . perhaps we could talk a moment? It'll be a pleasant break for me. Things are somewhat confused here today."

"Understandably," I said. "In fact, I didn't think you'd be open at all." We were in his office, a spartan, utilitarian box without a personalizing touch. The office of the former foundling looked institutional and overwhelmed—there was an enormous stack of papers and files on his desk. Everything but the gray-green file folders continued the monotonous beige color scheme, including Schmidt himself, whose fair skin and sandy hair nearly disappeared into his surroundings, like a hidden picture.

He settled on one of the two pale chairs in front of his desk, seeming ill-at-ease, awkward. I could understand why Wynn, so much more the showman, so much more expansive, had done all their publicity and promotion, and why I tended to forget the second name in Teller-Schmidt Learning Centers. "We'll certainly close for the funeral," he said, "but there are so many loose ends. The franchise owners, for example, need to know this doesn't mean we're out of business."

He was going to have to stop using *we*. His partner was dead and he was not royalty.

He returned to the business at hand: me. "In all honesty," Clifford Schmidt said, "I was pleased—and surprised—to see another Philly Prep teacher apply. I don't mean to speak harshly of your good friend, but Quigley is not the best spokesman for TLC."

"Well, I . . . he . . ." Schmidt's awkwardness was catching.

He drummed his fingers on my manila envelope. "I trust you do not share his . . . impractical approach to life." He stopped drumming and looked embarrassed. "Showing my bias, aren't I? I admit I'm a practical man. I care about the bottom line, the big picture. It's not romantic-sounding, but it keeps a business afloat." He studied me for a too-long moment. "Neil, on the other hand . . . But it appears that, despite his reservations, he encouraged you to join us." He waited for confirmation.

For Neil's sake, I couldn't admit that he'd very explicitly warned everybody off. "He made it sound intriguing." I hoped that covered all vague bases and pleasantries.

"Intriguing, eh?"

"And potentially profitable," I added with a smile.

"Ah." He tented his fingers and looked meditative.

We might have continued indefinitely except that my stomach growled. Audibly. I looked at my watch and spoke loudly, hoping he hadn't heard. "I'm sorry," I said, "but I'm running late." For sustenance. "Was there something specific you wanted to ask?"

"Oh, no. I didn't mean to detain you." He smiled, fleetingly, but with some charm. "Only wanted to get to know you a bit now that Wynn . . ." He sighed. "I'll have to—all the things he took care of and knew . . ." He stood up. "Oh," he said, "everything is so . . ."

So changed, so lost, so final, so confusing, I thought as I left the practical man trying to make sense of his mountain of papers and files.

MACAVITY CAN SMELL CAT FOOD STRAIGHT THROUGH THE tin, and he is particularly gallant and attentive whenever I come home bearing groceries. He purred. He preened. He groomed my ankle. If he ever learns to work a can opener, he'll have no further use for me, but until then, I appreciate the attention. I gave him an extra-long and serious under-ear scratching plus the promised gourmet treat.

I watched him eat with envy. I was suffering post-traumatic pastrami and soup loss and had never intended to diet quite this stringently. It was time to compensate. However, I can handle either a complicated life or a complicated cuisine, not both at the same time. Given recent history, dinner had to be a plate-size sedative. In fact, dinner, which was lunch, too, had to be breakfast. I scrambled eggs, toasted a muffin, and ate standing up while I listened to my messages.

Mackenzie's syllables were smudged. He was agitated, which served him right. He assured me that it was for the best for everybody that Lydia had stopped being a fugitive. He was more worried about me and my mood of late. "So why don't you join"—I perked up—"us"—I perked down—"at Nuevo. The place on South Street? Say seven-thirty?"

Fat chance.

Sasha sounded annoyed. "So where is she? It's four-thirty." Pause. "You know what I'm talking about, right? So I'll see you but if I don't, soon, I'm out of here." I'd forgotten to call her about Lydia. I would, as soon as I was finished eating.

My sister was all flutters and gasps about what had happened to Lydia's husband and how dreadful it was, and how horrible that she hadn't believed me when I tried to tell her.

But now she did. Believed that Lydia had committed murder. Score another one for me and my big mouth. "Call me," Beth said. "Meanwhile, Sam wants me to tell you that he—one of his associates, actually—is speeding her through the process as much as possible. Also trying to get her a bed in a very quiet psychiatric facility. I believe she's been there before. Call me."

I didn't want to talk to anybody. I had picked up *Mildred Pierce* as my dinner companion, and if her woes didn't take my mind off mine, I always had *Hunting and Trapping the Unsuspecting Male* or whatever it was called. Given all that plus a full container of Rocky Road, I was self-sufficient.

The only mail was a circular for neighborhood bargains and an envelope postmarked Boca Raton. Bea Pepper's clipping service in action. This time, a checklist for "planning your wedding early."

Surely this was a premature follow-up to the dating book. Then I had a thought. A nauseating one. Beth couldn't have actually . . . surely Bernard the oral surgeon fiancé was a joke between sisters. I was afraid he wasn't. Suddenly, even an imaginary man was a pain. I had to dispose of him, but how? What would sound best to my mother's co-players in the Greater Boca Raton Perpetual Gin Game? Should Bernard die tragically in an accident or of a rapid disease? But those options need documentation and possibly memorial services. Should he fall in love with somebody else? Turn out to be already married?

Like maybe Wynn Teller had been? Should I then blow Bernard away, as perhaps the first Mrs. Wynn Teller had?

Useless thoughts like moths inside a lampshade. I yawned, finished my eggs, and tapped my nails on the counter, amusing Macavity as I tried to decide what was the very earliest hour a grown-up person could get into bed, alone, without feeling embarrassed. I decided there was no time like the present, and was clutching the Rocky Road, spoon imbedded in its top, in one hand and the videotape in the other when the doorbell rang.

My peephole is angled toward the sky, so I did my usual verbal inquiries through the door. My caller was Neil, which fact did not make me feel comfortable, but I was also ashamed of being afraid of an old friend, so I compromised, opening the door a crack, the chain still bolted.

"I'd invite you in," I mumbled, "but the house is a mess! Not to mention me!" Easy to hide behind big, fat, female clichés.

"I wanted to talk with you at lunch," he said, "but you disappeared. Mandy, I feel like you don't . . ." He hesitated, and met my eyes with his sad gaze. I wanted to cry for the pressure he was under and for my doubts about him. But that didn't eliminate either of those things. It was very March winds doth blowish outside, even if it was only February, and my hand was freezing tight to the cardboard Rocky Road container.

". . . like you don't *trust* me anymore," Neil said, each word a sharp-edged rock. I felt like an ogre and let him in.

I discreetly put the Rocky Road back in the freezer—spoon still imbedded—and pushed *Mildred Pierce* under a napkin, ashamed of my spinsterly pleasures. As if Neil would have noticed that or anything.

"You know me, Mandy!" he blurted out. "Could you imagine me killing somebody?"

Hadn't we had a more subdued variation of this conversation at the top of the stairs this morning? And hadn't Neil told me why I should suspect him? I wasn't sure it would be politic or profitable to mention this change of perspective.

"I know it looks bad," he said.

"Why? To whom?" I asked. "Everybody's sure Lydia Teller killed her husband," I added bitterly.

"Not everybody, or why were the police at my house?"

His look was intent and unnerving. I became preoccupied sponging off the counter, searching for errant English muffin crumbs. Neil waited. "I give," I finally said. "Why were they?"

"You sure you don't know?" Then he shook his head, as if his own question had been ridiculous. His hair was thin and on the verge of scraggly, and fine strands lifted in the breeze his movements created.

"Why, Neil?" I repeated. "You think I sent them? You've been at war with the man for days. You've told everybody. Maybe that's why the police thought of you."

He stared at his shoes. He was on the opposite side of the kitchen divider, so I couldn't see them, but they must have been fascinating. Unfortunately, I was late for a date with Mildred Pierce, and short on patience. "Neil! You're scaring me! Stop that stupid staring, say something, and sit down!"

Maybe I sounded like his mother, or Angela, but in any case, he sat down on the sofa quickly, like something dropped from above. I suspected that he would have collapsed the same way onto the coffee table or the floor. "Why did the police come see you?" I put water on to boil.

Now he examined his hands, turning them palms up, then over, bending his fingers to examine the nails. "I guess," he finally said, "for the reasons you said." He sighed, letting air phut out of his partially opened lips. "Or maybe because they knew I was out there."

"There?" I whispered. "You mean Teller's? Last night?"

A jerked sort of acknowledgment and an open-mouthed sigh like a gasp in reverse while his head sunk so low it was nearing his knees. The teakettle shrieked and I rushed to silence it. Sometimes, the absolute best thing about cooking is that it gives you a series of emergencies that can busy your hands and divert your attention. "Why?" I remembered a phase my niece had gone through when she drove me crazy responding to every single question or remark with *why?* The entire adult world must have seemed as incomprehensible to her as Neil now did to me. "Why?" I repeated.

Neil raised his head and stared at me intently, as though I was the one who could answer the question. "If he'd just talked to me, treated me like a person . . ."

"Yes? What then?" I bobbled tea bags in boiling water and reminded myself that the police had visited, not held, him.

"Then I wouldn't have had to go to his house last night." Neil's forehead wrinkled at my stupidity.

I left the tea steeping, walked across the living room and assumed what I hoped looked like a lounging position close to the front door.

"I know I didn't say where I'd been when I came to school last night." He looked at me belligerently. "It wasn't like you had any particular reason to know, or anything, so why should you be angry?"

"I don't think I am." Nervous, for sure. Angry, not really. "I wasn't."

He leaned forward on the sofa. "I mean I didn't ask where you'd been before you were in the office, did I? Maybe you were out at Teller's."

"If you're suggesting I killed him, that's the most ridiculous—" I stopped myself. The lack of logic was frightening. "Neil," I said, pushing us back on track, if not exactly onto moral high ground, "where I was is not the question. We were discussing why the police came to see you."

"We were?" He looked honestly confused.

"So why did they?"

"Because I was there. Somebody must have told them." He stood up suddenly, looking disoriented. "I shouldn't have come here, you're right, it's not fair to dump my problems on . . . I'm just so on edge, I can't think straight—but I told Angela I wouldn't be long. Can't talk to her about any of this, about anything, really. She's nervous enough without it. It feels like the whole world is on my head."

"Ah," I said, "it can't be that bad."

He stared at me, openly incredulous. "It can," he said softly. "It is."

"Then . . . then I'll get the tea." It was herbal, and intense by now, deep green, aromatic with mint. I put his cup on the coffee table and said, as gently as I could, "Of course you can talk to me."

He looked at his watch. He looked toward the door. "Angela worries," he murmured.

"Yes." That was a chronic condition and no excuse. Angela had been a worrier before her marriage, before her allergies, before her pregnancy, before the financial difficulties, before the fire at her husband's TLC center, before last night. Just listing her more recent worries put me near an anxiety attack.

"Nothing happened last night." He left the untouched tea on the coffee table. "I tried getting an appointment and couldn't. The article said he always ate dinner with his wife. His secretary told me he had appointments that night, so I figured he wasn't going out to eat. I went to his house and warned him that I wasn't going to take it the way I was sure other teachers had." He waved his long arms for emphasis, his overcoat flapping around him. We had missed the let-me-take-your-coat phase.

"At first, all I'd asked was to go over my records. I was ready, willing, to assume I'd screwed up. But he was always busy being famous, and the longer that went on, the more I was convinced it wasn't my fault. The accounting was a scam, like they say it is with movies. Creative accounting. I told them that. They still wouldn't go over the books with me. Then I told them I was going to the guy who wrote the magazine piece, and to the D.A., and *they'd* go over my accounts with me."

"You told them?"

He nodded. "A jerk, huh? I wanted to be straight with them. I still thought we could work it out. Except then there was the fire. The *accident*. Which, of course, burned up all my records. I should have gone to the law without warning them, but you know, all through it, I was afraid I was maybe wrong, that they would explain things to me and set them right. When I went there, the day of the fire, the afternoon you saw me there, remember . . . ?"

"Yesterday," I whispered.

"God, really? Only yesterday?" He shook his head. "Schmidt accused me of burning the building for the insurance money and told me they were bringing charges."

The telephone interrupted him, but neither of us moved.

"I went a little crazy and said I was still suing, but now it would be a class action. All the franchisers, all the teacher-saps. I said I had copies of my records. Which isn't exactly true.'' He sighed.

That was all said during the second ring and a bit of the third, by which time I was able to reach and lift the receiver.

The woman's voice was unfamiliar. ''Neil Quigley?'' she shouted. I handed over the receiver. Neil flinched.

''Yes?'' he asked, and then he lapsed into noise rather than language, a symphony of sound blips until he clicked down the receiver, having become even more agitated than when he'd arrived, flapping his hands, his overcoat bagging around him. It was inappropriate to notice how much he looked like a scarecrow, but I did.

''What?'' I asked. ''I don't mean to probe, but . . .'' That wasn't true. I did mean to probe. Barge into my house, tell me about criminal acts, maybe even murder, then receive a cryptic call on my telephone, and I will definitely mean to probe. ''What happened?''

''Angela.''

''What's wrong?'' Even worrywart and chronically hysterical Angela wouldn't phone in a frenzy because a recipe had failed or Oprah hadn't been sufficiently entertaining.

''That was our neighbor.'' He was at the front door. ''She—Angela, not the neighbor—she's . . . we're in labor. For real. At the hospital already. That neighbor brought her in. I should have been there. Angela's going to be . . .'' He looked ready to faint. ''She's just about ready to . . . I'm about to become a . . .''

''Congratulations!''

He exhaled mightily and looked happily, fearfully, dazed. ''Right now,'' he gasped. ''She's having our . . . right now—''

He grabbed onto the doorknob, but for support, not egress.

''Hey, pal,'' I said softly, ''you're in no condition to drive. I'll call a cab.''

''Oh, no. No problem!'' He was becoming manic—and depressive still. ''Enough money worries already, can't afford a—wow, a baby. Tonight! I hope she's . . .''

All he needed was a serious auto accident to add to his

woes and perhaps somebody else's. "I'll drive you," I said firmly. "Your neighbor can bring you back for your car."

"Don't be silly. A baby! Can you imagine?"

"What hospital, Neil?" I pulled on my down coat against the blustery night outside. "Where is she?"

"Oh—out, where . . . Lankenau. Out City Line, you know?"

Joan Crawford waited on my kitchen counter. Later, I promised her. Men'll mess you up every time, she answered.

I was tempted to remind Neil that Angela was the one doing the hard work, but I was too busy steering him down my front steps. "Is that yours?" I pointed at a bland gray sedan that looked teacherly. "Better move it. Parking's illegal on this street."

He shook his head. "I'm around the corner. Legal until six A.M. Oh, God, it's for real! A baby!"

By the time we reached the hospital, Neil looked ready for a Breathalyzer test. And I'd always thought goofball fathers-to-be were comic strip inventions.

A sturdy and tolerant nurse came toward us smiling, and I passed Neil over to her supportive arm. "Quigley," I said. "His wife's in labor, but he needs intensive care."

Neil, hearing his name, jerked to attention. "Mandy!" he said. "You never explained why you called the police about me."

The nurse looked from him to me and back. "The police didn't bring you in, young man," she said. "This young lady did." She shook her head at me. Men! she mouthed.

"Have a great baby," I said, and I left.

I hovered around the lobby gift shop for a moment, drooling over seven varieties of chocolate bars. I summoned all my ethical strength and turned away, out into the chill clear night. The brisk air was intoxicating, as was my wonderfulness score. I gave myself points for braving the cold, ignoring Joan Crawford, escorting Neil, and, the most moral act possible for a contemporary woman, renouncing food.

My car was parallel parked at the curb only a few feet away. I stood on the sidewalk, fumbling with my keys, and felt, more than saw, a car approach. I looked up. A missable vehicle. Generic. A narc car, Sasha would call it. Designed to not be noticed. I looked back down at my key and unlocked my door, vaguely aware that the narc car was moving too fast for any parking lot, let alone one at a hospital. Still, one foot in the car, one foot out, I froze with the knowledge that something besides its speed was wrong.

That car. That gray car. But before I could understand my unease, the car screeched to a halt along the passenger side of the Mustang and I saw a ski mask, a black glove, and a gun. All aimed at me.

I unparalyzed, I ducked, I fell, but not in time, because I saw, or heard, or felt—all of the above plus tasted, I swear it—a flare of fire, a boom and a high whiny zing, the ongoing blare of my horn where my elbow was lodged and another boom and flash plus screams—mine and those of an instant crowd—a nurse in whites, an orderly, a woman holding an enormous bouquet—all rushing out of the large plate-glass doors as the ski mask burned rubber and squealed off into the night.

I pulled some parts of myself from between the bucket seats and unwrapped others from over the gearshift and extricated still more from inside the steering wheel, gingerly testing each before I moved it.

My scalp and face were, surprisingly, intact, although I could feel an angry sore spot in the middle of my forehead. Gearshift assault. I nervously approached my arm where I'd felt a bullet scrape by like a flying emery board. I explored for pain and the stickiness of blood. I was not prepared for feathers.

"She's not hurt." The disappointed lady with the flowers left in pursuit of the seriously afflicted.

I moaned. I was in one piece but my coat was mortally injured, spilling its downy guts over the car seat.

"Can you stand up?" The nurse shivered and rubbed her upper arms, and although moving a single one of my bones or muscles was close to the last thing I wanted to do, I didn't want her to die of exposure, so I began to extract myself from the car.

And that's when I noticed that my convertible roof, lacking

my ability to duck, had been newly, redundantly, aerated. I put my finger through the hole in the canvas, considered that my skin or vital organs could have been pocked instead, and thought I might be sick.

I wept and shivered, although there was plenty of down left to insulate me. Guns. Bullets. They were so casual about these things on TV shows. Bang, bang, you're dead. Let's watch something else now. But it wasn't like that. Not at all.

"Come inside. I'll call the police," the nurse said. She was the only one left.

I nodded. "Give me a second. I need air." I took another deep breath and nodded again. She shivered and patted my shoulder. "Awful," she said. "Lunatics all over these days." Then she made a beeline for the warm hospital.

I was seized by almost uncontrollable shudders. One of those lunatics had my name on it. I recognized that car now. It had been waiting outside my house. Probably, if Neil hadn't been along, it would have been all over whenever I walked outside. But Neil had been with me, so I'd been followed instead. There will be a brief delay in your murder, that's all.

Somebody, for reasons I could not fathom, wanted to kill me.

I bent and scanned the dark sidewalk. Then I pulled the emergency flashlight out of my trunk and searched all the way back in the foundation plantings. I worked as fast as I could, afraid the nurse would return before I found it.

But I saw the glint of the spent bullet and took it back to the car, where I slipped it into the change purse of my wallet. There was another one somewhere. The police could find that one. But I didn't want them to find me, to ask questions and waste my time. I had nothing helpful to say.

I could already hear the approaching whine of a siren, and I made my exit from the lot with a breath or two to spare before the noisy red and blue twirl of light passed me by.

And to think, a few minutes ago, when I was much younger, a chocolate bar had seemed the most dangerous thing I had to face this night.

Seventeen

HOME, WHICH HAD BECKONED LIKE AN OASIS, NOW SEEMED a trap. Did the driver of the gray car know he'd missed? Would he hie himself back to my door for a second chance?

Do not think about it, I counseled myself. The road to mental health is not in that direction.

The radio played songs of love—lost, despaired of, remembered. Very rarely rejoiced in.

I mulled that over through three blocks likely to be featured in a *Travel and Leisure* "Scary Inner City Destinations" feature. I passed a hotel no tourist with matched luggage had ever checked into, its walls covered with spray paint samples that ruined both architecture and atmosphere in one poof.

I stopped at yet another NO RIGHT TURN ON RED sign. There are about three corners in all Philadelphia where the right turn on red law is allowed to apply. The fellow who got the legislation passed must be the same guy making a fortune manufacturing signs marking every corner an exception to the rule.

I entered center city and approached the twinkling ALL-DAY–ALL-NITE—LONG-TERM AVAIL sign that meant home for the car, but my foot cast the deciding vote by staying put on the gas pedal. I pretended to wonder where it was taking me, although it became clear as we turned right—not on a red light, of course—toward South Street.

It wouldn't be the worst thing in the world to tell Mackenzie what had happened, even though I'd have to talk in front of the jinx. I couldn't hold off until Sunday, because my masked avenger might not understand he had to wait for her departure before once again trying to blow me away.

I parked and did my best to tidy myself as I bucked the wind en route to Nuevo, a precious designer restaurant of the sort Mackenzie abhors. Or did. Further evidence of Jinx contamination.

I spotted them the moment I walked in, even before I was guided in their direction by the host, Darryl, who had the air of a king in exile, barely suffering proximity with peasants such as I. Jinx was laughing, which was acceptable, but Mackenzie also looked amused, which was not.

I was acutely aware of my windblown, tangled hair, of the rising bump on my forehead, of the baby feathers drifting out of my right coat sleeve.

"Amanda!" Jinx squealed in a gush of Southern insincerity. Her beau's bemused expression changed to concern. He stood and pulled out a chair for me. I was surprised to see the table set for three, as if I'd honestly have joined them even if my life hadn't been threatened.

C.K. leaned over me while I settled in the chair. "Somethin' happen?" His voice was a murmur, for my ears only.

I was busy formulating my answer when Jinx, who hadn't blinked a single long lash at my feathers and bruises, filled the conversational gap. "We were havin' such fun reminiscin'," she twinkled.

I had no muscle memory of what it took to form a social smile. Besides, I didn't care how much fun they'd been havin'. My head ached, inside and out.

Mackenzie sat down and watched me, silently reiterating his question.

"We were so young," Jinx said. Then she giggled. "Of course, I was younger than the man!"

"Ummm." My smile felt more like a grimace.

I watched Jinx track a fluff of goose down as it left my

sleeve and floated on the accumulated exhalations of the diners before landing near her foot. Then her eyes met mine and she smiled overbrightly.

Mackenzie was not as discreet. "You're leakin', Mandy, and you have a bruise on your forehead and an interestin' new hairdo and what happened?"

The waiter arranged small dishes, each with different contents, around the table.

"We went ahead and ordered," Jinx said. "Hope you don' mind, but it's tapas, so it's for sharin' anyway." She beamed another toothpaste-ad smile. "Isn't this the cutest place? So new! Like its name. Nuevo's Spanish for new, did you know?"

"Somebody shot at me," I said. "Twice."

Mackenzie rose, as if my assailant were nearby and he was going to get him. In any other situation, without a goggle-eyed third party, I would have expressed my appreciation for his reflexes and sentiment.

"Goodness!" Jinx said.

"Out at Lankenau Hospital," I said.

He settled back down. "Were you sick? What were you doing there? Who shot at you? Have you had that bump looked at?"

"Good grief!" Jinx said.

I processed his questions in order, explaining about Neil and the baby and the ski mask, but of course that still didn't answer anything.

"Big cities are so scary!" Jinx said. "I'm so grateful havin' this man for a guide!" She patted Mackenzie's arm. "Oughta be more careful, Amanda!"

I ignored her. At work I have to be gracious about dumb responses, but not during my free time. "This wasn't random street crime," I said.

"What? You're sayin' somebody's gunning for you, specifically?" Mackenzie sounded incredulous. Obviously, brain death can also be a sexually transmitted disease.

"I told you! That car followed me!"

"You sure? Detroit turns out a hell of a lot of gray models."

"Honestly!" My indignation was restoring my normal bloodflow and appetite. I downed a small circle of ham and something delicious and garlicky.

"What kind of car was it, anyway?" Mackenzie asked.

Gray. Squarish. Four wheels. A few doors. Headlights. One of those.

"Great," he said. "Positive it's th' exact same car twice, but you don't have a clue what kind it was. There are crazies in the burbs, too."

"But—"

"Even on a hospital's grounds. You've had a real bad time lately, and this is an unfortunate coincidence. Some lunatic decides to blow away the first person out of the hospital tonight, and you're unlucky enough to be it. Thank goodness you're okay, that's all."

I took deep breaths and only broke the silence because I was sure if I didn't, Jinx would spout a perky homily. "It was the person who killed Wynn Teller. I just know it."

"Why?" That short word, distorted into a long, Southern *whaaahy* strained at the seams not only with extraneous vowels, but with irritation, disbelief, and self-control.

"Because whoever it is knows I'm getting close."

"To what?" He put a hand on mine, wise advisor style. "The person who killed Wynn Teller is probably still being arraigned. Havin' her bail hearin'. Findin' bail—which will be high because of the risk of flight after last night."

I pulled my hand away. "Lydia didn't do it. Maybe she should have, she certainly could have, and God knows she had reason to, but she said she didn't and she didn't."

Jinx swiveled her entire head toward whichever of us spoke, as if we were a tennis match. She nodded and raised eyebrows and displayed a lot of symbolic attention which I had a hard time accepting as real.

"Maybe," Mackenzie said, "you oughta hurry and go to law school real fast, so you can plead her case and convince a jury of that." He shook his head.

"I swear," Jinx trilled, "you people lead the most interestin' lives. Home's gonna seem drab after this!" She squeezed Mackenzie's forearm for emphasis.

"You have a big heart," Mackenzie said to me.

Jinx emphatically agreed.

"But facts are facts," he continued. "She's a nice woman who was pushed too far. Literally. But a lot of courts are more lenient these days. Used to be a woman who killed her husband was put away for life, but not so much anymore. An' there's more evidence than normal this time with that book of yours."

Jinx's head swiveled in my direction.

"Then why did somebody try to kill me tonight?"

"Because somebody was nuts. Don't be paranoid."

Had a figment of my imagination ripped through the car's roof and my sleeve? I opened my mouth, but nothing but astonishment came out. There is a moment, devoutly to be avoided if possible, when you realize you are well and truly alone on this planet, when you understand what the Lydia Tellers must feel too many times to count. "I thought you'd help me," I finally managed.

"Sure I will. How 'bout after dinner, we'll see you home and you'll lock your door behind us when we leave. Will that make you feel better?"

He had to be kidding. "You don't care, do you?"

Jinx looked nervous. Mackenzie looked surprised.

Maybe a bullet had, indeed, lodged in my brain, and that's why this scene seemed incomprehensible. Which reminded me. "Could you get this to the police out there?" I handed over the nonimaginary bullet, waiting for him to be impressed, even, perhaps, humbled.

"What's this?"

"I thought you guys learned those things in cop school."

"Why didn't you give it to the police right then?" It took a few seconds, that was all, and then his shoulders drooped.

"I think it's going to turn out to be from the same gun that killed Wynn Teller," I said.

"You didn't talk to the police, did you? You left."

I shrugged, although Gallic gestures did not suit the ambience of a Spanish tapas bar, but I was having this confusion problem. I didn't know what to make of anything, including myself. Was I being hunted down or had I been crazy for a while now, confusing wishes with fact? What if Lydia had indeed killed her husband, planned it, perhaps, had it all worked out—except that I ruined everything? What if—

"Unusual lookin' bullet," Mackenzie said. "I'm no ballistics expert, but this is different. Maybe bigger? Some old guns . . ."

"Is . . ." I had to swallow, to drink some wine before I could ask. "Is it possible Lydia Teller could be through the process by now? That she isn't still in jail?"

Mackenzie understood what I was really asking. "I'll make a call," he said. "Give me a while."

And then I was alone with Jinx and my throbbing forehead, and my ragtag mane, and my shabby, bullet-torn ensemble.

"Poor you," she said. "What a horrible thing, to be shot at!" She was so sympathetic, so completely mine, I understood the power of her practiced charm. "An' you're so brave and calm!" She shook her head, and her blonde hair swung slightly and resettled in its perfect smoothness.

"Is there anythin' I can do?" Jinx asked, blue eyes concerned. "Anythin' to make you feel better?"

"Actually," I said, "there is."

"Good." She did a flawless imitation of polite, dinner table ecstasy. "What is it?"

"The two of you go way back, don't you?"

She poked a manicured fingernail into the linen tablecloth. "Fifteen years, we figure. I was a freshman."

I quickly calculated. She was a year older than I was. I felt an irrational rush of joy, as if an additional twelve months of life were a major handicap. Talk about ageism. I was ashamed of myself for that, but all the same, I was having one of the worst days of my life, and I was more glad she was a year older than I was ashamed.

"So what can I do for you?" she said.

"Tell me his name."

She blinked. "Mackenzie?"

"Not that one. His first name. His middle name."

"You don' know?"

I shook my head and waited, but she seemed to have lost

the need to do anything to make me feel better. I tried to reactivate her compassion button. "It would mean a great, great deal to me. Especially today." I even smiled after that. A Yankee smile, to be sure, but emphatic.

"Wish I could," Jinx said. "But if he hasn't trusted you with it, it'd be a breach of confidence."

Bitch. "What's so bad about a breach now and then? It's just a joke, anyway. It's not like I'm going to publish it in the newspaper."

She shook the blonde coiffure again, smiling.

"In the name of sisterhood?" I said. Given enough stress, I'll even imitate Eve Wholeperson.

Jinx's expression was blank enough to suggest she'd missed the women's movement altogether, even as a subject in a history text.

"You're not going to tell me, are you?" I said.

She smiled, brilliantly, every gleaming tooth on display. "I couldn't, honey. Not to that sweet man. Besides, I always had my own name for him."

I closed my eyes. "Which was, is?"

"I call him Snuggles."

"I call that nauseating." I stood up. "Tell . . . Snuggles . . . I couldn't stay."

"But he's . . . isn't he . . . won't he be . . . what should I say?"

"You'll think of something, sweetie pie. I'm sure you always do."

I went out into the frigid night, coat dripping feathers, head aching, feeling even more intensely that dreadful revelation that I was in this alone.

Eighteen

TIMES LIKE THESE, STANDING AND SHIVERING ON A SIDEWALK, knowing that Snuggles and trouble would resume reminiscing and wineglass clicking while I leaked feathers, a person can use a friend. Luckily, I had a usable one only two blocks away.

"Where *were* you?" she demanded on the intercom after I announced myself. "Come on up!"

When she opened her apartment door, she looked beyond me, down the hallway. "Sasha," I said, "what's wrong?"

"Where is she? This isn't my definition of after school, Mandy. You said three-thirty, not eight P.M. I left a message hours ago. Jeez, I was afraid to leave." She looked like she had conquered the fear, because along with her black tunic with an enormous white lace collar, black tights, and snakeskin boots, she wore her camera on a black leather strap like a massive lavaliere. But then, you can never judge Sasha's destination by her ensemble.

"I'm sorry," I said. "I'll explain." And I did. "Of course, she's innocent," I said, but with less conviction than I'd had earlier. I'd have felt a lot better if I'd been sure that Lydia was still being unfairly detained. I knew I shouldn't have stormed out of the restaurant.

Sasha looked concerned. She is always willing to be troubled on my behalf—unless, of course, she is preoccupied with being troubled on her own behalf—which is one reason our friendship has survived seriously different personalities and interests. I wallowed in her sympathy for a moment, then decided to play on it. "Somebody shot at me tonight. Twice."

She was great. None of Mackenzie's rational observations. Within one minute, no more, she took the Lord's name in vain several times and asked for enough details to write a major news story. And not only that, she suggested that there was a silver lining—and it would be on top of my car. The insurance company would probably replace my convertible hood. I was cheered.

"Mackenzie thinks I'm paranoid." I had no shame. Sasha's ready to discount anything Mackenzie thinks anyway, and her emotions are always at flood level.

She reacted wonderfully, operatically, cursing him in a manner no English teacher would dare. Then she stood up. "Okay," she announced to an invisible audience. "Okay, then. We both need a change of scene, so we're out of here."

My turn to ask questions, but she said it was a surprise, something new for both of us, and that my coat and body should gather themselves up and follow, because we could walk there.

Outside, it was still bitter cold, still windy, but I was not still alone, which made all the difference. We walked, hunched against the elements, and I described, probably unfairly, my dinner date with the Dixie duo.

"Snuggles!" Sasha shouted in megadecibels. *"Snuggles!"*

I hoped Mackenzie could hear the hooting.

"Men," Sasha said, "have an infinite potential for being sickening. I have personally experienced nine million, twelve thousand and seven variations so far, and I suspect I'm only at the beginning of the list."

I followed her, as requested, dumbly and without question until we stopped in front of a once-grand, slightly down at its baseboards hotel. I fit right in with my lopsided coat—one arm plump and insulated, the other unstuffed and flimsy.

We went through the revolving doors, into a lobby designed with the space-wasting largesse of a dead era.

There was an announcement board which Sasha studied. "This way to the Grand Ballroom."

I peeked at what was playing there and saw only, NACHPA Festival. "Is that Spanish?" I asked her retreating form.

"Initials," she said.

"North American Chief Honchos Professional Association?" I guessed. She didn't whirl around and gasp with admiration. "Non-Agnostic Churches' Holy Prayer Alliance?" She kept walking. I hurried faster. "Nubile, Adorable, Cute Hustlers, Pros and Amateurs? Netherlands Antilles? New Amsterdam? Neuters, Abstainers, Cold and Hot Potatoes of America? Am I close?"

I wasn't. We had reached the open double, quadruple doors of an enormous ballroom filled with noise and bodies. I was handed a program for the New Age Festival of Conscious Healing and Personal Actualization.

Well, hey. I'd just read the results of a study that listed the three top desires of visitors to Philadelphia. In order, they were finding a bathroom, visiting the Liberty Bell, and running up the art museum steps like Rocky did. But here were scores of people seeking personal growth, not a toilet.

"Isn't New Age kind of old now?" I asked over the strains of Muzak played on synthesizer and trilling bells.

"Who are you, the delegate from Trend Central?"

"At least tell me when you joined this crowd," I grumbled.

"I'm trying it out. This guy I'm seeing said I should. You ever hear of tantric sex?" Her smile was somewhat smug.

"What guy could you possibly be seeing? Didn't you give up men forever last night? Decide to try clean living?"

She brushed away the suggestion with the back of her hand. "I probably meant I gave up men *for* last night. And this is part of getting into clean living." We drifted into the New Age carnival.

Sasha stopped at a booth that insisted upon the universal healing power of mung beans. She listened to the vendor hype legumes, but the whole time her eyes scouted the crowd.

It's an annoying trait, but she defends it on the grounds that she's a professional looker, as she puts it, collecting goodies for that lens of hers.

"Quick—stand over there," Sasha said. This was a familiar ploy. She'd position me near what interested her, then pretend to be taking my picture while she moved the camera slightly and captured somebody else altogether. She snapped once, then adjusted the lens and snapped again.

I caught up to her next to a Breatharian who subsisted completely on air. "I spent a lot of time today at the health food store," Sasha said. "No more MBAs, no more escargot at La Pomposity." It seemed cruel to discuss French food in front of a man who wasn't even connected to the food chain, but Sasha nattered on about organic vegetables and complementary grains. She stood on tiptoe, which made her taller than most of the crowd, and scanned the room. This was extreme behavior, even for her wandering eye.

"What are you looking for?" I asked as we moved on, undoubtedly to the Breatharian's great relief.

"You think these things actually heal you?" Sasha asked, lifting a watery pink crystal from a display.

The crystal healer looked anxious until the stone was put back in its velvet case and Sasha went en pointe again. "Who?" I asked. But I knew, without her answering. Tantric sex, that was who. New Age or old, Sasha has a good time.

"There he is!" She pointed at a pale, lanky fellow who looked like an outtake from a dour Ingmar Bergman film. There is no accounting for taste, the Breatharian's or Sasha's. "Lars," she said. "I'll be back." And she was gone.

I was traveling solo again. Alice in Actualization Land. I passed a jester, two magicians, a lion tamer, a penguin, and an enormous green pepper. Their costumes had a relevance I was too unenlightened to grasp.

A lot of attention, pamphlets, and therapies seemed devoted to dependents and co-, folks addicted to a multitude of things that sounded like fun. There were also globs of healing aimed at the child within, a concept that reminded me of that movie where space creatures incubate inside earthlings, then burst out of their bellies.

It appeared those kids within had heard about emancipation and needed to be freed. I'm all for equal rights, but I'm keeping the child within me in cold storage. For starters, who'd babysit it?

The other pressing problem of our age appeared to be loving too much. I'll be honest. I don't think it's possible. I think you can love stupidly, yes. Futilely, yes. But too much, no. I think people who hate too much need the workshops, but maybe I'm missing something.

My workshop of choice would have been what was called belly-goddess-dancing because I liked the costume, the hat with the spire and baggy pants over bare feet, golden coins encircling the waist and forehead. I felt better just thinking about it until I didn't feel better about anything. Abruptly, my muscles and mind both sagged and remembered that I'd been ready for bed hours ago, when it was still broad daylight.

If I could have found Sasha to say good night, I would have. Instead, I listlessly hung around Booth 419, which at least smelled good. To one side, a humidifier spewed eucalyptus steam, to the other, something grassy and soothing. "Nice," I murmured, with an uncomfortable sense that the aromas should mean something to me.

A passing woman handed me a flyer hawking a reflexology massage of my feet. "Ten percent off," she said.

"Does that mean you only do nine toes?"

She flounced on, but was replaced by Sasha. "I keep losing him," she said, eyes still doing up-periscope maneuvers.

"You sound like a country singer. And I'm awfully tired. I still have the key to your place, so you can stay. I'm sacking out."

"In a minute—one more pose for me, would you?" she asked. I obliged, like an automaton.

"They shouldn't allow picture taking in here. It's not professional-looking."

The voice carried like all seventy-six trombones, and I turned and saw the fuchsia hair and sausage torso, today in lime Day-Glo casing. And that's what the eucalyptus steam had meant. ''Hey, aromatherapy!'' I pushed through the crowd.

''You're ruining my shot,'' Sasha called after me.

But I was in pursuit of the missing link. ''Fay!'' I shouted. ''Mrs. Teller!''

She turned and craned and didn't seem to spot my raised hand until I was nearly next to her, and then she looked as if she might take flight. Straight up.

She was very short. The twins took after their daddy, I thought, and then wondered at what point I'd accepted Fay's claims about their paternity.

''Mrs. Teller.'' I put out my hand to shake hers.

She pulled away. ''The last name's Elias! Who are you?''

I obviously hadn't made as strong an impression on her as she had on me. ''Amanda Pepper.''

Her chin pushed out pugnaciously. ''Why'd you call me that other name?''

''I'm sorry, I thought . . . the other day, at the Learning Center, you said . . .'' My words dribbled off under the pressure of her peacock-blue squint. ''Didn't you?''

''You were there?''

I nodded. ''You told me I was an autumn. You told me about yourself.''

Her lids lowered like Technicolor shades drawn over her eyes. ''Me and my big mouth. Who are you and what do you want with me?''

It wasn't easy explaining what I wanted, since it was to entrap her, find a new suspect, so I fumbled, spluttered, and stumbled until she held up a hand.

''Enough already!'' She led me past physical fitnessland. Not the yuppie world of Nautilis machines or weights, cute workout clothes and aerobics. We were surrounded by Birkenstocks, yoga demonstrations, embarrassing testimonials to colonic cleansing, and free samples of peculiar foods. We walked slowly, working toward our real topic while accepting handouts. The tapas had given me indigestion and left me hungry, so I accepted all curative offerings from people whose wardrobes and edibles both were earth-colored. I scarfed sticky make-believe ice cream and tofu-gluten imitation sushi and a wheat-berry burger. I drank ersatz coffee made of obscure plants and munched salt-, sugar-, fat-, and taste-free cookies.

"They could call it Mock Donald's," I said. Fay didn't laugh.

We wound up at a juice bar unpopular enough to have available seats. It was in front of a booth occupied by a woman who channeled an Abyssinian potter.

"I use the name Elias for professional reasons," Fay said. "So my kids don't suffer. I am also a body worker, a masseuse—that's what kept a roof over us. Not the dirty kind, but you know how people are about masseuses. Elias was my maiden name." She blinked and bit her shiny pink lip. "So my big mouth got me in trouble, did it? All those people at the office heard me."

A giant carrot-waiter with a ferny green tuft on top and black Nikes at the bottom put a bowl of raw sunflower seeds on the table, handed us each a discount coupon for a juice extractor, and took our orders—guava muskmelon mash for Fay, mint tea for me.

"Listen," she said as soon as the carrot turned its tuft away. "Bottom line is, the case is already solved, so there's no reason for further conversation, is there?" Her brassy voice turned whiny and strained at the higher registers.

"I think there is. I think Lydia's innocent, and I don't think the case is closed."

Her face was a map of hard times and places, and the bright colors of her lids, cheeks, and lips like marks of desperation. She blinked hard and her eyes welled. "I didn't mean for it to end that way." Her chest puffed with an enormous inhale, which she held for a long time, then let out with a whoosh. "Not for him to *die*. I only wanted to scare him into doing something. I feel sick with guilt. To cause somebody's death—*his* death!" She sniffled.

My God—a holistic confession. Like that. And all I had wanted was a factoid, a clue, a hint. I welcomed the diversion of our drinks, delivered to the table by an orange waitfruit. "So, um, how did you—how did it happen?" Were there really such things as citizen arrests, or was that strictly comic book stuff? Could I convince her to do the right thing and turn herself in? Or physically coerce her to come with me—and, if so, to where? My car was parked down by the river. I imagined dragging the sausage lady behind me up the steps of a bus, and sighed and sank back in my chair.

She breathed shallowly and rapidly and wiped moisture from the corner of her eye. "Who knows exactly how it happened?" she trumpeted. People passing our table stopped and stared, but Fay was oblivious. "Horrible things happen all the time. Like that." She snapped two long purple nails together, then she fumbled in her purse, a carpetbag, and pulled out a lace-edged handkerchief and sobbed into it.

It was beyond irony to hear a confession of murder here in the citadel of absolute, optimum, permanent physical, mental, and spiritual wellness.

"I wanted him alive, making money," Fay said. "I wanted to murder him in court!"

I spotted the law across the way and tried for eye contact. He lounged against a zodiac sign, facing us, but although I winked and raised an eyebrow, inviting him over, he managed not to notice.

"Go on," I answered Fay between grimaces at the man in blue. "You wanted to use the law." So did I. I jerked my head and winked at the cop one more time.

"Something in your eye?" Fay asked.

I nodded, and blinked some more, rolling my eyes in the direction of the guard, who had X-ray vision, and therefore looked straight through me. I gave it up. "So tell me about last night." I tried to keep my voice casual.

Fay busied herself straightening the already-in-place neckline of her green ensemble. "I'm a survivor," she said. "He already near wrecked my life, and that two-faced no-good isn't pulling me into the grave after him now!"

Now what was this? A confession that she wasn't going to confess, after all? We sat in an awkward silence, then I tried to start her up again. I used the magic word. "Men!" I said.

It worked. She nodded. "Left me with tiny little babies. We'd been the two poorest kids working our way through State, but we had big plans. I was studying education, and I had this idea for centers for kids with learning problems, you know?'' Her expression had become dreamy and soft, and the young Fay was almost visible under the overbright pigments. Then she pushed out her chin and hardened up. ''Only I never got a degree. I got twins instead.'' She considered this for a moment, then nodded. ''I have to say, he did the decent thing by me.''

''You mean by marrying you?''

She nodded. ''Eloped one night to Jersey. A justice of the peace. Only . . . he was drunk.''

This was the business that concerned the twins, a possible problem with the marriage's validity. ''Lots of grooms are drunk from what I hear,'' I said.

''The justice of the peace was drunk, too. And I had morning sickness at night. I don't know if anybody ever sent in whatever you're supposed to.'' She sighed. ''But we were married. Wynn had a job by then. Teaching high school. I thought we were happy. But one morning during spring break, there's a twenty-dollar bill and a note that says *I'll call*. Which he didn't. Didn't come back to his job, either. Wrote letters instead. In Ohio, he said he was testing my idea, and that he'd send for us. From New York, he said it was *economically unfeasible*. He was bankrupt, depressed, desperate. I believed him.

''That postcard ended with *Sorry*, and it was the last I ever heard. I thought he'd killed himself. All these years, I figure I'm a widow, then I come to this conference and find out he's famous, making big bucks from my idea! Plus, he's a bigamist.'' She sat back and folded her arms over her puffy breast.

''Jeez, girl, what happened to you? I thought you were kidnapped.'' Sasha towered over us, a fleshy escapee from a Shakespearean spoof in her tunic and high boots. ''Expected to find your picture on soy milk cans from now on.''

''Sasha Berg, Fay Elias.'' Both women nodded at each other with no interest. ''Didn't mean to mess up your picture,'' I said, ''but I was so excited to see Fay that—''

Just then, Mr. Sighs and Whispers loped over, a shank of straight blond hair carefully draped over his right eye. ''You ready, Sasha?'' he asked with a disappointing twang. Maybe he was from Midwest Sweden.

Sasha saw something that intrigued her and turned, with her camera up to her eye, and Lars did a stupid double-take in my direction. ''Well, well,'' he said, ''and who is this?'' I wonder why men think it's cute to talk that way. ''Why weren't we introduced? I'm Lars Feldman. I'm an actor.'' He pulled out a wrought-iron chair and looked ready to settle down at our table. ''And you, pretty lady, are . . . ?''

''Sasha's best friend,'' I said. ''I think she needs one.''

''No offense,'' Fay said when Lars and Sasha meandered off, ''but where does your friend find her clothes?''

''The same secondhand sources she finds her men.'' Although Fay, who looked like a fluorescent hot dog, had no right to be a fashion Nazi.

She stuck her index finger through a curl and twirled it while her gaze became distant. Then she put down her hand and shook her head. ''Listen, the past is the past. The present is all that matters. I am his widow. Mother of his babies.''

''But about what you said. The . . . guilt, you know? About his death? That makes a difference.''

''Yeah?''

''I don't want to be tactless, but frankly, it doesn't matter if he was a bigamist or not. Given the, um, situation, what you did, you can't inherit from him. Now, as for Adam and Eve—''

''What're you talking about?'' Her eyes rounded, her mouth made a small scarlet O. ''Wait a—you're saying *I killed my own husband*?''

That summoned a crowd, even a lady with a placard about chakra cleansing. I leaned close and whispered. ''You said so! How guilty you felt about causing his death—you just said so!''

She put a purple-tipped hand to her bosom. ''My heart,'' she shrieked. ''I can't believe!''

The man in blue, the one I'd been vainly trying to entice, miraculously recovered from his coma and scuttled over. ''You all right, miss?'' he asked her.

His badge named a security firm, not the police. I had wasted a lot of eye-batting.

"My heart's going a mile a minute. Whoof!" Fay fanned herself.

The guard looked confused.

"That woman said—" Fay began.

The guard looked annoyed.

"I can't even repeat such things! If you knew what she said!"

"Your heart's all right, then?" he asked.

Fay shook herself back in place and looked up at him coquettishly. "She shocked me," she said.

His face wrinkled in a queasy grin that said "Women!" and he backed off warily.

"Then what on earth was all that guilty talk about?" I asked.

She looked solemn and near tears again. "I didn't want him to die, and I'm responsible."

"Look, Fay, this is where I came in." Maybe this was where I should get out. Join the recovery group for Women Who Sleuth Too Much.

"Wynn did me wrong, and that I don't forgive, but I never wished him *dead*." She looked appalled that the word had come out of her. "But I caused it all the same."

Her head drooped, her skin sagged, and I had no idea where we were or what was going on.

"Lydia is innocent, like you said. She pulled the trigger, but I was the one drove her crazy, appearing out of the blue, announcing she wasn't his real wife. I read in the newspaper that she has a history of not being screwed on too tight. I didn't know, I swear. I shamed her, drove her to it."

"No, no," I said. "Lydia did not pull that trigger."

Fay raised her penciled eyebrows. "Don't be ridiculous. I have reason to know she was very upset last night. Crazy, all right?"

"I know two of your reasons," I said. "They accosted me today."

"My children were there for legitimate purposes. There are millions at stake. Their rightful inheritance."

"Don't count on it." From what I'd heard, the business sounded as unstable as it was unethical, skimming profits, probably hiding them.

Fay recoiled a bit. "Millions," she insisted. "Although that's of no real importance to me. I'm more spiritual than the twins." She lowered her eyes and looked meditative, or perhaps a little disappointed in what she'd bred. Then her head popped back up and she eyed me sharply, belatedly realizing the implications of what she'd said. "Now don't you *dare* for one minute think my babies did anything like that!"

She and her enormous babies were getting on my nerves. I risked another fainting fit with a direct question. "You didn't happen to be out there with them last night, did you?"

She clutched her carpetbag in both hands. "There you go again!"

"All the same, where were you?"

"I was otherwise engaged . . . by . . . in a workshop."

I opened my program. "Come on, Fay, there isn't a single nighttime workshop."

"Well, it was a—a different kind. Not scheduled. And—none of your business!" Her cheeks flamed until they matched her hair.

I wondered who he'd been. The Breatharian? One of the carrots? Or had the roll in the tofu really been a trip to the Tellers'? Those fool twins needed guidance to do almost anything.

"The point is," Fay said, gathering up her carpetbag, "Lydia was pretty nuts last night. Crying and carrying on about her child being pushed out and my children pushing in. Made no sense."

"The twins told you all this?"

"How else would I know it? We were the final straw for crazy Lydia Teller, and she went over the edge. I'll die feeling guilty."

And with enough bad luck, I won't solve this and I'll just die. Now, I trusted no one. Lydia had lied, too, saying she'd been locked in a bathroom all night and had no knowledge of visitors. But the twins, or Fay, placed her there with them, engaging in a very visible tantrum. Lydia had lied. There was no way around it.

"He threw out my letters." Fay's face sagged with a heavy wistfulness. "He's a pack rat, but he didn't keep souvenirs of us. No reminders of who he'd been. I mean he *wanted* me, if you catch my meaning, but not as a wife. I was an accidental wife to him." She looked newly sad about it. "He always wanted class. Talked about it as far back as I can remember, when he was no more than a boy. He was going to be somebody special and marry somebody just as special. Like Lydia with her famous parents, like the article said."

She straightened up as tall as her small torso could manage. "And look where it got him. Or her, for that matter. He left a perfectly good woman and adorable babies so he could wind up with a no-good son and a classy wife who shoots him dead. Serves him right."

She seemed oblivious to the tears running down her face. Her eyeliner softened into a dark smudge, and her powder showed damp tracks.

"He pushed me around, too," she said, "like the news said he did to her. But he should have known. You can't dump on a class act the way you can on me. Well, she showed him, didn't she?"

Nineteen

"ABOUT YOUR STAYING OVER TONIGHT . . ." SASHA SAID.

Lars did not look like the path to clean living, but even so, for him, Sasha would risk my life, or simply forget about it for a few hours. "No problem," I lied.

"Will you be safe?" she belatedly asked.

"Sure. Definitely. Don't think about it." I did think about it, however, and decided that if the hearthside seemed too creepy, Macavity and I would check into a hotel. "But Sash," I said with a nod toward Lars, "I'm not sure you're safe. He's variation nine million, twelve thousand and eight."

She'd eventually remember her tally of rotten male types, but only after Lars had been added to the list of Mr. Wrongs. Where men are concerned, Sasha's learning curve is flat. Maybe that's true of all of us—breathes there a woman who listens to antiromantic killjoys?

I wondered if anybody had tried to warn Lydia Teller. I wondered if anybody besides Fay had even suspected who lived inside Wynn's charming exterior.

The winter night was an icy contrast to the bustling, light-filled heralds of the New Age I'd just left. On the bus, en route to my car, I talked to myself, insisting there was a logic to Wynn Teller's murder and that I would find it, and in so doing preserve the space between my shoulders and my chin. People stayed away from me as I mumbled.

I drove slowly toward my parking lot. But my self-assurances that I was smart and brave enough to handle this thing weren't enough to quell rising panic. I decided to check out my street surrounded by auto rather than only disintegrating, vulnerable down. If the gray narc car was even in the same zip code as mine, I wouldn't so much as slow down. Better to let Macavity diet a while longer than orphan him.

My home is on an alley with an attitude, bordered like a capital *I* with numbered streets. I approached it slowly, and slammed on my brakes at its entrance, causing traffic hysteria which I could only hope would drive the intruder away. Because there it was, a car illegally stopped mid-block. I couldn't tell its color at this hour and from this distance, but I could tell it was parked at Ground Zero, my front door.

My pulse pole vaulted above my target training zone into the seriously anaerobic—there was no longer any air in the car or my lungs.

The smell of gunpowder had decimated me. Just the sight of a car from which somebody had tried to kill me was too much to bear.

And its arrogance! At least the last time, it had lurked less obviously. Now, it didn't seem to care who noticed, including me. It made me feel impotent and doomed. Drivers squeezed around me, honking horns and expressing displeasure with fists and fingers. "Women drivers!" one man shouted, so upset he rolled down his window in the freezing night to insult me. "Women!" he bellowed.

I wasn't interested in challenging his sexist assumptions. I was interested in the driver of the car in front of my house. How dare he think he could be that blatant! Here I am, parked and waiting to off you, girl. Walk right on over, dummy. Who did he think I was, Little Red Riding Hood?

Unless it wasn't the wolf at all. I squinted. The car was dark. Not just nighttime and dim lamplight dark, but paint-dark. Too dark for a gray car at any hour. I breathed again as I made a left into my street and squeezed the Mustang half on the pavement between a set of hitching posts.

I tapped the driver's window. "Staking me out?" I asked.

He blinked, shook his head, and emerged, one long leg at

a time, unfolding and stretching. "Where've you been? I'm freezin' my—"

"Why didn't you use your key?"

"Din't want you freakin' when you walked in. Which seemed likely."

There was justice in his statement.

"Been shoppin'?" He tapped the canvas bag I reflexively clutched, the one that had LIFE!! JOY!! stenciled in silver script. The periods under the exclamation points were stars.

"At a seminar," I mumbled as I unlocked the door. "Where's Jinx?" I looked around, afraid she was lurking in another entryway, ready to rush in with him, like a thug.

"At the apartment." He sounded annoyed. I couldn't figure why. Macavity looked annoyed, too, but that was easier to understand.

"I'll make coffee." I tossed the LIFE!! JOY!! bag on the counter. A pink tablet slipped out. It had a multicolored message arching across its top: RAINBOW THOUGHTS ON THE LANDSCAPE OF MY MIND. I shoved it back into the bag before Mackenzie could spot it and make a comment. Then I noticed that the stupid book on getting dates was still out, another breach in my armament. I slipped the bag on top of that, too.

Mackenzie dropped his overcoat onto the suede chair. "Anything to eat? I'm starvin'. That wasn't exactly my idea of dinner."

There was comfort knowing Jinx had picked a dumb restaurant. There was less comfort watching C.K. pace the living room. I ground coffee beans and my teeth. Failure to settle in was a bad sign.

"We have to talk," he said.

Just once, I'd like that sentence to preface a discussion of something good, say world peace, or poetry, or how beautiful I look today.

I ducked behind my counter, theoretically in search of grub, actually because it was as far away as I could get from whatever we had to talk about.

My cupboard belonged in *Little House on the Prairie*. I had only the leftovers of domesticity fits: flour, rice, a sack of navy beans, a jar of pearl barley, some Chinese dried mushrooms, and nothing that crunched or snapped or took less than an hour to prepare. Why did they call those inert, useless things provisions when they provided nothing whatsoever? Chips provide. Peanuts. Frozen pizza.

"You've gone weird," I heard. Mackenzie was attacking me while I foraged for him. "You're like a girlie girl from a Fifties sitcom, and I don't get what's happened. Runnin' out of the restaurant tonight, out of the deli the other day. I can't get to you, talk to you. You act like I'm imposin', and you're mad all the time, too."

He said all of it without benefit of a single final *g* or hard vowel. I squatted behind the counter, translating swampese into Philadelphia. Meanwhile, I found a dusty box of cookies I must have hidden from myself. They didn't look worth retrieving, but I had no other option. "If somebody shot at you," I said as I stood up, "and I acted like it was a silly and meaningless event, would you get mad?"

He nodded a grudging acknowledgment. "The difference is, I'd say so. I'd treat you like a human who understood. I'd try to work it out."

I hate to be accused of something I'm actually guilty of. I took my time arranging a plate of cookies that looked like iced credit cards. I finally spoke, clipping my words as neatly as I could. "It would be easier for you to speak your mind to me or to work it out with me because I wouldn't have an old *flame* staying in my house, coming along for the ride and the talk and the working out. My old *flame* wouldn't be eyeballing us and saying, 'Goodness me!' every few seconds."

Mackenzie smiled, even tottered on the edge of a laugh before his expression sobered and soured. "That's what we'd better talk about," he said.

"Jinx? I'd rather talk about who shot me tonight."

His right hand clenched into a fist, but he spoke very softly. "I know you want to connect your attacker with this case, want to make sense of ever'thin' all in one package, but not ever'thin' fits all the time."

"It wasn't Lydia, then, was it?" I asked. "Was she still being detained?"

"Would you believe the phone was broken? Spent ten minutes and fifteen quarters findin' that out." He sighed. "But, it doesn't matter. A lunatic with a gun shot at you. There are too many of both those things around."

He made me so nervous and angry that I bit into one of the cookies, which made me yearn for tofu and gluten. "I never believed Lydia shot at me or at her husband. It was somebody else—the somebody who murdered Teller. It seems open and shut to you—and probably to the police, too, because none of you know all the facts. Or want to." I lifted the cookie plate and presented it to Mackenzie who, hungry or not, shook his head.

"Teller was a bigamist," I said. "His first family thought he was dead. He stole the idea of the centers from his ex-wife—his not-ex-wife—who wants what is hers. She found out this week—the day before he was killed. As did his children, who I know were in the Teller house the night of the murder." I took a deep breath. "As were other people, like a teacher from my school who was suing Teller for swindling his franchisers."

Now, finally, Mackenzie sat down, or rather sank down on top of his coat, which he then roughly pulled out from under him. Macavity, who'd been flirting with me, switched allegiance and began staking out Mackenzie's newfound lap. I wondered if female cats were as fickle.

"Give it up," he said in a near whisper. "Maybe she's a real nice lady, but she killed her husband. Lucky you didn't get there sooner, or she'd have blasted you away, the way those women do."

"What does that mean—*those* women?"

"It's the worst call, a domestic dispute. Woman phones for help, so you get hold of the husband, she gets hold of the gun and blows away the person tryin' to help her." He shook his head. "Women," he said.

"Lydia didn't—"

He sighed. "Mandy, most times the most obvious solution is the solution. Stop obsessing about it."

"It's all circumstantial!" I said.

He nodded. "True. But pretty serious circumstances. The

thing is, I'm upset somebody shot at you, but I think that was a separate, unrelated event. You watch, tomorrow she'll change her plea to guilty, or self-defense."

"Poor Lydia. First her husband victimizes her, now you. You collectively. Everybody."

"Try and remember that she killed somebody."

"She did not!"

"You're right. And also, everybody is nice and pretty and rich and goes to the country and lives happily ever after."

I ate another one of the cookies. I had nothing left to lose, including taste buds. "Your stubborn insistence that this case is closed leaves the real killer out there, gunning for me."

"Where's the logic?" Mackenzie asked. "If he's out free, not even suspected, why does he need to hurt you?"

"Because he doesn't know that. He just knows there's another story, another way of looking at this, and I'm getting hit on by one of the loose ends." I stopped.

"What?" Mackenzie asked.

I shook my head. I had an itch inside my brain, but I couldn't scratch it. Or identify what bothered me all of a sudden. "Anyway," I said, "everything was converging on Teller—his first wife, their kids on the one side—scandal plus major money demands, plus more from a teacher accusing him of creative bookkeeping and a class action suit against the company."

"Okay, and the tension built, so he did what those men do and beat up on his wife yet again, and she shot him."

"No."

"Nobody ever said life was fair."

"Somebody must have. Life should be fair every so often, or what's the point?"

Mackenzie shook his head rather wearily. "This isn't what I wanted to talk about."

My turn to exhale too loudly. "I know. You want to talk about old sweethearts." I was pleased that the teakettle let out its unholy scream at the very moment I alluded to Jinx.

Mackenzie excused himself—it had been a long wait out in that car, he explained—while I poured water into the filter and took the opportunity to listen to my phone messages.

I dreaded a threatening or frightening message, although it would be nice to have proof to show Mackenzie.

Perhaps whining students could be labeled threats. Seniors considered the final year of schooling nothing more than decorative packaging, the academic equivalent of frilly paper bonbon cups.

Josh Di Marco claimed he had injured his coccyx shoveling his parents' driveway. Now he couldn't sit in hard chairs—library, school, desk—and wanted 4F status as far as term papers were concerned. My students' creativity is exercised only on avoiding chances to be creative.

"Darling," the second and final message began, "we couldn't be more delighted."

I put cups down on the coffee table. Mackenzie stood on the bottom tread, head cocked to hear the message.

"Uncle Mike and I—"

"Omigosh—it's Aunt Lila!" I said. "She never calls."

"—we want to have you both to dinner. Your young man sounds dreamy, but of course, you deserve no less. Pick a date and let me know. This is cause for celebration."

Mackenzie looked both flustered and pleased. "You told her I was dreamy?"

My scalp went on follicle alert. Bernard! Bernard was growing like fungus.

And as if on cue, the telephone rang. I wasn't going to answer it, but Mackenzie raised an eyebrow and professional suspiciousness hazed my home. I lifted the receiver. "Finally!" my mother said. "You're home."

I was about to perform an emergency mythectomy on my own mother. But how? Did oral surgeons have occupational hazards that could do Bernard in? If the man simply ditched me, left me waiting at the altar, my mother would lose face with Aunt Lila and the entire Elysium Condo Square Dance and Discount Shoppers Association.

Mackenzie drank coffee and looked relaxed. He enjoys watching me cope with my mother. It's the same drive that makes bullfighting popular in Spain.

"Could the two of you come next weekend?" my mother asked. "I know it's short notice, but so is this engagement.

Besides, next weekend there's a Valentine's Day party right here at the condo. The plane tickets are our treat. What do you say?"

What could I? It's awkward for a thirty-year-old to admit having an imaginary friend. "Next weekend looks a little—"

"That's what I told Dad. You're young and in love and you must have your own plans for Valentine's."

What would she say if she knew the only plan I had for Valentine's Day was to still be alive?

"So Daddy and I will use the tickets and come up there," my mother said.

Which obviously was what she wanted all along, because this way she'd see her grandchildren in the bargain.

I envisioned Bernie in front of a firing squad. I wondered if he'd want a last smoke. "Mom," I said, gently, because she was having such a good time. "This is difficult to say, but—"

"I *knew* something was wrong! I told Daddy that if everything was okay you'd have called by now. What is it?"

"It's . . . Bernard."

"Who?" Mackenzie asked. "Who's Bernard?"

"Of course it's Bernard," my mother said. "Who else would it be? But what about him?"

"He's a . . ." I wanted to be honest and say a figment, but I was afraid she'd think that was some rarefied oral surgery subspecialty. ". . . a drug . . ." Fiend? Dealer? "Abuser," I finally said.

"Is this a student?" Mackenzie asked. "Mess with people like that and then wonder why somebody takes a potshot at you?"

My mother was equally horrified but for different reasons. That mother-of-the-bride dress in her mind was disintegrating. "Drug abuser!" she echoed, horrified.

I explained how his problem had begun with laughing gas and escalated, until now it was hopeless. Mackenzie looked incredulous, but I was really into the spirit of the thing. "I had no idea," I said, "but this afternoon I saw tracks on his arm and the whole ugly story came out."

It would please my mother to think that until this afternoon

I hadn't seen Bernard's inner arms, let alone other body parts. It was a small and virtuous repayment for the grief of the world's shortest engagement.

"Was it Bernard who shot you?" Mackenzie asked. "You're coverin' for him?"

I kept waving at him, shushing him, trying to hear my mother.

"Oh, darling, how awful," she said. "I just don't know about men anymore. They can be so disappointing, can't they?" She described a no-good seventy-eight-year-old Lothario breaking the hearts of the widows of Boca Raton. "Maybe you should get help for Bernard," she suddenly suggested. "They do wonders at Betty Ford, and think of the famous people he'd meet."

I wasn't sure if this suggestion was a result of her generous nature, or a desperate attempt to salvage a fiancé. A little cleaning and Bernard would be good as new.

I therefore had to bury the man deeper, beyond the farthest reach of my mother's charity. "It's not only that," I said, hoping I sounded on the edge of heartbreak, "turns out he *never went to dental school*! He's been drilling under false pretenses."

And that did it. Bernard was history. I weakly agreed I'd live to love again and that, yes, that book on getting dates had some clever ideas, and I declined her offer to fly north and hold my hand, and then, in a voice only half as animated as it had been, my mother said she needed to make other calls, including, to my enormous relief, Aunt Lila.

I felt cruel, not at all pleased by my ability to disappoint her. I even felt dreadful about defaming the figment and found myself hoping his practice wouldn't suffer.

"Bernard." C.K. rolled the syllables around, giving them a peculiar Scottish-Southern burr, as if the ghosts of distant Mackenzies had materialized to disparage Berrrnarrrd.

"Forget him. He doesn't exist." I came back into the living room with the carafe of coffee and refilled our cups.

"Boy, when you're finished with somebody, you're really finished, aren't you?" Mackenzie eyed me warily. "I'll bear that in mind. And you're pretty high and mighty about my entertaining a houseguest while you're messing with a—what was his drug of choice? Or is your contempt reserved for former *flames*, as you put it, and current druggies don't count?"

"He's a *joke*! He's nothing!"

"You are one harsh woman. The man has problems, but—"

"I don't want to talk about him." Bernard wasn't the joke—I was, to have been involved in such a pathetic game.

"Okay," Mackenzie said. "Then let's talk some about why you keep acting like Doris Day in a bad movie, and a worse snit."

I shrugged and nodded at the same time, an if-you-insist grudged agreement. Mackenzie put down his cup and stood up. Maybe because of his slouch, I am always surprised by his height, especially when I am being loomed over and interrogated.

"You could be nicer to the woman," he said. "I know she's dull, but her father and my mother are cousins, and the family said she needed this break, so what could I do?"

"You think she's dull?"

He looked surprised. "What? Yes. Of course. Don't you?"

I felt an almost giddy relief. "I thought you and she—"

He cruised the room again, running his hand over the mantel, the windowsill, the back of the suede chair. Mackenzie's as good as a feather duster on his fidgety strolls. "I assumed you'd understand. You work with adolescents. I was nineteen and she was seventeen and the attraction wasn't intellectual. It wasn't particularly physical, either, but it was incredibly, intensely, *available*. At that age, that seemed enough. For a few months. Then, even back then, it wasn't. Unfortunately, our parents stayed related, so we've seen each other through the years at Christmas and anniversaries and her wedding. That's all."

He sat down on the sofa near me and took one of my hands. "I don't much care for knee-jerk assumptions," he said softly. "Particularly from you. Like you weren't seeing me, just generic male evil." His free hand approached my bruised forehead, stroking the air near it, as if he could magically heal me.

"Bernard was literally a joke Beth made up, but my mother took it seriously. I had to bump him off."

"Tonight, after you ran away," Mackenzie murmured, "I decided that you didn't believe men and women could be friends."

"This hasn't been the best week for that kind of belief," I whispered. "It's stupid, I know, but the final straw was when she admitted she called you Snuggles."

"What?" He looked as if he expected to find me drooling and cross-eyed. "Who said that? Snuggles? Me? *Me?*" He laughed out loud and shook his head so vigorously his gray-brown curls danced. "Where'd you ever get that idea?"

So there were some plots the great detective did not even suspect. I felt almost sorry for Jinx. "I got the idea from somebody who only pretends she believes men and women can be friends," I said.

He isn't dumb, not even after four days with Jinx. "She's leavin' tomorrow," he said.

"I thought not until Sunday."

"Changed her mind after dinner. Remembered something. I don't know why, all of a sudden like that, but I admit I didn't try to talk her out of it."

I knew why. Because she didn't know his name, either, and she'd never called him Snuggles and because he left her to find me and because she was dull, but not stupid. What she remembered were that the pickings would be better elsewhere.

"Her flight's at five," he said. "Maybe we could have dinner—real food, too—after I drop her off?"

"Pick me up at school? I'll be selling junk."

"So," he said, his voice low and a little husky. "Do you believe men and women can be friends?"

I was willing to be convinced.

Let me say that there is nothing more comforting than a bodyguard, especially one who takes a keen and extremely personal interest in the body he's guarding.

Mackenzie left at dawn, by which time I wasn't shaky, terrified, or angry anymore.

Not even when I realized I hadn't marked a paper or checked a lesson plan since a few lifetimes ago, and that before and since Wynn Teller's murder I'd done nothing but make things worse. Not even when I put on my coat, and enough feathers for a small throw pillow escaped and I had to go to work with a Band-Aid over the rip. Not even when I opened the door to a heavy grayness that hissed *snow*. Not even when I realized my car was still on the curb and decorated with a big, fat parking ticket on its windshield. Not even when I acknowledged that I still had no idea who had tried to murder me yesterday.

Well, maybe a little when I thought about that.

Twenty

I INTERCEPTED A NOTE THAT ANNOUNCED *MISS PEPPER HAS a hickey on her forehead!* I tried to imagine the passionate scene that would result in a bruise in that locale, but the only kind I could think of was a Wynn Teller kind of passion that left a woman as disfigured and discolored as Lydia had been. Which more or less ended the post-Snuggles euphoria.

I wanted to make sure the note writer understood that bruises weren't signs of love, but she was anonymous, her sex known only because teensy open circles dotting *i*'s are not yet an androgynous affectation.

The morning plodded ahead normally, as if all was right with the world.

Maybe it was, or as all right as things can be in a not all right universe. The morning *Inquirer* chortled WIFE CHARGED IN TLC MURDER with salacious, unhesitant delight. Everything was settled to everybody else's satisfaction, justice meted out.

But I wasn't satisfied about who shot me or why. I wasn't satisfied about why Lydia—the goodie—lied. I wasn't satisfied about Adam and Eve and Fay. Or Neil.

Everybody was crazy except me.

But that's exactly what crazy people thought, wasn't it?

Except if I was aware of the manner in which crazy people thought, I wasn't crazy, was I?

I grumped my way down the stairs, past the office, toward the faculty lounge. "Yo!" Edie Friedman said. "News update." She gestured back toward the office. "I eavesdropped. Angela's *still* in labor. She's setting the all-Jefferson varsity hard labor record." Her expression turned wistfully hopeful and I tensed. "Did you see Neil's sub?" she asked. "Kind of cute and literary, with the beard and the glasses."

We were nearly in the lounge when I realized what she'd said. "Jefferson?" I asked. "Jefferson Hospital? Are you sure?"

She nodded and opened the lounge door.

"Not Lankenau?"

"Jefferson. The humongous brick place where they take sick people and ladies having babies? Want me to walk you down there? Honestly, Mandy!"

I replayed yesterday afternoon as best I could. The odd visit, the phone call from a strange woman, the offer to take my car—but I had made the offer, hadn't I?

I had thought the person in the car on my street left me alone because Neil was there, but perhaps Neil had been there because of the person in the car. As in a setup. A cohort with a gray car. Why else take me miles away?

Because the right hospital was in the city, crowded, obvious. The wrong hospital was in the green, rolling suburbs, on a quiet campus with outdoor parking. The better to shoot somebody and get away.

I shuddered. It was also possible that Neil could have gone out another exit from the hospital, could have raced to that car, waiting for him with his cohort.

I'd fallen into a lethal farce, one with real guns. And when I noticed what was going on around me in the teachers' lounge, the farcical feeling persisted.

Déjà vu all over again. Only today it wasn't schnecken, but turkey and lettuce on pita with a side of tomato. "I bought two on purpose," the biology teacher said. "I didn't want to have to go out and buy anything today. What is this, some kind of revenge because you thought I snatched your mother's cookies?"

"I didn't take your sandwich!"

This was too boring for an encore.

"My cup has been moved again," Potter Standish—*Doctor* Potter Standish—pronounced. There is always a natural hush after his inane edicts, because his uninflected tone mimics a newscaster with major late-breaking news.

"This is no longer a trivial matter," he intoned.

Pompous Potter, but all the same, the disappearing acts were getting creepy. Formerly amicable coworkers suspiciously eyed each other and held on to their food stocks like peasants in a famine.

"Jean Valjean's back to his tricks," I said. "Only now he's stealing the sandwich filling, too." Only Charlie Pickles, fellow English teacher, snickered, and Charlie Pickles was a pedantic oaf.

"Where is this John fellow?" Potter demanded.

"In *Les Miserables*," Charlie said from over in the corner. "He's the poor sap sentenced to nineteen years for stealing a loaf of bread."

"Is he out yet?" Potter asked.

"It's *fiction*," I said.

"No wonder." Potter turned back to study the coffee cup arrangement. "Fiction," he said with as much contempt as a monotone can muster.

The lounge felt overheated, overcrowded, and overexcited. Everyone looked on the verge of screaming "J'accuse!" I decided to do something useful with my lunch hour. There was a whiz of a seamstress a few blocks up, and perhaps she could perform first aid on my coat. A flesh-toned Band-Aid was not very subtle or secure on a navy sleeve.

Without its downy contents, the injured sleeve was scant protection from the cold, but the rest of me felt decently insulated, and there was nothing like a walk to encourage thinking.

I checked for the gray car, but to tell the truth, I was no longer positive of its color. There seemed a lot of near-possibilities: blue-silver, or taupe, or beige. I wondered if Edie knew what color car Neil drove. I wished I paid more attention to those things.

The square's Formerly Taller Women were meeting elsewhere this noon, but there was a full contingent of homeless souls waiting on benches until shelters opened. I can never resist a moment's worry that they were once English teachers in private schools with no tenure or pension plan.

I was nearly across the square when I saw her. Her pretty royal-blue coat made her stand out because it didn't fit the general attire or the bruised and defeated rest of her. "You're out, then," I gasped.

Lydia Teller looked chronically frightened.

"What are you doing here?" I sat down on the empty portion of her bench.

"Waiting."

"For what?"

"For . . . ummm . . . you. To thank you. For your kindness. I forgot how schools are, though. All the people. I decided to wait until afterward."

"That's hours from now. You can't sit out here all that time, and anyway, there's no need to thank me." No reason, either, if we were honest.

"I was just going, actually. To have coffee somewhere and wait," she said.

I didn't believe her. Here, she blended in with the lost people. In a coffee shop, her mustard and mauve and gray-green bruises would attract attention. The poor cameo face had a Richard Nixon five o'clock shadow of bruises, not quite as livid as they'd been, but still sufficiently horrifying.

I touched her hand, hoping to comfort her. "Are you upset about going back to that house? Do you want to stay with me awhile?"

She shook her head, her lips tight.

"Then is there some other way I can help you?" I asked.

She shook her head again. "You've already done too much."

I didn't dare ask what that meant. Instead, I offered to hail a cab for her.

"Oh, no, I drove. I'm parked right there." She waved without looking. There were three vehicles at the curb, a tangerine Trans-Am, a white and green van with MICKY'S DRY CLEANERS stenciled on it, and a sedan the color of fog.

I changed the subject even though she didn't know it. "Was it very terrible with the police?" I asked while my eyes reverted to the narc car.

"It would have been without your brother-in-law. If he and his colleague hadn't taken care of everything so well, I would have had to stay there all night."

"And you didn't?" I took a deep breath of the hostile air and tried to make my question sound innocuous. Girl talk. "And how quickly did that brother-in-law of mine get you released?"

Her eyes wandered vaguely, pausing only when they looked up at the bare branches arching over us. "I'm not sure. It was almost dark. When would that be?"

Afternoon is when that would be in darkest February. Early enough to toddle down to my street then trail me out to the suburbs and avenge herself on the woman who had ruined everything for her.

I wondered if I saw madness along with bruises on her battered face. I also wondered whether there was an antique, but lethal, weapon in the commodious purse on her lap. She clutched its handle with both hands, like a woman waiting for a bus.

Perhaps it was time to stop protecting her and begin protecting myself. Push her a little, test her. "I saw the young man who says he's Adam Teller, Wynn's son. Right here, actually. And his sister."

"Wholeperson," Lydia muttered.

"They said they were at your house the night Wynn . . . Wednesday night."

Lydia stared at me blankly.

"They said you were upset, too."

"How couldn't I be?" she said, surprising me. "They act like they're his only children—if they're his children at all!"

"I thought you were upstairs the whole time," I said quietly.

"After that. After them, I ran upstairs. They put Wynn in a fury. He hurt me. I ran upstairs."

"And their mother was there, too, wasn't she?" I said, testing it out. "Fay . . . Elias."

"Her. You'd think a family could decide on a last name, wouldn't you? Who does she think she is, barging in on our dinner hour with those two oafs, claiming to be his true family, like I wasn't real, like Hugh wasn't real, making things worse than they already were!" Lydia began to cry. "First the man with the lawsuit, then them! One fight after another!"

Oh, I wish, I wish she had stuck to her locked-in-the-bathroom, don't-know-a-thing story, had remained my unsullied, blameless heroine. I wish, I wish I could find the person to believe.

She tightened her lips and looked out from exhausted eyes. I felt terrible, for both of us.

"Actually," she said, "I was upstairs just about the whole evening, like I said. Up and down for a while, then just up there. I knew I was safe until the people left. He never hurt me when people were around." She scowled and clutched her purse even more tightly. "Except if the person was Hugh," she added in a whisper. "But of course, that's different. Hugh's family."

That went right up there among the most chilling sentences I'd ever heard.

"So I'm sorry if I confused you before by saying I was in the bathroom, because of course I was, but not maybe every minute. Not exactly."

I thought of the Greek philosopher Diogenes, who'd traveled with a lantern in search of an honest man, and who'd then founded the Cynic sect in Athens. Lydia was probably one of the people he interviewed along the way.

"If they hadn't descended on him like locusts, none of this would have happened. You had to know how to handle him." She looked very sad again. "Not that I did."

She needed counseling, needed to get it straight where responsibility and guilt should be assigned. As soon as I was positive she wasn't going to kill me, I'd mention it.

"Like vultures, they were, after his flesh. Picking, picking." She looked at me carefully. "That's another reason I went into the bathroom. I couldn't stand them, and I knew Wynn couldn't and that he'd be furious."

"Was anybody still there when you went upstairs for good?"

She nodded. "All of them. Except maybe the teacher about the lawsuit." She wrinkled her forehead in thought. "No, maybe he was there, too. I can't remember. I was barely downstairs at all."

"Was your husband for sure still alive when you locked yourself up?"

"Please." Again her eyes welled up and over. "This feels like the police again. When I came downstairs way later, he was . . ." She shrugged and released the pocketbook long enough to brush away the tears. "You believe me, don't you? I thought you believed me!" Her voice was low, but with a desperate edge of hysteria.

"You never heard the gun go off?"

"Please." She shook her head.

Of course she'd heard it. I simply couldn't figure why she wouldn't say when, or by whom, unless as I increasingly feared, she had herself fired it. "Go home," I said softly. "You need rest. And I need to get back to work."

She nodded.

But next period, while my class had a pop quiz on "Stopping by Woods on a Snowy Evening," I looked out my window and Lydia was still there, out among the homeless waiting for shelter. Or for me, she'd said. I automatically leaned forward and opened my mouth, as if to call out, although whether to warn her or to frighten her away I couldn't have said.

Twenty-one

IF YOU SIT DOWN AND FIGURE IT OUT, YOU'LL FIND THERE are a handful of hours during all of high school when learning is possible.

Ninth grade drowns in a hormonal swamp. As has been mentioned, twelfth grade is a wash. In any grade at any time, attention spans snap when atmospheric conditions are too exciting, as when it rains or snows, or does neither and is perfect, including all of spring. All Mondays are lost to laments at another week's beginning, and all Fridays are treated as early weekends. During first period, students are too bleary to think; during the period before lunch, they're too hungry to think; and during last period, they're exhausted. Days and sometimes weeks are spent preparing for and recovering from vacations, and in those few slivers of time with no other excuse for goofing off, kids get sick.

The flu was the excuse-of-choice for half the senior class today. There was a big concert at the Spectrum tonight, and they needed to be rested for it.

The loyal remnants of the class and I were reviewing, at their request, the mechanics of assembling their term paper notes. I launched into a well-worn monologue. "The researcher is a detective," I said. "The question that needs answering is the mystery, and clues are scattered all over. The truth is in fragments, pieces that in themselves might not seem relevant or important. The research sleuth finds and assembles the pieces until they form the whole picture and answer the question.''

Two pigeons landed on the windowsill. I forgot to mention that learning also stops for wildlife, however prosaic the species. I droned on above the giggles of my students, ignoring them and the pigeons, who had mistaken my sill for a motel. Luckily, from what I've unwillingly observed, pigeon foreplay is pretty much for the birds, so it wasn't all that long before the hope of tomorrow was watching me again.

But their bored faces made it clear that after the avian live porno show, an illustration of how to cross-reference a note card was an anticlimax in several senses.

''Then we break the topic down into its questions, its subcategories, so that when we find an interesting tidbit, we can decide where it belongs, and can see where we need more information. . . .'' My voice dribbled off, but the class didn't seem to mind, so I stopped a moment and thought.

Unlike my students, I was really listening and hearing. My familiar detective–research paper analogy had suddenly struck me, and I mentally filled three-by-five cards, trying to put together my own clues.

Somebody coughed, and I returned to teaching, discussing coding the cards so they'd know who said what, then moved to coding cards for the sub-subjects on their outlines. ''Say there's a category called Arguments Against or Evidence Proving whatever—the existence of Atlantis, or Elvis, or reincarnation,'' I said.

Evidence. What would go on those three-by-five cards? The book. The corpse. The bullet. The motive. The beatings of Lydia Teller.

I went on automatic pilot, answering a question, even making sense, I think; but my mind was now fixed on what had started this nightmare: the beatings of Lydia Teller and what might have ended it, the last beating of Lydia Teller.

At what point during the night of the murder had it happened? Lydia said that Neil's lawsuit and Fay's claims and Adam and Eve's harassment pushed Wynn to the explosive point, that he hurt her. But she also said he wouldn't do it in front of anybody. So she was beaten after they left, after she claimed to be locked upstairs.

Neither Neil, nor Fay, nor Adam and Eve had mentioned bruises, not even after the news said that Lydia Teller had often been victimized. Surely, even if everybody else were oddly oblivious, Eve Wholeperson would have seized on such an obvious case of brutality.

"Allow for surprises," I told my class. "For information not on your outline, something you couldn't have anticipated, something that doesn't agree with what you thought was so. Be flexible." There was a collective, tolerant sigh. The assumption that they would rush off to a dusky stack where they'd make discoveries in obscure texts was ludicrous, but we humored each other because we all knew it was an inflexible given of the curriculum that I present this to them.

They listened, their minds undoubtedly on tonight's concert. And I spoke, my attention stuck on Lydia's bruises.

Dead men don't beat their wives. Wynn Teller had vented his frustration with his life, his double whammy of professional and personal pursuers, on Lydia, and then he'd been killed.

Somebody doubled back.

Or somebody new entered.

Or, what made the most sense, Mackenzie had been right all along and Lydia, beaten and desperate, pulled her grandfather's gun off the wall and well and truly ended her misery.

The class snickered. I realized my hand was up, the chalk still on the board where I'd written *Neil* and *Fay* with arrows pointing at them, and *hurt after?* and *lying?*

For the rest of the hour, I tried not to chew gum and walk at the same time. Except when I kept teaching and looked out the window one more time. And again saw a woman with a royal-blue coat and a gray, unpretentious car, and all too probably, a gun in her black leather purse, waiting.

Waiting for me.

THE NOT-A-GARAGE SALE BEGAN ITS PREVIEW AT THE END of the school day. Philly Prep was justifiably afraid the students wouldn't reenter the building on the weekend and would spend their allowances elsewhere. So Friday afternoon was dedicated to their wallets. To my astonishment, the students willingly accommodated this cynical ploy, behaving as if the sale were a treasure hunt. Tim Clark showed me his favorite earring—a fly-fishing lure—discovered at the sale a year ago. Mirri Langdorf said this was where she'd found her Spanish mantilla. "My signature accessory," she added with pride. Sackett Smith had discovered an ancient camera with a bellows. It didn't work, he explained, but it was so radically great he kept it on the dashboard of his car.

The book stall was to the right of MUSIC, another lonely category where round black disks of varying rpms waited in vain to be adopted. Records and books had become collectible oddities. I had become old.

I had little to do besides watch America's youth find accoutrements, which I did for as long as I could. Then I decided I had more important things to stare at, like Lydia, presumably still out there waiting for me. I asked Charlie Pickles, a sort of seller at large, to cover for me.

I peeked into the office as I passed it. Helga, still at work, gazed affectionately at her computer screen. Maybe she was delving in that mysterious *ogzmic* file of hers. I turned the corner toward the staircase and, for perhaps the first time in history, my reaction to Helga was a smile.

But a short, aborted one that turned into a choke and came out a rasp that had meant to be a scream. I was hammerlocked from behind. I kicked backward—with difficulty, as I was on the first step—and twisted my entire body away. The hand let go and I fell, hard, onto the steps.

"Did I scare you?" Neil Quigley looked surprised and goofier than ever, holding a Mylar balloon that said IT'S A BOY!

"Congratulations," I gasped. My feet were every which way and my rear end hurt. I stood and limped to the marble foyer, from which I could more easily escape.

He reached in his topcoat pocket. I put my hands up over my face and pushed at the glass inner door. "Here," he said, putting something in my hand. I stared at a thick cigar that you just knew was particularly odiferous. It had a wide baby-blue band repeating the balloon's message.

If you ask me, there'd be more justification for exclamation points and amazement if there were a greater variety of possibilities. If there were a chance of giving birth to a halibut, a Corinthian pediment, or even a full-grown man. But with a fifty-fifty probability, a mere two choices, why such astonishment? "And the baby's at Jefferson," I said.

"What?"

"Where's your baby?"

"Did you expect me to have him on me?" He patted his pockets and laughed nervously. I got some satisfaction because my question apparently frightened him the way various characteristics of his did me.

"Well?"

"I expected you to ask his name, or his size, or how Angela's doing," he said.

"Well, I'm asking *where* Angela's doing."

"She's still in the hospital." He looked very troubled.

"How come Jefferson?" I backed another step away.

"Mandy?"

"We went to Lankenau. You had me drive you there. It's not even in the same direction. How come?"

"Oh, boy," he muttered. He offered me another cigar, but I declined. "I'm embarrassed. Her allergy doctor's at Lankenau, and her first G-Y-N was there, and I drove her there a million times, but two months ago, when things got complicated, she switched to a specialist at Jefferson and she took the bus for those appointments, and yesterday I . . . a failure of memory?" His shoulders slumped, so that with his balloon, he looked like a sad clown painting on velvet. "I acted like a dope, didn't I? And it was worse after you left—you should have seen me insisting she was there, practically storming the maternity ward." He laughed, then grew solemn. "Angela didn't think it was funny. How Daddy Went to the Wrong Hospital is going to be the first story she tells the kid."

As soon as he said the word *daddy*, he blushed. "He's a cute little guy," he added softly, and he blinked hard.

I knew that daddies could kill, but the odds were against a sentimental one carrying a Mylar balloon, who couldn't remember which direction to head under stress. Still. "What color is your car?" I asked. His cohort might have been a clear thinker.

Neil's turn to back off. "Green, same as ever. Do other men have their cars painted while their wives are in labor? Is it a custom I forgot?" He smiled nervously.

I smiled for real for the first time.

"Look," he said, "I can't help noticing that bruise on your forehead. What happened? Has a doctor seen it? You're—forgive me but you're acting pretty weird."

"Me? I'm fine, but you're pretty weird, not even telling me his name and who he looks like and whether he has hair and how much he weighs and how Angela's doing."

The baby had amassed an amazing amount of statistical data in his two hours of life. I aimed Neil toward the gym, fleetingly remembering that I had meant to do a Lydia check, but deciding that if she was freezing out there, she could continue to do so. There was a gratifying burst of applause when Neil entered carrying his balloon.

I returned to selling books and watching the new father hand out cigars. I'm glad it wasn't Neil, I thought as I transacted a sale. I always knew it couldn't have been. But of course, I had also always known it couldn't have been Lydia, because it was too horrible to think of a life so trapped that the only way out leads to prison. I didn't want it that way, but I was beginning to accept it.

Forty-five minutes and similar nonstop thoughts later, I again turned the book business over to Charlie Pickles. He looked peeved, but then, he generally does. I said I had to leave for a call of nature. I did. A call of my nature.

Once in the hall, I reached into my shirt pocket and realized I had left my classroom keys at the book stall. I started back, then wondered what I'd tell Charlie Pickles. Besides, I didn't need a second story panoramic view, only a glance.

The gym had high wire-meshed frosted windows facing the alleyway. Across the hall the auditorium, which sided on the square, had clear but impossibly high windows. The only first floor lookout seemed the one from the principal's office, guarded by the hound from Hell-ga.

I turned back toward the staircase, planning to try doors until I found an unlocked classroom, when I remembered the window backstage. I also remembered my stashed treasures: the wholesome and not-so-wholesome books, and Sasha's cape. Two birds with one etcetera.

I went up the stage steps and back behind the curtain. My memory hadn't failed me. The cracked tan window shade was up. I peered out. The only person I saw across the way had dreadlocks and a red backpack, and the gray car had been replaced by a purple and white finned number. Lydia had given up on me. I could breathe easy for a while.

It felt so good not to be afraid, I laughed with relief and went in search of my goodies.

This is where I fell on Monday, I remembered idly.

So, for symmetry's sake, that was where I fell on Friday, too. Down, splat, with a thunk and a clatter, bruising whatever places had been spared on my staircase flop and whatever sense of dignity I had left.

I was surrounded by moldering upholstery, heavy velvet curtains, and a partial backdrop of celestial blue with fluffy white clouds. Musty, maybe, but peaceful as can be. I climbed to my feet and looked around more closely, carefully retracing my steps. And then I saw the cane—a showy sort that Martha Thornton might use for a tap dance, red and silver candy-striped, and realized that I had done the thunking and splatting, but it had done the clattering. Which had to mean it had been propped up.

Like a trap. Like something else had been rigged Monday, had tripped me the same way Monday.

I stood very quietly. I would grab the books and the cape and be on my way. Except that the books had been moved, and were not on the chair but on a nearby table, as if a housekeeper had come in to tidy. The chair had been turned to face another chair. To make a bed, I thought. And Sasha's cape was flung like a throw or blanket over one of them. At the other end, a small carpet was rolled into a pillow.

I thought I heard a shuffle, movement, but it was only my

own heartbeat gone wild. I very carefully tiptoed to the end table and picked up the stack of books.

There were too many and the top one was unfamiliar. *Great American Plays: 1950–1960.* PROPERTY OF PHILLY PREP LIBRARY was stamped inside.

I tried to convince myself that it had been here all along, left by an absentminded player long ago. I looked around more carefully and realized the furniture arrangement was not quite as haphazard as I'd first thought. The two chairs together. The end table next to it.

And on the floor at its side, a carton removed from onstage. I knew that was so because this one still had a shipping tag addressed to Sasha Berg.

But its contents weren't from Sasha anymore. Not the three white yogurt cups and lids, wrapping paper from various sandwiches, an empty pudding container, apple cores, banana peels, or the small plastic bag of uneaten celery sticks, which seriously annoyed me. You should have to eat everything you steal, including vegetables. Especially vegetables.

"The Phantom." I didn't think I had said it, let alone said it loudly, but the words flew up above the sets and expanded into the cavernous maze of ropes and supports. I belatedly clapped my hand over my mouth.

Wait till that silly commercial art teacher heard that her schnecken hadn't been an inside job. Some poor but clever street person had figured it out, found a way to nest back here and forage at night.

And in the daytime? Like right now? I was suddenly in that nightmare where you have to flee but can't. My feet grew and melded to the stage floor and had nothing at all to do with my brain or my needs.

Get out, I told myself. Get out, I told the intruder. Sad, but you can't be here. I thought of the children. He could be dangerous. I thought of myself. "Help!" I cried. "Help!"

"No!" a voice thundered. Low, rumbling, frightening. I fought to catch my breath, squinted, looked and finally saw an enormous bulk halfway behind the flat.

I couldn't tell who he was or if I knew him. I couldn't tell much of anything.

He reached around the canvas backdrop. Now things were clearer, especially his hand silhouetted against a backdrop of cumulus clouds, and two other things.

First, that was a gun in his hand, and second, I was in deep trouble.

Twenty-two

"DON'T SHOOT!" I SCREAMED.

I knew that was an incredibly stupid, not to mention useless, thing to say, no matter how loudly. Still, that idea held top priority in my mind, followed closely by a completely hysterical inner voice shrieking, *Gun! Gun!*

There was no response. He kept all but his weapon and a small slice of himself behind the bilious sky and clouds. Every few seconds, he'd poke his head out, checking my whereabouts. He moved so quickly, head out and back in a flash, that I didn't think he could see anything. I couldn't make out much of him, except bulk, a black beard, a knit cap. The generic homeless man from the square, in out of the cold. And armed.

The stairs and a possible exit were too far. He'd shoot me if I bolted. Instead, I used the time between his bobblings to retreat inch by inch, until I was at the other edge of the backdrop. Only then did I consider how easily a bullet had zipped through the canvas hood of my car and wonder why I was behaving as if canvas painted to look like heaven was a magic shield. I stood still, hoping he hadn't noticed the shift enough to activate his trigger finger.

We seemed stuck in a silly version of the classic standoff, and no posse would ever ride over the ridge of the footlights and end our impasse.

My call of nature had become a permanent summons.

The man at the other end of the backdrop was probably desperate. He had nothing left to lose, considering life on the streets in February, particularly after this warm haven with refrigerators full of yogurt and fruit. A cafeteria to invade at night. Furniture, indoor plumbing. This was not going to be a voluntary evacuation.

I looked around for a solution. Above my head, ropes looped and hung like twisted vines. I tried to imagine myself leaping up, grabbing one and swinging toward him, kicking my feet and—I failed. I couldn't imagine it.

Me not Tarzan. What I could imagine was a variety of humiliations—missing, tripping, losing hold, slamming into the backdrop next to me, enraging the man with the gun, and managing to get myself shot while simultaneously smashing my own face.

"Please," I said. "There's no reason for violence, for that gun. Put it down and come out and we can get you some help."

"I didn't do anything!" he bellowed.

I never said he had. His response therefore worried me a lot.

"Leave me alone!" he shouted, which was ridiculous. He was found out, and he knew it. He was trapped, and he knew that, too.

And so was I, and I knew it, too. Only I didn't have a gun, which didn't bode well for my side of the trap unless I learned to dematerialize, and learned it quickly. I tried to move my thoughts beyond self-defense into active aggression.

One good, solid, everything-you've-got shove, I told myself. Backdrop to the gut, winding him.

Which is what I did. I pushed, hard, and heard a satisfying *whooof!* as the wooden frame tried to bisect him from the forehead down. He lost his balance and backed up, grabbed the set, fell.

And dropped the gun.

I raced around the wobbling, toppling backdrop and slammed my foot on it. He was disarmed and I was on the verge of breathing freely again.

I carefully picked it up and pointed it at him. "Okay, come with me," I said in my gruffest law and order voice.

He straightened up, looked at me, and laughed.

Nobody did that to John Wayne. "Hey!" I said. "This isn't a joke."

"Miss Pepper! I can't believe it's you." The bearded giant looked honestly happy, as if we had bumped into each other at a delicious party. "The fact is," he said, "it's not real."

"What?"

"The gun's a fake. A prop I found back here."

Sure, sure. I'd seen those movies, where the dumb villain is duped into distraction. Only thing this bearded critter didn't remember was that it was the bad guy who got fooled, and I was the good guy. "Come on," I said. "I hate to do it, but you can't keep living back here."

There was a rush of peripheral movement as a flurry of blue whirred my way and grabbed my blouse.

"Don't you touch him!" it screamed. "Leave him alone!"

"Mom!" the beard said. "Hey!"

He walked toward me—toward her, too—with such a complete lack of anxiety, I knew he was telling the truth about the gun. I looked at my weapon.

"Calm down," he told the woman.

I aimed at the floor and pulled the trigger. There was a small bang and a familiar whiff. A very impressive cap pistol. I dropped the entire business in my skirt pocket and tried to hide how stupid I felt. Not particularly about the gun—all I know about guns is that I want to avoid them. But I like to think I know something about people. Especially when they tell me about their protective son who always and forever left his boarding schools to come home and save his mother. Especially when I knew the son had just come home and been told by his father never to come home again. Especially when the mother of that son keeps a vigil outside a school her son had once attended, a school that for the same week since the son had been told to disappear had been missing all manner of small objects, mostly food.

So it had been Hugh. Poor Hugh. It should have felt better to have it not be Lydia, but having it be Hugh was no improvement. At least now I knew why she'd lied, insisted she never heard the shot or knew who was there. Knew why she felt guilty for not having killed Wynn, why she was willing to go to jail in her son's place.

Lydia Teller breathed in hard, ragged gasps. "Oh, please," she sobbed. "Let him come home, live in his own house again. Let him finally have a normal life. Please!"

"How normal will it be with his mother in jail for a crime she didn't commit?"

Hugh Teller, so hairy and tall I would never have recognized him, looked surprised. "You didn't?" he asked.

Even in the gloom, I saw her eyes widen. "How could you of all people say that?" She looked ready to cry.

"Mom," Hugh said. "This is important. Tell me the truth."

She spoke slowly, and breathed hard between phrases, as if each word were heavy and painful. "I heard the shot from upstairs. I was in . . . I ran into the bathroom after he . . ."

Hugh seemed as surprised as I was. "You were? You didn't?"

"I thought he would kill me this time. Blaming everything happening to him on me, like he always did, but it was worse that night. The worst ever." She sounded frightened even of the memory.

"I know that part, remember?" Hugh said. "I was the one who told you to get out, that we'd leave together, but you wouldn't." He shook his head as if still angry with her refusal.

"You were there?" I asked, but Hugh kept his attention on his mother.

"It wasn't you?" Lydia whispered. "You really, truly, didn't fire your great-great-grandfather's gun?"

What a quaint way to put it, as if she couldn't say what had happened directly even now.

Hugh shook his head.

It wasn't you. It wasn't Hugh. My mind played the stupid refrain back and forth. It wasn't Hugh, who thought Lydia had done it, or goofy Neil, or Lydia, locked in the bathroom, thinking her son had fired the shot she heard.

"I went down later, when it was quiet," she said. "You were gone, and he was . . . on the kitchen floor. I didn't know what to do. I couldn't even fix the back door because I'd have to walk over . . ." She shook her head. "I put on *Oklahoma* and I thought about what to say." Her voice became dreamy, drugged-sounding. "I thought about you as Curly. I thought about you running away, safe, maybe all the way to the real Oklahoma where nobody would find you. It calmed me down, made there seem a point to it all. I was going to wait to call the police for a long, long time. Until you were far away and safe."

"You should have known I would never have left without getting you out. I told you that. That's why I didn't leave Sunday like he said. That's why I didn't leave Wednesday."

"I thought you had gotten me out by . . . firing that gun," she said.

"I thought you had gotten yourself out."

They viewed each other with amazement and relief. They'd protected each other, finally, even if it was for a crime neither had committed. It was the nicest thing I'd heard about that family so far.

"How did you wind up here?" I asked.

"I've always been fond of the stage," he said.

"This is not the time for jokes, Hugh."

"Seriously, every hiding place from my childhood was outside, and cold. I didn't even have a car to sleep in—I had to do my big rescue efforts by public transportation, believe it or not. Plus I needed a place I could take her to, at least for maybe one night, until we could get away from him. And then I remembered a story. In fact, I remembered it from your ninth grade class."

Nice to know that literature can be useful. I waited.

"Instead of looking for a place where nobody was," he said, "I'd go where there were lots of people. So many, nobody would notice me."

"Here? With that woodsman's beard?" For some reason, nobody at school had chosen that particular hair aberration.

"I was going to shave it, but I couldn't find a razor anywhere in the building."

My elbow hurt. I rubbed it and remembered. "You set traps, just in case somebody wandered back here, didn't you?" I asked.

"Sorry about that. But the very first afternoon, there were like a million teachers all over the stage. I hadn't counted on that. I thought of it like a doorbell, just so I'd know somebody was coming."

I forgave him, although my knees still ached.

"Lots of days, I'd prop the door and sit out in the square a couple hours. Amazing how invisible you can be if you decide to. Nobody noticed there; nobody noticed here. If I could have shaved, I bet I could have sat in the classes. 'The Purloined Letter,' remember? Everybody's looking for it, and it's on the fireplace mantel in front of them all along."

Like I said, Poe is always a winner.

"Wednesday night, I came back here and watched the TV in the faculty lounge and found out he was dead. I took the radio from the gym office and heard later Mom had turned herself in. I was really surprised. I couldn't believe she'd ever hurt anybody, no matter what they did to her. I watched, my whole life, and she never fought back, except when he tried to go for me. Then I heard she was out on bail and I called and said not to worry, but she did. She came here."

"I couldn't stand thinking about him hiding, scared. I didn't know there would be people staying after school."

They both looked at me. Hugh looked hopeful. Lydia was her chronically frightened self. It was going to take a lot of time and help to get past that.

"This is the truth," Hugh said. "My mother ran upstairs. She knew he wouldn't hurt me—bullies don't when you're bigger than they are. We were having the worst shouting match. He was ranting about the bible, for some reason."

"About Adam and Eve," I suggested.

"Yes. And then on and on about somebody else—he had a lot of names for that somebody—upsetting the apple cart so that now every single person he counted on was against him and he couldn't trust anybody anymore. Not a living soul. That's exactly what he said. It was insane—we were fighting, but it had nothing to do with me or anybody I knew.

He was drinking the whole time and then, suddenly, he was out of steam. Past the point where he'd go up and hurt her again. In fact, pretty close to passing out. And I left. And that's all."

"Then the question is, who came into the house after Hugh?"

"The question is, who was left?" Lydia asked with the mildest hint of black humor. And then she looked meditative and sad, and I could almost read her thoughts. If she was no longer protecting Hugh, who was she protecting, and whose jail sentence would she serve?

"Why don't you enjoy your reunion and try not to worry about it for a while," I suggested. "Go home."

"You aren't going to tell the principal?" Hugh asked.

"I don't think this comes under the normal rules, do you? Besides, the staff can do with a little mystery, with the legend of the hungry poltergeist."

"My car's around back," Lydia told her son. "In the alleyway."

"Hurry, before you get towed," I said, and, after gathering up a few possessions of Hugh's, they took their leave.

The Not-a-Garage Sale population had exploded, mostly with parents peeling children off the booths. Neil's balloon still bounced above the crowd, but it was tied to the cashier's stand.

I scanned the room for Mackenzie's salt and pepper curls, but couldn't find them. I sincerely hoped this didn't mean that Jinx had delayed her departure. Neil, engrossed in conversation with a light-haired man, saw me, called my name and waved. I saw his friend begin to turn toward me, and fearing they would invite me to join them, to hear more birth and labor statistics, I turned away and nearly bumped into Sasha.

She carried a bulging LIFE !! JOY!! canvas sack. Portrait of a New Age ecologically correct flea-market maven.

"I found two more frames," she said. "Not to mention a fantastic hat." The latter looked like a veiled stack of rattan pancakes, but happily, Sasha knows what she likes and invites you to view it, not editorialize on it, so I didn't have to admit that it made her look like a charwoman in a British mystery.

"I'll wear it tonight. With these." She pulled out a pair of fairly intact black lace gloves that would give her frostbite. "Lars will love it."

Heroically, I kept silent. Lars's deficiencies would become apparent on their own as surely as did images in Sasha's darkroom trays.

"Where've you been?" she asked. "I was looking for you."

"Should have looked backstage. The most amazing thing just happened."

"Tell me en route to the exit," she said. "If I don't leave, nothing amazing will ever happen to me. He'll be at my place in fifteen minutes."

The school hallway wasn't nearly long enough for the entire story, and certainly not for what I'd hoped, some fresh insight into who, then, had killed Wynn Teller.

"My money's on dopey Wholesperson," Sasha said. "For some obscure ideological reason. Anyway, let's talk tomorrow. You going out tonight?"

I nodded.

"Good," she said. "I was afraid you might be moping for J. Edgar. J as in Jinx's, as in property of, you know."

"We have a lot of updates to take care of," I began, but she opened the glass inner door, releasing the vestibule's freezing air, so I stood behind it, watching her like a prisoner through the clear thick barrier. "I'll give you a call tomorrow."

"Not too early." Winter whistled through the door opening. Sasha scowled.

"What?" I said.

Her nostrils flared. "If I didn't have to get going," she said, and then she shook her head. "I have a score to settle. I haven't forgotten."

"What? Did I do something?"

"You? Him! I could swear that was Mr. No Show, the CPA creep who stood me up. Behind you. Please tell me he isn't your date tonight."

"Mackenzie is. Jinx left. There was nothing between them." I turned to see the man who'd stood her up, but saw only trouser cuffs turning the bend in the staircase.

She released the inner door, blew a kiss and left. No avoiding the bookstall now, but there wasn't that much longer to go. I took a deep breath, set my shoulders, and resolved to diligently unload used books on all passersby until the day's session ended.

Which turned out to be one more fine and unhonored resolution. "Mandy?" a voice called from above.

I looked up. "Neil?" He bent over the top landing. I could see his thinning hair and one shoulder. "Could you give me a hand?" he said. "I have this . . . problem."

Ill-timed periods and pregnancies were referred to that way, but neither condition seemed likely to apply to Neil Quigley.

"I can't talk about it from up here," he said.

A delicate social problem? Maybe his pants had ripped and he thought all women knew how to sew. Maybe he'd been asked to prepare a speech, say something about his baby and needed coaching from the oral book report lady. Maybe he couldn't remember which hospital Angela was in. I walked up the staircase, mystified. From the landing midway, I could see that Neil looked rather green. Maybe he was ill, afraid to go back to being the center of the crowd.

It is amazing how many theories you can create walking up one flight of stairs, especially when it's double-wide and double-long.

Amazing, too, how once upstairs, all the theories dissipated and I was able to instantly diagnose Neil's true problem.

Not a split seam, not a virus, but a sandy-haired man standing against a classroom door where he couldn't be seen from below, pointing a silver-chased old-fashioned ivory-handled gun at him. At us.

And just as immediately I knew that this time, this gun, this threat, was for real.

This was serious. Dead serious.

Twenty-three

I LOOKED AROUND. NOT ANOTHER SIGN OF LIFE ON THE entire floor. No one below. The merry shoppers were using the gym's outside exit.

"Clifford made me do it, call you up here. I feel awful, but I didn't know what else to do," Neil said. "The gun and all . . ."

Clifford. Clifford Schmidt. The Sneeze. The surviving partner. "You're the one," I said before I censored myself.

"I am?"

I'd meant the one Sasha had seen. The one whose cuffs I'd glimpsed ascending the staircase—the better to wait and entrap me. He probably had his gun at Neil's back all along. The one who'd stood Sasha up Wednesday night. The night Wynn Teller was murdered.

"Why'd he want me up here?" I whispered to Neil.

"Enough!" Clifford said. "You two don't have anything left to talk over. No more lawsuit, no more anything except a tragic end to the entire mess." I didn't understand much, except that it didn't sound healthy for me, and I suddenly remembered our brief conversation the other afternoon and how he'd complained of loose ends he had to clean up.

I tried to remember what else had been said in Schmidt's office, but it seemed vague and insubstantial. Something about Neil and practicality?

Clifford waved his gun like a traffic policeman's baton, directing us into Neil's classroom, a fit setting, I feared, in which to become a footnote to history. Stay tuned. Story at eleven.

I wondered if Cliff appreciated the symbolism of the event. I wondered, had my own room been unlocked, whether I would have found literary overtones to this ambush. And then I wondered if I were showing early signs of dementia.

"Listen," I said, "you're making—"

"—a big mistake. I know. I saw those movies, too," Clifford Schmidt said. "But this isn't a mistake. It's unfortunate, but you have no one to blame but yourselves. You stir things up, wake up sleeping dogs, and you can't complain about what happens next."

"I don't even know what you're talking about!"

"Of course not." He closed the classroom door. Neil and I stood awkwardly, like gangly students on the first day of school. "Okay," Cliff said. "You, Quigley—over here." He indicated the desk closest to the door. He pulled a folded piece of paper out of his pocket, and then a clean sheet. "Copy this," he said. "Word for word. Make it look nice, it's your confession."

"I'm not going to—" Neil began.

"If you aren't writing by the time I finish this sentence, I'll shoot her, and my typed note will have to do. Your call."

"They'll trace the typewriter," I said. "They always do."

Cliff looked mildly amused. "Did. It's harder to trace a laser printer. I'll take the chance."

With an imploring glance at me, Neil started writing.

"You, over there!" Cliff pointed to the window wall. I sat where he indicated, in the front row, and hoped that if I barely moved or breathed or made noise, he might forget about me.

He was one of the people Wynn Teller had told his son he could no longer trust. His partner, but what had been going on?

"I'm sorry about this." Cliff rubbed a palm over the barrel of the gun. I could have almost believed he was holding a toy, or a very fancy cigarette lighter. It was lovely in its own way, with the silver design, the sort of thing the cowboy in the white hat carried.

Even I could understand why guns like that one would be passed on to Lydia, and how any friend of the family or business partner would be apt to know about such a collection.

"Nothing personal," Clifford said. "Merely survival."

"We aren't referring to my survival by any chance, are we?" I muttered.

He had a mean, dry chuckle.

If I lived, I vowed to have a serious talk with Sasha. How could she have accepted a date with him in the first place?

"A man works a lifetime to build something up," Schmidt said. "He can't sit by while people ruin it, can he?"

"It hasn't been a lifetime. You're barely forty, I'll bet." Actually, he looked closer to fifty, but flattery never hurt anybody, especially a man with thinning hair. "You have years and years—"

"I'm not interested," he snapped. Maybe he was only thirty-five and I'd insulted him.

"What good do you think this'll do you, Cliff?" Neil asked. There was a desperate quaver in his voice, and I was embarrassed by his attempt to ingratiate himself. You don't call the man trying to murder you by his nickname.

"A whole lot. I'll have an income, to mention one fairly basic item. Without your interference, TLC will go on, thank you. You don't have much muscle left, do you?"

I thought he was referring to Neil's physique.

"It burned," Neil said softly.

"Oddly enough," Cliff said, "my books look just fine. I wouldn't have done this, but you won't give up. You should have stopped once the place burned down. It's really too bad."

He relaxed, almost strutted, relocated nearer to Neil, the better to intimidate him.

"Been a lot of pressure on you. I'm sure your coworkers will remember how disturbed you seemed this week. And then, alas, your wires sprung and you killed the man you had wanted to sue when you didn't have a case anymore. And now, filled with remorse, and maybe still a little of the crazies, you shoot your partner over there—''

''His what?'' I said. ''Me? Are you talking about me?''

''Be quiet. You don't think I understood why you were suddenly appearing at the office every single day?'' He didn't even look at me when he said it. ''You shoot her,'' he said to Neil. ''And yourself. End of one very sad story. When we rebuild, we may name the place the Neil Quigley Memorial Learning Center. How would that be?''

''Why did you kill him?'' Neil asked. ''At least tell me that. You must have known all along what was going on. You're the one with the business background.''

It was okay for Neil to act like this was a talk show, but I was afraid that in lieu of a commercial break, I was going to be blown away, so I listened with half an ear and searched for an escape with all the rest of me.

I stretched. Clifford watched with a little manly interest, then must have remembered I was a short-timer, as he ignored me again. ''I was never for his style,'' he said. ''He wasted money left and right—splashy TV ads, a PR firm on retainer, bills for business entertaining that would choke a horse, the clothing, the car. Even crazy gifts for his wife every so often—fur coats, trips.''

Lydia. I'd thought this was all about her, and it wasn't. Even in this drama so central to her life, she was a bit player.

Schmidt was enjoying his diatribe against Teller. He puffed up and orated to the two of us. ''He acted like this was Hollywood. We were on the verge of bankruptcy. I said cut back, cut out, but the showman insisted we'd be dead without the image. It was too easy an idea to copy—he had to be the symbol of quality and prestige. I was trapped. If I sued him for his stupidity and stubbornness, I'd destroy the business.''

That sounded more ethical than destroying him and saving the business, but I kept that to myself. I was already afraid I was about to become a bad odor they tracked down on Monday morning.

''I went along—what choice did I have? And then your wife got sick and you got antsy.'' He glared at Neil as if every single thing that had happened was because of Angela's environmental allergies. "And then, when I got you under control—"

"The fire? You burned down my center and you call that getting me under control?" It was a breakthrough in assertiveness for Neil, even if his forehead was beading with sweat.

"And then that woman flounces in!" Cliff's face was flushed, his temper up. "Another goddamn wife!"

Of course. Another wife, another claim, would mean the books were going to be inspected and challenged by all sorts of lawyers. The game was up.

"And Wynn says it's lucky we're not making a fortune now because maybe, when you get right down to it, she really did think of the idea." Clifford looked apoplectic, cheeks red and veins bulging. "Then," he said, "two more of them pop up—his kids, they say. Like a circus car pouring out people!" He looked at both of us as if he expected sympathy.

I stopped stretching, stomped my foot and stood up.

"Hey! What're you doing?" Clifford asked.

"Foot's asleep." He shrugged, so I rocked on it, forward, backward, until he stopped paying attention once again, and I sidled toward the windowsill. I don't know what I expected—perhaps a conveniently placed fire escape? But Neil's side of the building faced an airshaft. There was nothing below but debris and cement. I wondered how many really unfixable parts broke on impact if you fell from the equivalent of the third story. Damn that double high first floor.

I sat on the edge of the windowsill, looking around. Shame on Neil not to have a broadax or cannon or rifle. What else was history all about?

But there was only the same tan squatty desk I had in my room; the same standard-issue four-drawer green file cabinet; several maps of the world; pictures of JFK, Martin Luther King, and Bobby Kennedy; and articles pro and con gun control. Unfortunate choice of bulletin boards at the moment, I thought. It was more pleasant to contemplate a nearby picture of a crusader and a knight in full regalia and a display, WHAT IS NEWS? comparing the front pages of *The New York Times*, *The Philadelphia Inquirer*, and *USA Today* for the week of February 4. An insufficiently lethal room.

"He was cracking," Clifford said. "Drinking more. I was afraid what he'd say to reporters. The signs were everywhere. I didn't have much of a choice, did I? If you'd seen him the last time I did, you'd know how far gone he was."

"It won't work, Cliff," I said. "You're forgetting something."

Neil looked heartened and interested. I wanted him also to look at our positions. We flanked Cliff, more or less, I behind and to his right, Neil in front and to his left. If we could coordinate a rush, if Neil would take the dare, we had a chance.

"Well?" Cliff said.

"Fay," I replied. "She's his widow now and entitled to half the business."

Clifford shrugged.

"If you set up Neil as the murderer and kill him, how will you get rid of Fay? Because you want to, don't you? Shouldn't you save us—at least Neil, and certainly the gun—until after everybody else is gone?" I wasn't sure what I was talking about, noise was all it was, although I aimed for a semblance of logic. Mostly, whenever Clifford looked away, I goggled my eyes and tried to put Neil on alert.

He was as peppy as disintegrating compost, sweating and scribbling his stupid confession. Whatever happened to old-fashioned heroes? Was it an absolute requisite of liberation to be forbidden irrationally brave maiden-rescuers when you truly needed them?

"Stop making goo-goo eyes at him," Clifford said. "You should be ashamed. Him, with a pregnant wife and all. I knew you were in cahoots first time I saw you together. I knew why he was bringing you into the operation, why you came back the day after the fire, too. You two weren't giving up. I saw him in your house, too." He looked proud of his achievements. I could imagine him back in high school, the belligerent little foundling boy, unpopular, ungifted, and terrified he'd be that way forever. He was right, except that TLC had been his fairy godmother, his path out. Until Wynn began bleeding it, endangering him. Until Neil caught on and Fay bopped in to compound his problems.

It was always the same, except for a few details. Neil had been correct. It was all about self-defense. Somebody's life was in danger—the fill-in-the-blank part was how *life* was defined. All the rest was justification.

"Nice gray car you have," I said. "Did you follow me home from your office yesterday?"

"I didn't have to. Your address was on the résumé you left."

I looked up at the classroom clock. Somewhere in this very building—if he hadn't already left—a man was being stood up by me. "I have a date!" I shouted, jumping off the windowsill. "And I keep my dates, unlike you!"

"What?" Cliff wheeled toward me, his back to Neil. I raised my hand, palm up—the universal teacher sign, I thought, to stand, but Neil blinked and trembled and gulped like a flounder.

"Only date you have is with me." Cliff turned away. I gritted my teeth behind him, waved expansively this time for Neil to stand up, made two fists and brought them in together, suggesting, I hoped, Cliff's unfortunate self in between us.

Neil looked like he might weep. I resigned myself to finding other options. Running across the room in front of Cliff or out the window were suicidal choices. That left attacking and hiding with no visible places to do either. One of the above, none of the above.

All of the above.

I relaxed my arms, shoved my hands into my skirt pockets, and touched something more solid than my hips.

We had reached a point where any idea was worth a try. Cliff was monitoring the suicide letter, which seemed so long, it must have begun with how failures in toilet training accounted for Neil's murderous turn. Or maybe Cliff was planning to sell the note later, as a novel.

"Stick 'em up!" I screamed, pulling the gun out of my pocket and pointing it. I jumped sideways, meaning to imitate old Errol Flynn swashbuckler movies, but looking more like a nervous crab. Nonetheless, with a little additional scuttling, I was shielded by the file cabinet.

"A gun?" Neil whispered when he could speak.

"I always pack a . . . pack a . . ." I couldn't remember whether it was really *heater* or not. "A woman can never be too safe. Her most precious possession and all that. Do they teach you to shoot straight in business school, Clifford?" I snarled from behind my bunker.

Oh, please, I silently begged Neil. You got me into this. He thinks I'm your partner. Act like one. Get me out of this. Do something. Anything. Bore him to death, but don't leave me to clown myself to oblivion.

Clifford glanced at Neil, who began writing again. Then at me, then back. Every time he looked away, I screamed.

"Don't get hysterical," he said.

"Why the hell not?" I'd be any cliché I damn well pleased. Maybe I'd do Mae West next. It wasn't his call.

Neil sat, quiet as algae.

"I'm gonna blow you to smithereens," I shouted.

I'd missed all this, growing up as a girlchild without a toy gun. It was kind of fun, actually—as long as I pretended that Clifford's gun also shot words, not bullets.

"It's over, dumbo." My throat hurt from screaming, but if shrill female sounds unnerved him, I'd scream until I stripped the entire system in my throat. "You're losing everything. You were seen entering the house that night. There was a witness."

Neil looked heartened by the news. I didn't break his happy mood by adding that witness Patsy had seen only umbrellas.

The news galvanized Clifford, however. He advanced. "No reason to wait," he said. I pulled my weapon closer. Another step, and then another; he approached me from the other side of the file cabinet and we both did a funny sideways shuffle in order to aim our guns. Clifford lifted his and cocked it. "Neil!" I screamed. "The door!" Clifford was near me, his back to Neil.

"What about it?" Neil asked.

Perhaps he only moved in epochs and dynasties.

Clifford's gun, lovely ivory handle and silver chasing notwithstanding, made its way around the file cabinet until no matter how hard I contorted or pressed against the wall, the barrel aimed at one of my favorite parts. I could see Schmidt's trigger finger pale at the edge as it exerted pressure. I had perhaps a second or two.

All right, I told myself. Go for it. If the mountain wouldn't come to Mohammed, Mohammed could pretend it had. "No!" I screamed. "Neil, don't! Don't! Oh, my God, my God, watch out!" Even I couldn't imagine what Neil might have been doing to provoke me that way, given the preexisting situation. Neither could Clifford, whose finger didn't change direction as quickly as the rest of him did. His shot boomed, blasted, deafened, but the bullet hit and fragmented the blackboard, then ricocheted through a windowpane and out, presumably into the rough stucco side of the next building.

"Yay!" I screamed. "Helga, do you hear that? Property damage! Property damage!"

"What?" Clifford looked more than a little confused, turning back from an even more bewildered Neil. "What?" he shouted again. "What?"

It's too easy flustering a rigid jerk like Clifford Schmidt. Simply remove the laws of logic as he knows them. React when nothing's happened. Laugh, like now, when nothing's funny.

My giggling nearly started him foaming at the mouth. "Stop that!" he shouted. "I'm going to kill you."

I did my best banshee imitation. "Not if I get you first!" I raised my trusty pistol and aimed it directly between his eyes. He ducked behind the file cabinet, as I had hoped he would, and I pushed with everything I had. Pushed once and forever and hard, wishing I had joined the gym as promised on New Year's Day. Wishing I'd worked out, built my pecs, could push harder.

But I pushed hard enough. Cliff shouted, scrambled, but not in time. A great metal oblong tottered, drawers sliding first, a sharp edge gouging his jaw—years of history papers, curriculum materials, and, it appeared, old bologna sandwiches tumbling onto him along with a five foot column of metal.

''My legs!'' he shouted. ''God, my legs.'' He was trapped, half under it, half out.

And now, *now*, Neil's system activated. He stood up and took a step forward. ''We're going to live, aren't we?'' He sounded dazed.

And the classroom door opened and in came Mackenzie, sideways, whipping around the molding, arm straight out, holding a gun. What a week for weaponry. ''Drop it,'' he said.

''I already did. On him.'' I held up my gun, pulled the trigger and said ''Bang, bang'' as a cap exploded. Schmidt groaned even more.

''Oh, my!'' Helga squeaked from the doorway. ''The blackboard!''

''It was all Mandy,'' Neil said. I thought he was turning me in for destruction of property, but he was praising me. ''She teased him and distracted him and got him to fire into the air. You planned that, didn't you?''

I nodded. It's lovely having somebody else brag about you now and then, while you remain becomingly modest, doing an ''aw shucks.'' I forgave Neil a whole lot of wimpiness for this gesture.

''Get me out,'' Clifford said. ''My legs are crushed.''

''Talk about a restraining device,'' Mackenzie murmured.

''Idle hands are the devil's work.'' I put his laser-printer page on the floor, clean side up. ''Should I dictate?'' I asked. ''Or can you remember everything—all the way back to the crooked business, the fire, the murder, the attempted murder of yours truly.'' I looked at Mackenzie. ''Meet Mr. Random Violence,'' I said. And to Clifford, I added, ''And tonight. Tonight was really annoying. And why. And whatever else I left out.''

Helga examined the broken window and the toppled and messy file cabinet with great anguish.

''I'll call an ambulance.'' Neil was suddenly a take-charge kind of guy. ''I'll call a glazier. I'll call Angela.'' And he was gone.

Mackenzie read Clifford his rights. Clifford's clamped mouth emphasized his right to remain silent, but his hand was willing to communicate, moving the felt pen over the page. I walked away with Mackenzie—out into the hallway where the air was less charged and didn't smell of gunpowder.

"Was this in the book your mother sent you?" Mackenzie asked. "Catch a killer, get a date?"

I didn't get to answer. "Yo!" I heard from below. I looked over the railing, the way Neil had a short while ago. Or had it been hours? I couldn't tell.

"We met your *friend*," Rita said. "He's looking for you." She put up a thumb. Mackenzie could live, I suppose. "Alllll riiight!" she shouted up.

Colleen, next to her, nodded agreement. Of course.

"The kids have taste," Mackenzie said.

"It isn't Clifford, is it?" I asked softly.

"What isn't?"

"Your name."

He looked pained.

"Okay, then, one more try." Might as well take advantage of his tolerant and benign mood. "C.K., do you sometimes put on a red cape and become *S*?"

"Do I seem mild-mannered? Or the kind to strip in a phone booth?"

"I guess I knew that. Superman would have arrived way earlier."

"What I am is hungry," he said.

What I was was exhausted. Maybe hunger was in there, too, but I'd get to it after all my systems—muscular, skeletal, and nervous—returned to normal. "This week has been the most—"

"—boring five days of my life," Mackenzie said. "Might have to give up on Southern hospitality. But the night is young, this is a big city, and anything's possible. How about a little excitement?"

"Of all the unobservant, unempathetic ideas you have *ever* . . . !" The words that followed did not reflect well on my education or profession, but I think they made my stance on redundant excitement pretty clear.

"Good," he said.

"Good?"

"I just wanted to offer options. I hoped you'd choose the two pizzas I have in the car, plus the bottle of fine red wine and a tape—Joan Crawford at her worst. That's what I call really exciting."

Halfway to the car, he stopped and said, "And I'm sorry for not listenin' to you better. For too many knee-jerk reactions. I was way wrong."

So when all was said and done, even the things said and done this particular week, it was evident that there were still a few good men around.

Now that's what I call really exciting.

One

It was a dark and stormy night. Honestly. Earlier, it had been a dim and stormy day. Demonstrating no originality, March had indeed come in like a lion—a wet, angry one who blew ill winds every which way.

And here I was, not home cuddling by the fire with whatever was available—a man, a cat, a book—but driving in the rain with my mother, wearing my sister's panty hose and fulfilling social obligations that were not mine.

I clutched the steering wheel and thought about the difficulty of raising parents, particularly mine, particularly today.

My father had overreacted, overprotected, and overparented me into this pickle. Generally speaking, my father is so quiet that any woman near him (namely my mother) gets the urge to scream, simply to compensate for the sound deficit. His favorite way of interacting with the women of his family is from behind the shelter of his newspaper.

All the same, this afternoon some late blooming swashbuckler hormone kicked into his system and he suffered an attack of galloping, completely unnecessary heroism. As a result he lost his mobility and I lost my Sunday night.

We had all been in my sister's living room, enduring the sometimes elusive pleasures of a Long Parental Visit. Bea and Gilbert Pepper, a.k.a. Mom and Dad, had arrived four days earlier. Since then I'd been puzzling how to once and for all establish the concept that I was not willing to be a child for as long as Gilbert and Bea were willing to be parents—i.e., forever, i.e., right now.

It was hard pondering this delicate issue or anything else in the din of family. Everyone—except my father—talked at once, and the chatter was compounded by background music: my niece Karen's recording of Mother Goose done rap style. I remembered how unfond I had once been of the endless, enclosed hours of Sundays, and I remembered why.

I allocated twenty more minutes to this visit, by which time my exit wouldn't seem abrupt or overeager. The good thing about teaching English is that the bad thing about teaching English—endless papers to mark—provides a perpetual excuse to split.

Once I knew there was a definite reprieve ahead, I relaxed and tuned back into the conversation.

"I do hope the messenger delivered the gift in time," my mother was saying. "I've never done this before." She had read, in *People* magazine, of tributes arriving via messenger, and had decided that was the appropriate style when gifting a Somebody. Apparently, the host of the party she was attending tonight fit that category. "And not too soon," she continued. "What if it arrives before Lyle gets there? Would the hotel accept it?"

Everybody murmured reassurances, just as everybody had fifteen minutes earlier, the last time she'd worried over the matter. Only Karen, dancing to her barked-out rhymes, seemed unconcerned.

My Floridian parents had braved the last gasps of a Philadelphia winter to attend the fiftieth birthday party of a man they said was an old friend, but whose name I'd never heard. I don't keep close tabs on my parents' social life, but the invitation confused me, particularly since the birthday boy had sent them their airline tickets and was treating them—and all his other out-of-town guests—to rooms at the small hotel where the party would be held.

I was amazed by this stranger's largesse, so that now, when the conversation again veered toward the party, I poked around for more information. "Mom," I said, "explain why I've never heard of Lyle Zacharias."

"I told you," my mother said. "We've been out of touch for a long time."

About then my niece yelped. That's all it was, a minor blip, a five-year-old's reaction to bumping an unimportant body part on the coffee table.

But my father must have heard something primitive, a summons. He levitated, saying "Whooah!" or "Oh, woe!" and frantically, as if Karen were sinking into quicksand with only her teensy nose still poking out, he attempted to swing—without benefit of a vine—across the room to rescue his granddamsel in distress.

There were suddenly a lot of other sounds, too. Karen's infant brother, Alexander, keened. Their mother, my sister Beth, said, "Dad?" My mother said, "Gilbert! What on earth are you—" and even I stood and cried, futilely, "Watch out!" Only Karen, her bump forgotten, said nothing whatsoever. She was too busy boogying again.

Meanwhile, half of my father landed on one of her former musical selections and, almost immediately, his swash buckled. Down onto a pink plastic record went his right foot, skating straight ahead. His left foot, however, stayed put, pending further instructions. The rest of him flailed and looked bewildered, like a cartoon character running on air over a chasm.

The family attempted a save, but by then he'd achieved a split Baryshnikov would envy. He made another, sadder and less heroic "Whooah" and collapsed, the rug-skating leg tilting where it should not.

IT'S AMAZING HOW MUCH TIME AND PLASTER TAPE AND MEDical staff it takes to set a fracture. As wet gray day slid into wetter, darker night, we hobbled back to Beth's house. The party my parents had flown hither to attend loomed.

My mother bit her lower lip and looked like the frantic heroine of a silent film. My father grinned wickedly. His painkillered pupils were pinwheels. A whole new Daddy on dope. I told him he'd look sexy on crutches at the party.

My practical sister—who, being married, had a permanent companion, and who was therefore in no danger of being deputized as Mom's date—reacted immediately. "That little hotel might not have an elevator, Mandy! After all, it used to be a boardinghouse. How would Daddy get to his room?"

"We could call and find out." I was snappish, but only because I knew what was coming. I tried to stop it, but it was as effective as putting a hand up to stop a boulder rolling downhill. "And if there's no elevator, Mom and Dad can come back here tonight."

"Gilbert," my mother said. "Lyle wants you, not me, at his party. He wasn't part of my family."

Did that mean, then, that this Lyle person, this Somebody, was a secret part of my father's family? The black sheep? That sounded almost interesting. "Who *is* this man?" I asked again.

My father beamed. Sedated, he was more placidly impervious to female noises than ever. I couldn't believe my mother wanted to be accompanied by a space cadet, but the need for an escort has made lots of women drop their standards.

"He's a producer." My mother tossed the words my way. An answer, I realized. Lyle the mystery man was a producer.

My mother's attention was again wholly on my father. "Gilbert?" His answer was the downward flutter of his eyelids.

"Broadway?" The word *producer* is so mysterious. What does it mean? What does one do? If it's real, why isn't there a college major called Producing?

"Television." My mother woefully considered her comatose husband.

"What kind of—"

"*The Second Generation.*" Beth looked sheepish. "It's on every afternoon. Something to do while I'm feeding the baby."

My mother eyed her older daughter with concern.

"Don't worry," Beth said. "Dr. Spock does not object to watching soaps while nursing."

I could almost see my mother scan the Dr. Spock data base in her brain. He'd been her guru, and the final authority during our growing years, and she still idolized him. But we weren't talking about pediatricians. We were talking about producers, and I steered my mother back to the topic.

"Years ago, Lyle had a show on Broadway," she said. "A great big hit. Then it became a TV series, and that's how he got into the field." She turned back to my father, who was awake, but just barely. "We really have to go. Everybody will be there," she said. "And I've already made all those tarts and messengered them."

That was it, I was sure. She'd done a jet-set thing as per *People* magazine, and she wanted—and deserved—the acclaim for both her baking and her au courant presentation. Tarts seemed poor reasons for dragging a semiconscious man on crutches to a party, but as I knew who his stand-in was likely to be, I said nothing.

"The queen of hearts, she made some tarts," Karen chanted. There were collective frowns as we were reminded of her nursery rhyme collection, and in fact, of the infamous pink record that had resulted in this impasse. Karen didn't notice. "All on a summer's day!" she continued. "The knave of hearts, he stole—"

"How can we accept plane tickets from the man and then not go to his party?" my mother asked.

"I didn't ask him to invite me." My father spoke slowly. "You're the one who insisted we accept, even though you didn't like him, either, after. . . ."

"You're too harsh," my mother said. "Be tolerant. Think about how much he's suffered. He's reaching out to us now."

She didn't deny my father's accusation that she disliked Lyle Zacharias. But her overabundant supply of guilt and do-goodness would demand that she celebrate the birth of a man she wasn't fond of, if she thought he'd suffered in some way.

"You go," my father urged.

"Alone?" My mother's jaw dangled. No date for a party?

I deliberately ignored the wide-eyed flares my sister was hurling in my direction. She escalated to a *psst* that I was forced to acknowledge. Behind my mother's back she mouthed, silently, a question. It didn't take long to decipher it, although I wished I hadn't.

She had pantomimed, "Do you have a date tonight?"

I didn't. I was supposed to. We had planned to go to the movies, like normal people. And afterward we were going to buy hoagies stuffed to the brim with saturated animal fats. And after that, who knew?

However, normal people aren't homicide cops, and neither are the folk who keep homicide cops busy. This morning, just before I toodled out to the suburbs for Sunday brunch, C. K. Mackenzie had called in his regrets. Our date was off because it was his turn on the wheel to be assigned, and a fingerless corpse had been found on a brick-littered lot up in The Badlands near Germantown Avenue. Recently, the city has tried quashing drug dealers by demolishing their lairs. The de-digitized corpse had been left on the rubble of a former crack house. Mackenzie would undoubtedly work well past a normal shift.

Philadelphia does not give its police compensatory time off. Instead it pays overtime, which is no time at all. This policy enlarges wallets, shrinks social lives, and allows significant others to experience only the *others* part. After nearly a year of nearly knowing Mackenzie, I was still much fonder of him than of his job, and I still didn't know what to do about it, since the two appeared only in combination.

But the point was, I didn't have what anyone might call a date tonight. As if she had overheard my brain synapses, my mother turned. "Mandy!" she said with an air of discovery. Sometimes I look at my mother and see myself, gently distorted as in, perhaps, a kindly fun-house mirror. She is smaller, rounder, her features not truly mine, but definitely their source. We both have precisely the same auburn hue on our heads, although hers is mostly chemical. She achieved the match by holding up swatches of my hair—my head still attached—to every box of chestnut, auburn, brown, and red dye in the pharmacy.

Unassisted nature made our eyes the same confused green, which a seriously yuppified acquaintance described as the color of overhandled money. But whatever their tint, there is a horrific optimistic innocence in my mother's eyes that I hope is missing in mine.

"No," I said firmly. "I have things I absolutely must—tomorrow is a workday and I have papers and—"

"It'll be fun."

"Not for me. I'll drive you there, I'll pick you up, but I really don't want to go to—"

"A once in a lifetime chance."

"For what, Mom? Please."

"Show people. Household names."

In my household the names were Amanda and Macavity Pepper, and I already knew them. I shook my head. I'm adulation-challenged. I lack the celebrity-gawking gene, the part of the DNA that makes people line sidewalks and stage doors in hopes of glimpsing a famous face. I don't even understand the urge. And even if I were into such behavior, in this case the household name produced a soap opera I'd never seen. The potential thrill quotient was absent.

"Just for dinner," my mother said. "Okay? We won't even stay late. Who knows? Maybe you'll even meet somebody. Those actors can be very handsome, you know."

I envisioned my mother scanning the room for potential son-in-laws, then climbing on a chair and auctioning off her single daughter-overstock to the highest bidder. The closer I crept to thirty-one—and I was now only days away—the more panic-stricken she became. "Please, Mom!" A whine I thought I'd outgrown along with my training bra was back in my voice. I reminded myself that I was a mature woman with a mind and life of my own.

My mother raised her eyebrows. "I only meant you might meet a man who spends his time with people who are still alive, unlike your policeman friend." She laughed warmly, maternally, slyly.

Like I said, she was getting desperate. "I don't know Lyle Zacharias," I said. "I never heard of him before today. Whatever your ties to him might be, he's not connected to me in any—"

"Cindy was Lyle Zacharias's first wife."

I looked at my sister. She looked at me. We both looked at my mother. My father, on the other hand, looked away.

"Who," Beth and I said in unison, "is Cindy?"

"Cindy." My mother spoke loudly, as if our incomprehension was a hearing problem. "Of course you've heard of her. She was your father's foster sister."

Repetition of the name made it seem dimly familiar, part of ancient hazy childhood impressions, but nothing more.

"You even met her. They lived in New York and we didn't see them much, but you did meet her."

"You've never talked about her," I said with awe. Bea Pepper, the Scheherazade of family gossip, she who trolled all lines for a nibble twenty-four hours a day, the village chronicler of Philadelphia, had remained silent about a foster sister of her husband's?

"I'm sure we were invited tonight because we'd be the only people there who knew Cindy and that time in his life. A tragic time." She sighed and stopped looming over my father and, instead, sank onto Beth's chintz-covered love seat. "Right, Gilbert?" My father appeared to be visiting outer space, and to be having a good time there.

My mother put her hands up. "He doesn't like to talk about it." Whenever she is truly upset with my father, she speaks of him only in pronouns. "Lyle kept a gun in his house. For protection. They lived in New York, after all. We told him it was a bad idea, dangerous. Then one day—it's so horrible—Cindy's little girl found it and killed her mother with it."

"Accidentally." My father's blissful obliviousness had been replaced by a perturbed expression. Cindy was making it through the drug barrier. "They have laws some places for that now. He'd go to jail nowadays for leaving a gun where a three-year-old child could find it." He shook his head, still appalled.

"When did all of this happen?" Beth asked

My mother began her infamous circular computations. "Let's see, it was just after Uncle Lewis' seventy-fifth birthday, so when would that be? He and Aunt Gloria had a big anniversary party—their silver—the same day as your first birthday, Mandy, and I remember he married late in life, he was a famous bachelor around town, which means that by then he must have been—"

"For heaven's sake!" my father said. "Cindy died nearly twenty years ago."

When I was ten or eleven. How could I have missed an accidental homicide in my own family? What else could have occupied my attention back then when puberty hadn't even kicked in? Beth looked equally baffled.

"Well, it happened in New York in their home," my mother said. "You barely knew her, anyway. She never lived near us. Besides, you were away at the shore at the time, visiting Grandma. What was the point of going out of our way to tell you terrible news about somebody you didn't even know? Parents are supposed to protect their children from bad things when they can. That's what we did."

I appreciated the sentiment, but I nonetheless felt uncomfortable. Family secrets jutted like hard-edged foreign objects under the smooth skin of our lives.

"What happened to his little girl?" Beth asked softly.

"Betsy?" my mother said. "She wasn't Lyle's, biologically. Cindy was one of those flower children. And then she became one of those flower mothers. The flower father was nowhere to be found."

My father looked away from us, as if he still found Cindy's history embarrassing.

"Did he keep her—the little girl—Betsy, after . . ." Beth's voice dribbled off.

My mother shook her head. "He was all to pieces, beside himself. Hattie, Lyle's aunt, who raised him, took the baby. Lyle couldn't be around her. Your father and I talked about adopting her."

"Look," my father said, cutting to the chase, "the . . . um, natural father was back from Vietnam by then, and when he found out what had happened, he took Betsy. He wouldn't speak to the family after that."

My mother stood up. "And we weren't so much better. Never really tried to see Lyle after that, poor man."

"He should have kept the baby. Besides, he did fine without us." My father sounded uncharacteristically hostile.

"I hope nobody ever told that little girl what she'd done," Beth said, provoking a long, heavy silence.

My mother finally broke it with a pragmatic return to the issue at hand. "I still think it would be wrong to stay away from his party. He wants so much to make peace finally. Did you see the invitation, girls?" She walked to the hall table and rummaged in her pocketbook, returning with a large, cream square.

At first glance it looked quite standard. Heavy stock with bold engraving. It might have been a wedding invitation, except that it was so verbose, like nothing I'd ever seen before.

> Most of life moves double-time, too quickly to see each individual frame or even to make sense of it. But the half-century marker is a time to pause, take stock and seriously consider the course. I'm very excited about my next fifty years as I switch from one rodent image (the rat race) to another (the country mouse).
>
> But now, before I move on, I want to believe that you—and I—*can* go home again. Please join me back where my voyage began, to celebrate the points along the way where our lives touched. You are a part of my story, and I of yours, and the only birthday present I want is a chance to see my life in front of me, whole, in your faces, to heal what needs healing and to drink a toast to auld lang syne.

Beth let go of her half of the invitation. "Forgive me, but I think it's weird," she said. "Slightly creepy. Inappropriate. Sounds like he has a lot of enemies, for one thing. And then—oh, maybe he just needed an editor, a more careful choice of words. But the way he said it—seeing his life before him—that's not a birthday wish, that's what's supposed to happen to a dying man."

It wasn't like my sister to be morbid, so her words struck with extra impact. Which is not to say they deterred my mother.

"You'll go with me, won't you? It could be awkward," she said to me, "without your father there. It's important."

And because of the need in my mother's eyes, the image of a long-dead flower child and the odd wording of an invitation, I wound up borrowing panty hose and a cocktail dress from my sister and going to a party for a man I didn't know.

And that, in turn, meant that later in the evening I was there to witness it when, just as Beth had suggested, Lyle Zacharias got his wish and saw his life pass before his eyes. Exactly the way a dying man is supposed to.